AMISTAD

An Imprint of HarperCollins*Publishers*

Dear Reader,

Joe McClean and I are thrilled to share our labor of love, *Sins of Survivors*.

There are a thousand reasons why people love a great story, but a consistent truth comes from the sage advice of Mary Poppins—"A spoonful of sugar helps the medicine go down."

There are great documentaries and even wonderful textbooks about redlining, prohibition, organized crime, racial integration, union labor, the auto industry, Joe Louis, jazz, and all the other things that added together equal Black Bottom, Detroit . . . but we don't always want to be preached at or taught a lesson. We don't want to be forced to take our medicine.

That's where the sugar comes in—forbidden love, cover-ups, betrayal, sex, corruption, murder, and family. The Carter brothers, Jasper and Ben, become kings after a brutal and ruthless rise; but staying on top reveals two paths. The first says the world is a dirty place, and if you need to get a little mud on your hands to protect your family, that's what you do. The other path risks all you've gained as you gamble your influence to help drag your entire community to a safer harbor. What would you do? Are you sure?

It's an honor for Joe and I to share this thrilling and emotional story set in the realest of worlds—the indispensable and tragically demolished Black neighborhoods of Black Bottom and Paradise Valley. It is our hope that others out there in the world can enjoy, appreciate, heal, and grow as much as we have from the sweet medicine that is *Sins of Survivors*.

Thank you,
Blair Underwood

SINS OF SURVIVORS

ALSO BY BLAIR UNDERWOOD

Casanegra: A Tennyson Hardwick Novel

In the Night of the Heat: A Tennyson Hardwick Novel

From Cape Town with Love: A Tennyson Hardwick Novel

South by Southeast: A Tennyson Hardwick Novel

BLAIR UNDERWOOD PRESENTS

SINS OF SURVIVORS

A NOVEL

BY JOE McCLEAN

BASED ON CHARACTERS CREATED BY

TIAKA HURST AND JOE McCLEAN

AMISTAD

An Imprint of HarperCollins*Publishers*

HarperCollins books may be purchased for educational, business, or sales promotional use. For information, please email the Special Markets Department at SPsales@harpercollins.com.

FIRST EDITION

Designed by Yvonne Chan

Library of Congress Cataloging-in-Publication Data has been applied for.

ISBN 978-0-06-331678-2

$PrintCode

TK

CARTER FAMILY TREE

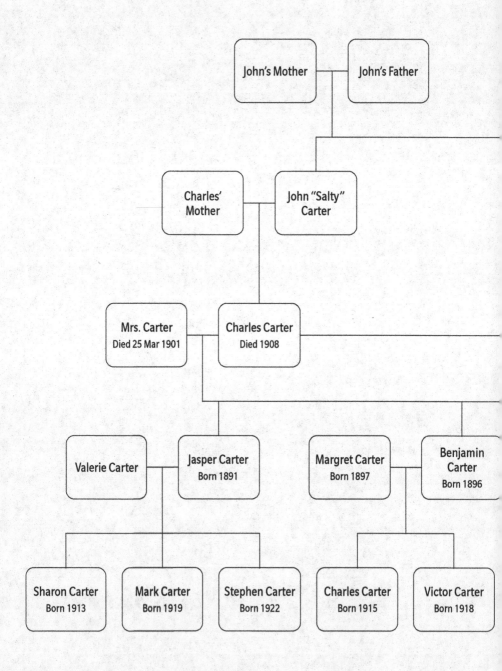

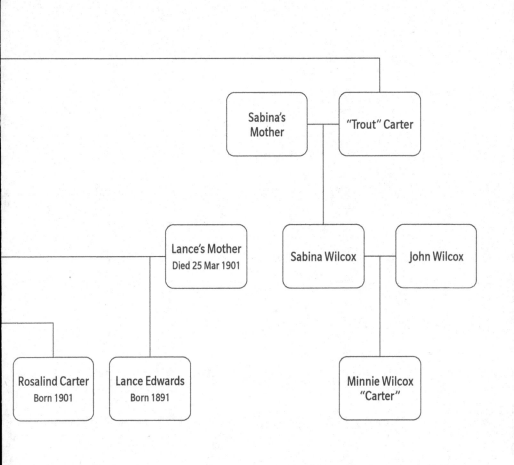

PART ONE

CHAPTER ONE

The long dirt road bustled with hundreds of men ready for work but daring not to. It had been three weeks and two days since any of them had crossed under the wooden arch that announced the entrance to the PRATT COAL & COKE COMPANY, and it was only yesterday when federal marshals showed up to keep order. The year was 1908.

Racially integrated picketers marched in their threadbare, coal-stained work clothes and caps, carrying signs with messages as black and white as they were, occasionally yelling and chanting their slogans.

"The UMW says NO to the Big Mules!"

"Keep the magic in Magic City!"

"United we stand, divided we fall!"

Down the road, away from the action, the landscape was littered with smokestacks and a smattering of support shanties. Rail tracks. Mining cars. Get just a bit farther off and segregation began to show, predominately Black on one side of the road, white on the other. Groups of men waiting to relieve their picketing brethren with re-invigorated excitement huddled together to laugh at one another's stories while others stood silently reading newspapers. Behind them stretched tent cities, their homes away from home during the strike, nicer on the white side but not by much.

Just before the road became desolate on its way back to Birmingham was Pratt City, which wasn't a city at all but a small string of connected buildings: a general store, a large gathering place with a sign above the door that read MINOR'S HALL, and a pharmacy with an ice cream parlor on one wall. It was here at the pharmacy that three Black teenagers loitered around one of the posts holding up the porch.

One of these boys, the round-faced twelve-year-old Benjamin, sat quietly, staring poignantly off into space. At a glance, he wouldn't be noticed, but if roaming eyes paused just long enough to light a pipe or drag a rag across a sweaty forehead, one might catch the glint in the child's curious eyes, which always seemed to leave a patch of out-of-place wrinkles on his otherwise baby-smooth forehead. His father, Charles, once described Benjamin's youthful intensity as the roots of a weed desperately forging and clinging to the inside of the boy's skull. "One day it'a take root and grow into a oak strong enough for all our kin to climb out of Jim Crow."

Benjamin's seventeen-year-old brother Jasper—lean, clean, and spry—squatted low next to the third kid, Lance, also seventeen, where they secretly rolled a wooden die on the plank porch floor. Jasper had a glint in his eye too, but it was accompanied by a sly smirk that turned the whole look into something visceral, with a tinge of trouble.

No sooner had the die come up four than Jasper grabbed the two pennies from the floor between him and his friend.

"Hot damn! You cheatin' me, Jasper?"

"How I gonna cheat you? The dice got six sides. You got one, three, five. I got two, four, six. It don't get more fair than that!" Jasper explained with exaggerated contempt as his slower friend attempted to tally the fairness on his fingers. "You want your penny back, Lance, then throw another one in the pot."

The fate of two more pennies placed between them rendered Benjamin invisible. The young gamblers didn't notice when he stood up, and they certainly hadn't seen how much his glare had intensified. Slow, deliberate steps carried Benjamin across the pharmacy's porch. A magnet attracted to the human soul had him in its grasp.

Jasper snatched up the die and two more pennies with barely enough time for Lance to register that yet another four had been rolled.

"That's three in a row," Lance complained.

"It's my lucky day!"

"Show me that dice, Jasper."

Deeply hurt that anyone would question his good name, Jasper quickly flashed each of the cube's sides with a delicate sleight of hand to distract his friend from seeing the sequence: one, two, three, four, four, six.

"Shit, Jasper! Now I gotta win at least one roll if I want lunch!" Lance smacked another penny on the floor, but Jasper's bet didn't follow. "Come on, now. You can't do me three in a row and not gimme a chance to win it back."

Jasper wasn't paying attention anymore. Time, for him, had slowed to molasses, and he was honed in on his brother and his brother alone. He knew the right thing to do was leap up and give Benjamin a lashing, but something inside him must have needed answers as badly as Benjamin did, and for once it seemed his kid brother had more nerve. Benjamin's eyes were glued to the water fountains on the wall.

Each step closer amplified Benjamin's curiosity. He took special note of the single pipe that came up through the floorboards. Tracing the pipe with a rare and peculiar focus, he furled his brow more when the pipe came to a *T* and split in two. The left pipe ran parallel to the porch floor for eighteen inches, then took a 90-degree turn up the wall, where Benjamin was met with a crusty spigot hanging over a rusted basin corroded with grime and mineral deposits. A small placard was nailed to the wall above the fountain. COLORED.

Benjamin's eyes carefully followed their way back to where the water pipe curiously split and this time proceeded to the right. It mirrored the left but found its way to a pristine chrome basin with an ivory handle. This much more appetizing fountain had a matching placard with a different word. WHITE.

Benjamin was now in a face-off with the fountains, and time had come to a full stop.

"Hey, Jasper." Lance was no longer begging a shark for a fair shot, no. All that mattered now was nudging Jasper to stop his certifiably insane brother. Unfortunately, the sound waves were physically unable to swim their way through the thickened atmosphere.

Watching his brother inch closer to the fountains, Jasper wanted desperately to be the one who was man enough to take a stand, but this little runt beat him to it. Subconsciously, that was the moment Jasper anointed himself the protector of his father's sapling of an oak tree.

Benjamin was now less than an arm's length away, and his intention was plainly visible. There were only two physical objects left in the universe: Benjamin and the "white" drinking fountain.

He stepped up.

He twisted the ivory handle, letting water flow in a beautiful arc before it splashed into the shining basin.

The wrinkles in his forehead released.

He bent at the waist, and his lips touched the tepid water.

It splashed and bounced around the inside of his mouth like a miniature, slow-motion tempest, finally whirlpooling at the back of his tongue.

Then Benjamin swallowed.

Like a spark running out of fuse, reality burst back into action, and from this moment on, the lives of the Carter brothers would be a lively, never-ending string of exploding firecrackers that refused to let them slow down, take a breath, or relax.

A white teenager who seemed to have appeared from heat vapor violently yanked Benjamin back and shoved him stumbling off the porch.

"I know you can't read, nigger, but it's pretty obvious which one belongs to you." Andy's ragtag clothes said his family was no better off than Benjamin's. It was melanin alone that gave him the privilege to use physical violence against a younger, darker boy.

All eyes within reach, Black and white, snapped to attention. Now it was the bystanders' moment to be stuck in Benjamin's time warp as they watched the confrontation the way that Jasper had watched its instigation. Jasper freed himself from the limitations of slowed time, leapt up from his rigged dice game, and slammed his chest into the white boy.

"My brother read just fine, Andy."

Andy was scared. His privilege didn't seem to be able to protect him from getting pulverized. In fact, now it felt like a handicap, because Jasper already knew he'd catch hell for his actions, so why not make the crime worth the punishment by pummeling Andy's face even harder? Lucky for Andy, Charles Carter was close by.

Charles bolted onto the porch from within the pharmacy. Black, strong, and domineering, the man was built like a machine, but he'd already broken into a thin film of fearful sweat because of this skinny white kid. His callused Black hand pulled back on Andy's shoulder, maneuvering himself between Jasper and his son's locked target.

"Don't touch me! You don't get to touch me!" Andy squeaked belligerently.

"Back off, Jasper." Only three words, but father and son spoke far more with their eyes. Charles clearly demanded and desperately pleaded for obedience while Jasper sternly refused to let anyone talk to or touch Benjamin that way. How could Charles begin to explain or justify that, at this juncture, one of his children defending the other was the wrong path? He didn't understand or even believe it himself, but Charles knew from experience that doing nothing was the least painful and disruptive option before him.

Charles repeated himself. "Back off, I said. We don't want no trouble!"

Jasper took a couple steps back, not in defeat against Andy but with the understanding that he was no match for his father.

"Andy! Get your ass down here, boy!" yelled a white miner from the edge of the street.

The hollers of his quickly approaching father, Andrew, ended Andy's test run of manhood and revealed a snot-nosed tattletale. As he scurried off the porch into his father's shadow, Andy ratted, "Benjamin was drinking from the white fountain!"

Andrew surprised his son with a solid slap to the back of the head. "Get outta my sight. Causing trouble." Then he slowed his charge a few steps from the pharmacy porch, looking up at the three Carter men.

Feeling as if the world's collective injustice had befallen him, Andy looked around indignantly, landing on Charles last and rubbing his shoulder where the Black man had touched him in his effort to prevent the foregone conclusion of Jasper knocking the kid's teeth out. Milking his imagined shoulder ailment for every drop of sympathy, Andy glanced up to his father. "Daddy, that man . . ."

"Git along now!" Andrew raised his hand with the promise of another wallop, and Andy scuttled off down the dirt road.

Every person within sight, still frozen, stared at the porch of the

Pratt City pharmacy. Black onlookers had tinges of pained under-standing in their faces for what they knew the near future may hold. Whites looked on with the strange expression of *Now look what you've gone and done.* After all, they were poor and societally abused too, so if they let something like this slide without repercussions, they'd lose the last thing they had of any value—the ability to feel elevated by holding someone else down.

Andrew slowly climbed the steps, pursing his lips and glancing at Benjamin. He looked Jasper up and down before his final step landed him in front of Charles, man-to-man, father-to-father.

"We sorry, Andrew. I didn't hurt the boy. I just pull him back to get between 'um. Trying to stop trouble before it start."

Andrew's face contorted with internal struggle. What was the stronger move? Was it compassion or a corporal show of force to ce-ment this man's position on a lower rung? He took one step closer to Charles and spoke in a voice the onlookers strained to hear but could not. "We're one and the same in the mines, Charles. And we need the colored folk on our side during the strike."

"I know. I know."

"But up here?"

"I know. I'm sorry. My boys are sorry." Charles's eyes were forced to the floor by Andrew's hard glare. Finally, the white man turned and walked off, granting Charles the freedom to stop holding his breath and setting Father Time back in motion for Pratt City. When Charles lifted his gaze to watch mercy personified walk away, he spoke to Jas-per with a calmness that bred fear in the boy. "Get your brother back to the tent."

Neither boy moved. An eternity had passed, but only moments prior, Jasper had scammed his friend Lance for pennies because the great unifier for humankind seemed to be holding others back if it meant you could get ahead.

"Go!" Charles snapped.

Jasper grabbed his brother by the arm and dragged him down the steps. Benjamin was still in shock, and his brain wasn't yet sending perfect signals to his feet. "Jasper..."

"Walk, dammit." Jasper yanked Benjamin with a jolt, forcing his shorter legs into lockstep with reality, but his face was still lost somewhere in the dust cloud they kicked up behind them.

"It didn't taste no different, Jasper."

"I know, Benny. I know." Jasper looked around and caught two white miners pretending to go back to their own business but delivering residual side-eye. "The taste ain't the damn point."

Benjamin spun his head around to find his father still standing on the pharmacy porch in the wake of their near disaster. Nearby, Lance stood with his mouth agape before finally snapping out of it and pointlessly checking his pockets for more pennies. They all belonged to Jasper now.

"You get enough?" Benjamin questioned his brother.

"Got extra too. This one's for you." Jasper slid the last penny he won into Benjamin's hand. "Save it up."

Benjamin's face lit with pride and joy. "Thanks, Jasper!"

Jasper did not relent his quick step back to their tent or his grip on Benjamin's upper arm. That didn't bother Benjamin none, though. He studied the penny in awe; a Native man's head on one side and the words ONE CENT surrounded by wheat on the other. He'd never had a penny of his own before. It was a single grimy copper coin, but it felt like success.

No, that wasn't quite it.

No.

It felt like freedom.

Money felt like freedom.

Cheap labor was the backbone of profit making, and the destitute

Southern population was easy pickings for the Northern steel companies who owned them—or, rather, who owned the mines. The hypocrisy was not lost on journalists, who pointed out that a mere forty-three years prior, the North had won a war to end slavery and ended up in a more productive method of capitalism—pay people enough to make them grateful for their freedom but so little that climbing out of poverty is a mathematical impossibility. Uprisings could be easily fractured, and worker retention was as high as before the War of Northern Aggression. Forty-three years. Most of the men on strike in Pratt City had not yet been born when a famous actor avenged the South with a single-shot derringer. To them, this was a story their grandparents told, nothing more. Forty-three years. The blink of an eye and an incomprehensible cosmic span at the same time.

Rough burlap was yanked down over the whole world, and the veil of night hid the assailants. Inside the sack, the sound of the boy's heavy breathing was amplified, and his pulse was a pounding bass drum, but despite the internal cacophony, every sound outside was crisp and sharp.

"If the lawman ain't gonna put 'em in their place, somebody gotta!"

The man's unfamiliar voice belonged to one of the shadowy figures barely visible between the thick threads of the loosely woven fabric.

"Be strong! You the man of the family now, you hear?"

That voice he knew. It was his father's. Charles Carter. Somewhere out in the darkness. *What does he mean "be strong"? Where is he going?* Benjamin pushed and stretched his limbs as hard as he could, but the bag would not give. The only tool he had left was his voice. "Daaad-dyyy!"

The glow of a small torch burst to life, and Benjamin's breathing gained pace!

"This one's yours, Brother Andrew," said the voice Benjamin couldn't place.

Benjamin pressed his eye against the sack, desperate to peer through the weave, but alas, he was only capable of following the orange glow that flickered through the walls of his cloth prison.

"Andrew, I did your boy no harm." Charles's voice was calm and pleading as the small flame slowly inched in his direction, but in the very next words he spoke, Benjamin could hear the quiver in his throat. "Jasper. Jasper, listen now. . . ."

"Shut yer yap, nigger!"

"Jasper. You do as your daddy says now. You take care of your brothers and your sister. You their daddy now." Charles's voice was getting louder and faster as the glowing ball of light got closer.

"Daaaddyyy!" Benjamin's scream invited a solid hit by something unseen. A flash of light behind his eyes was followed by a high-pitched ring that took over the sound of the beating pulse in his ears. Now lying on his side, trying to focus on the orange glow, one thought filled his brain: *He said "brothers." More than one. It's true. Lance is our brother.*

"You their daddy now, Jasper. I have faith in you. The Lord has faith in you."

"It's gonna be easier if you just be quiet now, Charles." There was fear and pain in Brother Andrew's voice too, but there was also steadfastness.

"You strong, Jasper! You stronger than me!" Charles was crying.

Andrew was losing control now. "Shut your mouth! Shut it!"

Jasper must have been nearby, but Benjamin didn't know where. He wasn't speaking.

"They'll need you, Jasper. Don't let me down, you hear? You hear me, boy?"

"Shut! Your! Damn! Mouth!" The fiery glow started moving faster.

"I hear you, Daddy! I hear you!"

"Goddamnit! Stop yer trap!"

The flame leapt from the place of Andrew's yelling and sailed through the air in a mesmerizing arc, leaving a golden trail. A comet blazing through the night sky, promising torturous ruin upon the Carter family.

Upon landing, it ignited an explosion that engulfed every shadow. Charles's horrifying screams rang out, echoing into the night!

Jasper screamed too, but his was different. There was no fear. No sadness. It was all rage. "Nooo! Daddy!"

A violent struggle broke out, and all recognizable voices became indecipherable grunts. Benjamin couldn't tell who was taking hits and who was delivering them. It was then that all sounds began to dim.

"Grab that little coon! Git 'em!"

Benjamin was slowly losing consciousness to the sounds of his brother fighting for his life, the agony-filled screams of his father, and the sight of the explosive, blinding light that settled into the shape of a glowing cross, shining through the fabric.

BANG! A shot rang out, and desperate men charged. *BANG! BANG!* With each gunshot, a body fell, and another man's voice vanished into the night. The only sounds left were the faint, guttural moans of Jasper and Benjamin's father burning at the stake.

BANG! And then there was silence.

From that moment on, Benjamin was drifting in and out. He couldn't be sure the order of events or how long they took. Running footsteps. His body was lifted and carried over someone's shoulder, still in his sack. He landed with a metallic thud in the back of a pickup truck. Benjamin heard the engine rev and tires spin in the dirt. His consciousness faded as the truck sped away, and his father's cross, shrinking with distance, was forever burned into his retinas.

Blackness.

"Wake up, Benny."

This gentle voice was soothing in comparison to Benjamin's dull, throbbing headache, his cheek now adorned with a swollen purple egg. Benjamin's eyes fluttered open to find daylight—no idea how much time had gone by. His view was consumed by the familiar face that belonged to the gentle voice. Jasper Carter. He was still physically seventeen years old, but having taken the lives of villains and graciously delivering mercy to the man whose shoes he'd now stepped into had aged him beyond the year of his birth—1891.

A bell was ringing—from where, Benjamin didn't know.

Jasper repeated himself with more vigor. "Wake up, Benny!"

Something was urgent. Benjamin squeezed his eyes shut and stretched his neck, half to relieve himself of slumber, half to push off his pain. *Where is the damn ringing coming from?*

"Wake up, Ben!"

He opened his eyes, and his brother was gone.

So was his youth.

Lying in a tangled lump of sheets next to him in their bed was Margaret, Ben's wife of twenty-three years. "I'll never know how you sleep through that noise."

Ben rolled over, reaching to cover the hammer and bells of the ringing alarm clock on the bedside table. Finally, peace. Quiet. The hour on the clock was in reference to the current year of 1937, but the boy who drank white water and altered the course of his family forever still had his round, baby-smooth face at the age of forty-one.

CHAPTER TWO

Her eyes were still crusty, her hair hidden under a nightcap, and her breath was a topic Ben had only ever mentioned one time, and that had been enough to learn his lesson. A year younger than Ben, Margaret was just at the age where one starts to feel their bones when they get out of bed in the morning. She tossed off the sheets with a sigh, then threw her legs over the edge and stood. Ben watched her shuffle to the bathroom, eyes half-closed, absentmindedly scratching an itch under a breast, and he had the same thought he'd had every day since the first moments they spent together: *How is it possible to be this lucky?*

Ben lay motionless on his back with his eyes open, staring at nothing.

The room was fifteen by fifteen feet, with a row of five windows, side by side by side, giving the illusion of a single large one. The walls and ceiling were decorated with colorful hanging fabric that gave off a slightly bohemian feel. At the corners, where the cloth didn't completely cover the walls, one could see its purpose was to hide cracked and peeling wallpaper.

A rocking chair with frayed upholstery sat in front of the windows, unused since Victor, their youngest, was a toddler. A matching dresser and armoire with worn, ornate woodwork crowded in the four-poster bed that Margaret insisted was too big for the room. She was right, but for Ben, it simply hadn't registered as important against all the other responsibilities balanced in his brain.

Sunlight was creeping into the room, and a rooster crowed somewhere outside. This was followed by the hollow gurgle of a flush that wasn't refilling. There was no avoiding it any longer. It was time to rise and shine.

Ben rubbed sleep out of his eyes while he listened to Margaret jiggling the handle of the empty toilet. He could almost predict the squeaks that followed of the turning faucet handle absent the sound of flowing water.

"Water's off again," Margaret called from the other side of the door.

Ben propped himself up on an elbow, pausing for the briefest of moments before continuing his journey out of bed. He used the physics of weight distribution and a roll more than any muscle. Then it was his hands on his knees, not the strength of his back, that hoisted him to his feet. His shirtless physique was pudgy, just enough out of shape to be unassuming.

"Jasper ain't so crazy after all. Conant Gardens sounding better every day." Margaret had a way of saying things in a roundabout way that was very different from Ben's straight-arrow nature.

"It'll come back on. Always does," he lobbed back.

The floorboards squeaked as Ben stretched—arched back, arms raised high, a morning quiver up his spine. He stepped to the dresser and opened the top drawer for an undershirt and socks.

He pulled on his slacks, buttoned his shirt, and tied his wide tie. The day's routine had begun. He looped the laces of his shiny, two-tone leather shoes and topped off his snazzy duds with a tan porkpie hat adorned with a checkered ribbon that he lifted from a coatrack flanking the door. Ben stood in front of the armoire's full-length mirror for a final look-see. *Not too flashy, just the right classy.*

He looked down at the bedside table with the alarm clock. Waiting next to it, a silver wristwatch with a leather band and an Indian head penny from 1908.

Ben pocketed the lucky penny and slid the timepiece onto his wrist—7:36 a.m.

He called through the bathroom door, "I only have a few stops before I get to you, baby. See you soon."

With that, Ben opened the bedroom door and exited immediately into a stairwell. He quickstepped down into his home's main living area. It was an eyesore. Down here no one had taken care to cover the ugly, peeling, water-stained wallpaper.

"Ain't no water s'morning."

Ben didn't know exactly who the voice came from because it was normal for extra bodies to be sleeping on the sofas or the floor of his living room. Usually friends of Charles or his nephews. Victor, more reserved and who sometimes struggled to fit in, rarely had friends stay the night. "It'll be back," he told the voice. Then, as he made his way to the front door, Ben recognized the familiar-shaped lump under the blanket on a sofa chair. "Stephen!"

Ben snatched up the cover, revealing his wiry fifteen-year-old nephew, who, dressed only in boxer shorts, recoiled from contact with the air beyond his disturbed cocoon.

"Get up, boy! What are you doing here?"

"Your place was closer to my last delivery, Uncle Ben," Stephen explained through slammed-closed eyes.

"You think your daddy cares where your last delivery was? Get moving!"

Ben watched as the teenager got up and stumbled through the room to a dirty sink hung on the wall outside the bathroom door and spun the faucet's handle, already having forgotten there was no water.

Ben dragged open the window curtains by the front door, and every corner of the room filled with sunlight and groans. Ben couldn't help but crack a smile, proud of himself for jump-starting their day.

A small oval mirror hanging by the front door offered Ben a brief glimpse of himself. He adjusted his hat to just the right degree of crooked, smoothed his jacket, took a deep breath, and opened the door.

His smile grew as he stepped into the world.

His world.

The world of Black Bottom.

Hastings Street was Black Bottom's main thoroughfare, which was where Ben liked to be, right in the middle of it all. Although poor, his neighborhood was vibrant. It was active and alive, as if the place was a living, breathing resident of itself, but much of Black Bottom was also in disrepair. The whites in control of greater Detroit's politics, as well as those at the state level, wrote off the residents of Black Bottom due to their Black and Brown skin, but it was their policies, those white people's policies, that created Black Bottom in the first place.

The US government established the Federal Housing Administration three years prior, in 1934, to help solidify the slipping foothold of the housing market. The new government agency insured low-interest loans as a boon for home construction to get people back to work during the sluggish recovery from the crash of '29. And it worked—for white people. The FHA adopted thinly veiled racist policies that labeled Black and immigrant neighborhoods as "undesirable" locations for the government's investment. This meant FHA loans were systematically withheld from the residents of Black Bottom. No access to affordable loans meant new construction and costly repairs simply didn't happen. It meant zero opportunity to gain or improve your individual creditworthiness and far too many options to hurt it. Bad credit was an easy, bureaucratic way to tell Black applicants that they didn't qualify when they attempted to move into "desirable"—meaning "white"—neighborhoods. Thus, a chapter of America's "undesirables" took up residence in the only places society would allow them.

Ben knew where he lived. He understood why he lived there. However, Ben's smile was an ever-present fixture on his face. This was home, his home, and the white men didn't realize the gift they'd given to Detroit's Black mecca. When a person is forced to fend for themselves, they do just that. With no help from the government, no ability to move into neighborhoods where God forbid a white person might see a Black person in a local shop, Black Detroiters learned to do for themselves. No access to lawyers? Black Bottom would cultivate its own. Only third-rate medical care, you say? Black Bottom had seventeen of its very own physicians. Not allowed in white-only restaurants? Hem in your favorite slacks give out? No agency to call after a death in the family? Black Bottom boasted ten restaurants, eleven tailors, four undertakers, and they even had their very own candymaker—all Black owned, Black run, and Black patronized. Black Bottom was created by racism, but Ben knew it also acted as proof to Black and white alike that an all-Black community was capable of running every aspect of its own society. In fact, they were brilliant at it. Sure, the South Side of Chicago was an exciting and enticing Negro neighborhood of the day. The City of Big Shoulders was inventing its very own exciting style of blues, but if musicians relied on tips playing the Maxwell Street Market, they'd starve. And, yes, New York's Harlem was an important Black enclave too, but when the Dandridge Sisters, Duke Ellington, and Count Basie were gigging at Harlem's famous Cotton Club, only white patrons were allowed to hear them play. Black Bottom was different—hell, it was better, and Ben Carter wanted to scream it out, celebrate it, and push it forward.

The easiest way for Ben to show what he meant was to invite someone as his personal guest to the prize jewel of the Carter family empire—Geraldine's, the family's ritzy dinner-and-jazz club. Geraldine's was technically in Paradise Valley, just north of Black Bottom, but there wasn't one without the other. It could be said that Paradise Valley was the entertainment district of Black Bottom. Ben saw the future in Paradise Valley because it was here where Blacks and whites congregated together as integrated guests—the first place anywhere in America as far as he knew—all made one by their love of good booze and better music. That said, he took great pride that the music this mixed crowd came to hear was Black. There would be no equality until the world saw the undeniable contribution of his race, and Ben wanted to do his part to showcase his beautiful community. He loved Paradise Valley. He loved Black Bottom. He also wasn't shy when he preached that there was no spot as hip, no jazz as hot, no club as with it as Geraldine's.

Black Bottom was undeniable because it was Black. Black Bottom was vital due to its Blackness. Black Bottom was important, and that's what put the smile on Ben's face and pep in his finely dressed step.

This morning was no different. Hastings Street was already busy with cars and a colorful bevy of beautiful Black pedestrians starting their day as Ben hopped down his porch steps and onto the sidewalk. People always happily greeted him with a shout or a smile, sometimes both.

Black Bottom businessmen passed and tipped their hats.

Three kids on bikes—and one trying to keep up on foot—scurried by. "Morning, Mr. Carter!"

"Gonna be a hot one today, Mr. Carter. Make sure you be drinking water," called out Willie-Joe, a shirtless man with too few teeth, as he wheeled his large junk cart across Hastings.

"You too, Willie-Joe! Try to find some shade if you can!"

Two women talking over the fence between their yards smiled and whispered as he strolled by. Bernice was the more forthcoming of the two. "Looking sharp, Ben. Looking sharp."

Ben spun to the ladies as he continued on his way. "Don't go causing me any trouble, Bernice. I'm a married man, and you're too young for me, anyhow." She was not. She was twenty-five years his senior, and she loved his attention.

When Ben turned the corner onto Congress Street, his mint-condition 1937 Cadillac Series 70 came into view. It was easily the newest and nicest car on the road, no question. A man in his midfifties and built like a tank leaned on the driver's side door with his head buried deep in a newspaper. His impossibly square jaw, shaded with razor burn, was the dominant feature on his face, and it gave him a look of rugged danger that he used to his advantage. These days it was hard to remember a time when Hank Malveaux wasn't Ben's right-hand man, but their kinship had begun because of an undeniable resemblance in physicality and demeanor to how Ben remembered his father, Charles Carter. And the more Ben got to know the man, the more he saw one of the few truly decent men the world had to offer, one who just never got a break. Ben was that break for Hank. Did Ben absolutely need a chauffeur? No. A bodyguard? An errand boy? No. These things were nice, but the reason Ben kept him on the payroll was sentimental. The man who reminded him of his father deserved a break.

"Good morning, Hank. How's it coming?" Ben stuck out his hand, fingers wide.

Hank stood to attention, folded the paper under his arm, and greeted his boss with a handshake and an understated but genuine grin. "Slow but steady, you know. I still need the pictures more than the words," he said as he opened the back door of the Series 70.

"You just keep at it. You'll get it. I promise."

"Yes, sir." Hank tipped his head as Ben lowered himself into the car. "I put the stock pages on the seat for ya." Once the door was shut, Hank climbed the running board into the driver's seat, and soon they were turning north, back onto Hastings Street.

"How's your mama doing, Hank?"

"She always says she's doing fine, but I worry about her. Got another rent hike, so we might be moving her again."

"You let me know if I can help."

"Oh, I can't ask anything more than you already do, boss. We'll make it through. We always do."

From high above Ben's Series 70, it was indistinguishable from every other car. From high enough, all things seemed equal. The birds had the perfect view. With Black Bottom directly below, it was just another neighborhood in America's fourth-largest city, the only American metropolis with Canada to the south. The skyscrapers in downtown Detroit climbed high, just to the west, and the sun glistened off the Detroit River as it flowed between the two nations. It wasn't until people were close enough to fuss over the tiniest of details that any trouble really began.

Five blocks up, the Series 70 turned left onto Clinton Street, where a line of five annoyed Black men spilled onto the sidewalk out from under a canvas awning painted with red block letters: CARTER DRY CLEANING. When the car pulled to the curb, Ben hopped out in a hurry. Hank jumped out too, but Ben settled him back with a gentle wave and a reassuring nod. The men waiting on the sidewalk posed no threat, and Hank eased back into the car.

One of the men in line called out as Ben passed by. "I know that girl's working it, but that don't get me my duds in time for the matinee."

Ben shook the man's hand not unlike a politician and replied, "I'll have a look and see if we can't get you on your way. We want you to look good!" Then a string of bells chimed as Ben opened the door and disappeared inside.

The customer immediately turned to another man in line and pointed out what they were both thinking. "White boy gonna go have a look and see if he can't get me on my way." Then they laughed heartily at the man's exaggerated impression of Ben's college-educated, "white" way of speaking.

The customers inside moved out of Ben's way as he stepped up to the counter. He craned his neck to catch wisps of a figure in the back, running to and fro, racing to catch up with what, by the looks of it, was an already stressful day.

"I'll be with you in a minute, but just to let you know, we're running a little behind," called the wisping figure in the back.

"I was under the impression that having my name on the sign out front came with customer service privileges," Ben hollered back.

Sharon's head popped out from around the corner to find Ben's smiling face. "Hey, Uncle Ben. One minute." Then she disappeared for half a second before returning with a clean suit. Twenty-four years old, Sharon was Jasper's oldest child. Not just that, she was the oldest of the five cousins in her generation of the Carter brood, and even on days without a line out the door, customers knew Sharon was made of equal parts business, attitude, and gumption.

Ben inspected his suit, and he was not displeased in the slightest.

The next customer in line couldn't help speaking up. "I guess you gotta know somebody."

Sharon spun on the man like a snapped whip. Tilted head and hand on her hip, she said, "Don't you start nothing. When you buy your own dry cleaner's, you can cut the line too!"

The customer nodded his head and pursed his lips, impressed by her commanding sass. "Careful, Ben. Turn your back for half a shake and the sign out front'll say 'Sharon's Dry Cleaning.'"

Sharon was already in the back, hard at work again like a little hurricane.

Ben hung his suit on a nearby wall hook, raised the hinged countertop, and joined Sharon in the back. In the commercial portion of the little shop was a series of three washing drums and two dry tumblers—all noisily spinning with large rubber belts, solvent pipes with pressure dials and valves, loaded clothing racks, and hinged arms that swung overhead, bringing steam down rubber hoses to irons at two pressing stations. Since she was running everything on her own, it was hard to believe Sharon wasn't more behind than she was. In the farthest corner, under a table for folding clothes, Ben rolled aside an overloaded supply cart of spray bottles, brushes, and hemming tools to reveal a small floor safe. Sharon watched him from her station behind an industrial ironing board.

"You ain't gonna be happy, Uncle Ben. Just because we got a line outside don't mean business been good. A certain someone, I ain't naming who, is a little soft if you ask me. Says I gotta clean some people's rags for free."

Ben finished thumbing a small stack of cash from inside the safe before he tossed his response over his shoulder. "Call me soft if you want, but a man has a better chance of finding a job if he looks the part. Help a man find a job and he'll be back to pay the tab. You'll see." Ben pocketed the money, closed the safe, and pushed the cart back into place, intentionally ignoring the rolling of Sharon's eyes that he knew was on full display behind his back.

"You gonna stay and help?"

"I have too much to do before I meet your daddy this evening. Where's your mama?"

"She ain't feeling well."

"She was sure feeling well last night."

In already familiar Sharon fashion, she tilted her head and threw out that hip of hers. "Feeling it last night is exactly why she ain't feeling well this morning!" Sharon went right back to her work, angrily pushing and dragging a hunk of steel connected to an electrical cord over a pin-striped pair of slacks.

Momentarily motionless, Ben stared at his niece across the room. He understood her complicated anger at her mother, Valerie. He'd felt it too over the years, but there was also no denying where Sharon got her electrifying vim and vigor. Sharon was a living reminder of the brilliance of the Valerie of yore. He knew that must be hard on Sharon, but under the pressure of their current workload, Ben couldn't help wondering if a tinge of anger was the right ingredient to add some needed speed to her work.

"You know, Uncle Ben, I'm basically running this place myself. Don't take advantage of me just because I'm a Black woman."

Ben's dumbfounded stare cracked into his contagious smile. "Baby, I take advantage of you because you're my niece. Being Black or a woman doesn't have anything to do with it."

"Uh-huh."

"The fight for better working conditions within this family is a long way off, but you keep fighting the good fight." With that, he and his smile were gone, and Sharon continued to press the pants, possibly for someone who couldn't pay.

The door's bells announced to the customers waiting outside that Ben had jumped them in line to get his freshly cleaned suit, and he was met with a choir of teeth smacking. Fortunately, he didn't have the privilege of paying any attention to them because he was quickly met with an ominous look from Hank, who was waiting with a raised hand of caution to personally escort him back to their vehicle. Ben was unable to put his finger on anything amiss, but he knew better then to ignore Hank's suspicions.

Just as they got to the back of their car, Ben caught his body-guard's menacing glare toward a parked 1933 Model 40 Victoria, custom green, with its grill practically on top of their bumper. As Hank opened Ben's door, both doors of the Victoria opened, and three men climbed out, on a mission. Hank grabbed the back of Ben's arm to physically lower him into the car, but he resisted. Without looking Hank in the eye, Ben gently touched his hand to let him know the men were allowed to approach. Even still, Hank stood over Ben's shoulder, making sure his presence was felt by their unexpected guests.

All three men were dressed in their finest zoot suits and broadest smiles. Too friendly. Something was up.

"Slip me some skin, Ben! *Ooo-wee!* You looking togged to the bricks!"

Ben wasn't impressed that Leon Bates, about his same age, was pretending he'd never seen nice clothes before. "I need to look good on payday," Ben said.

The second man, Shelton Tappes, a dozen years younger at least, traced his fingers over the sleek curve of the Series 70's front fender. "That's one hot Caddy. '36?"

"'37," Ben corrected him with a straight face.

"She pretty, Mr. Carter, but you know Ford pays Black folk more than GM."

Polite yet stern, Hank removed Tappes's fingers from the vehicle. Then, keeping his eyes on the men, he pulled out a hanky and buffed the spot that had been touched.

"Leon, you wanna tell me who this Abercrombie is and why he thought it was a good idea to touch my tin can?" Ben knew Leon, and the most important thing to know about this man was that Jasper Carter didn't approve.

Leon had helped organize Negro involvement in the sit-down

strike at the General Motors plant in Flint, which Jasper had described as "doing the peckerwoods' heavy lifting and getting none of the credit." When Ben argued that the six-week work stoppage had led to a 5 percent pay raise, Jasper responded with oozing sarcasm, "And they got permission to speak to one another on their lunch breaks. Oooh boy, we movin' up in the world now, ain't we?" Ben didn't have a response. Talking on lunch breaks was an actual "victory" that came from months of planning, death threats, and the personal intervention of the governor of Michigan. Progress that slow made it easy to question the value of the whole movement.

Leon was in politician mode. "Don't mind the kid none. How's Margaret doing? You best watch that one. She a dish."

"Stop selling me now and say what's your story."

"All right, Ben. All right. To the point. A businessman. See? That's why we came to talk. This here is my associate, John Conyers." Leon motioned to the third man, and Ben shook his hand. "And the 'Abercrombie' here, who meant no disrespect to the Caddy, is Shelton Tappes, one of the newest and most energetic members of . . ."

Ben cut him off. "The UAW."

"Yes, sir, the UAW." Leon tried his best not to become deflated by the disdain in Ben's voice.

After a quick look over each of the men, even the young Tappes, Ben asked, "Don't you think Black Bottom has enough people looking for work? Besides, I got three words for you: 'Memorial Day Massacre.'"

"It ain't like that," said Leon.

"What ain't it like? Chi-Town cops shot and killed ten union protestors, and they clubbed a bunch more into the hospital. And they were white. You know who else was white? Those boys handing out leaflets at the Rouge plant who got their asses beat on the overpass. You think Black men gonna get it better or worse?"

"In Flint . . ." Tappes interjected.

"You think you learned something in Flint? Well, so did the opposition. You got lucky in Flint."

"Ain't no one said anything about a strike," Leon said.

"Not now, fellas, I just ain't got time." Ben started to lower himself into the back seat, and Leon touched his shoulder to stop him. This mistake was met with the lightning-fast, ironclad grip of Hank's fingers wrapped around Leon's wrist.

Leon threw his other hand up in surrender. "Okay, okay, okay. We all friends here." But even though he was still at Hank's mercy, Leon demanded this moment to level with Ben. "It ain't fair what Ford doing, Ben. You know it."

Ben nodded at Hank to let the poor man go. "No, I do not know it. Know why I don't know? Because your associate here just said he's paying 'Black folk' more than GM. Sounds good to me, so what is it exactly you're looking for?" Sarcasm was a trait the Carter family had perfected.

"We looking for your support." There it was. Leon laid it all out on the table.

After a brief moment to let it sink in, John Conyers finally spoke up. "You're connected, Ben. You and Jasper know a lot of important people."

"Knowing people is one of the reasons my family is still in business. It's hard times! Hard on everybody."

"Harder on us, Ben. Ain't no denying what Ford done for our people, but that's not license to take advantage." Conyers made a good point.

"I think Reverend Bradby might argue that point, and so would my brother."

Conyers quickly made it apparent that he wasn't afraid of a fight. "Bradby is in Ford's pocket. Hell, so is every other damn preacher in town. I hope your brother Jasper is smart enough to understand that!"

The men huffed at one another in the silence that followed. The customers in line outside the dry cleaner's were all watching. The things said here could get around, and everyone knew it.

Ben was upset with himself for even mentioning his brother at all. One thing he was sure of was that if these daring union men had felt they could go directly to Jasper, they would have bypassed Ben altogether. Were these men crazy? Was it even possible to get a foothold in the Black community if you opposed the church, specifically Second Baptist? After all, the preachers were only doing what they thought they needed to in order to survive.

Henry Ford worked with Detroit's preachers like they were his Black employment agency, and he made no qualms about including "anti–labor union" as a necessary job qualification. This gave Black preachers the ability to hand out jobs to parishioners, and when word got around that all you had to do was attend Sunday services in a particular congregation to get a job, the pews filled up. Wasn't this a win-win situation? The inhabitants of Black Bottom had an avenue to good-paying jobs, the tithing baskets got heavier, and the unrelated side effect was that people heard the Word of Jesus. Lordy, have mercy, hallelujah! Was it wrong if Henry Ford was buying political goodwill? Was it wrong for a preacher's wife to want a new Sunday hat? So what if Ford had an army of workers too loyal to realize they were standing against their own rights to safe and proper working conditions? Weren't union men all communists anyway?

Jasper didn't believe in the salvation of mankind through any savior's blood but his own, and Ford's relationship with Black Christians was fine with him. Ben didn't want to admit it, but he was on the fence. Maybe that's why these union chaps were trying to butter him up. Maybe they could smell his weakness.

That's when Shelton Tappes showed Ben why these older men let him tag along. "We gotta learn to see past the ends of our noses, Ben. We gotta stop looking for what helps us right now and pay more attention to the community as a whole."

This kid was a leader, Ben could see it, but there was nothing more to say. "If you'll excuse me."

"We don't owe Henry Ford a damn thing," Conyers said loud enough for the onlookers outside Carter Dry Cleaning.

Ben climbed into the car, and Hank closed the door. Without taking his eyes off them, Hank rounded the car, climbed the running board, and closed himself behind the steering wheel. The three men were searching one another's eyes for their next move when the engine cranked and purred to life, but the car did not pull away.

Ben's window rolled down. "Ford employs more Blacks, with better pay, than any man, white or Black, in the whole damn country."

Leon answered with an equal amount of calm authority. "But he pays us less than whites. Works us longer. In less skilled and more dangerous jobs. We don't want to strike, Ben. That's a last resort. That's why we want your help."

Ben simply looked up at the men. Then Conyers played their last card. "We know you and Jasper have ties to Governor Murphy."

Stern-faced, Ben stared into Conyers' eyes as he pondered their proposition. "Have a good day, gentlemen."

The window rolled up, and John Conyers, Leon Bates, and Shelton Tappes were left speechless as they watched the car pull away from the curb and continue east down Clinton Street.

CHAPTER THREE

By 9:00 a.m. Rose Winston had been up for hours. Her husband, Thomas, had been due to see his first patient at Henry Ford Hospital at 8:00 a.m. sharp. Though she always woke up an hour earlier than Thomas to do her hair and makeup before he opened his eyes, today was special. Today she went above and beyond her already meticulous routine. Every hair on her head, every crease in her outfit, had been placed with exacting precision and double-checked with a prayer that she'd make a good impression on her first day of work. A job. At noon that day, Rose Winston would join the workforce.

Currently, however, she was sitting on the floral-print sofa in her immaculate living room, knees together, hands folded on the lap of her dress, a wide, formfitting belt across her stomach assisting her perfect posture, a wide white collar fanned over her navy blue blouse, a single button undone at the neck, accentuated by a string of pearls, not too ostentatious, her inky dark curls pinned on top and framing her face on both sides, and this morning, rather than her regular Merlot shade of lipstick, she wore Tango Red, which made a statement, not whorish but bold. She had sat there, lost in a continuous run-on string of thoughts since the second her husband had walked out the door at 7:32. It was at that moment that she became paralyzed by the excitement of her own daring behavior that had brought her to this point in time. She had stood up for herself, which made her proud, and she felt her head balancing higher on the tip of her spine. There was also a thrill in simply not knowing what to expect. Every day of the last eight years, her life had felt repetitive, leading nowhere. Now there was at least something different to look forward to. Even if she ended up hating the job, the office, the people, the commute, she would no longer be faced with Thomas's weekly inquisition about how she spent her previous allowance.

It felt like freedom.

Work felt like freedom.

In many ways, her life with Thomas would make the job of photographers for *Better Homes and Gardens* magazine too easy. Not only did Thomas come from money but now he was a surgeon and earning his own income. From the very start, they had nothing to worry about financially, so the $275 a week Thomas brought home from the hospital was simply extra. Extra in a time and place when most people were forced to make do with less than even the most basic of necessities. How dare Rose complain about a lack of contentment. Medical school at Pritzker was paid off; their four-bedroom, two-bathroom home on Birchcrest Drive, in the upper-class neighborhood of the University District, was a gift from Rose's in-laws, and when Thomas bought her a custom two-seater Detroit Electric from the Anderson Electric Car Company, they became the only two-car family on the block. Thus, Thomas had been confused when Rose said she wanted to join the tens of thousands of American women who had joined the workforce since the economic collapse.

She approached him with a well-thought-out argument that she had little faith in but one she hoped would swing the needle of

Thomas's permission in her favor. Having secretarial experience before Thomas opened his own practice, she argued, could save them a bundle because she would be able to run his office. She had been able to tell from the glaze in his eyes that he wasn't yet convinced, so she smacked him with a quote from First Lady Eleanor Roosevelt, who she'd heard speak back in September of '35 at the ribbon-cutting ceremony for the Brewster Homes: "The battle for the individual rights of women is one of long standing, and none of us should countenance anything which undermines it." In truth, Rose didn't know exactly what the quote meant, but Thomas blinked, and the glazing was washed away. Rather than disagreeing or needing to understand her logic, Thomas simply allowed his wife to do as she pleased. It was that conversation which had spurred his decision to place the order for a Detroit Electric. The dainty electric cars only went fifty miles on a charge, which was more than adequate for Rose's commute downtown, but the selling point for him seemed to have been that "electric vehicles were more suitable to women"—whatever that meant.

In a momentary out-of-body experience, Rose caught herself smiling. She was still sitting alone in her picture-perfect house, staring into space with a grin. She felt silly and worked to turn the corners of her mouth back into a straight line. As in life, sometimes the smallest action creates the biggest change, and the act of repressing her smile allowed her heart to fill with fear and doubt. She was unable to pull the brakes on her melting expression, and her lips plowed right through straight-faced and into a concerned frown.

Rose and Thomas met in '29, and it's possible the only reason Thomas's father, Bernard, had agreed to the match was because the world was falling apart. No one knew what 1930 had in store or if there would be a 1930 at all. There had been countrywide mass confusion, and it was through the nation's downfall that Rose found herself set for life. It no longer mattered to the Winstons that she came from the humblest of beginnings, because all people had recently become humbled. Both law and medicine ran in the Winston line, and for some reason, the stock market had always made them nervous, preferring an earned dime over a gambled dollar. This meant they had not been hurt nearly as much as most others. They took a hit because society had less money to spend, but doctors and lawyers were needed no matter the country's financial forecast.

The crash manifested itself by forcing Bernard Winston to sell his vacation home in New Baltimore, on the north shore of Lake St. Clair. Edith, Bernard's doting wife, had to cancel plans to visit her father in London in the summer of 1930. She could have gone in 1931 but not in the comfort she desired, so 1932 it was. For Thomas and Rose specifically, it meant social dinners out turned into house parties at their place.

Neda, their domestic help, was a woman in her sixties, Black of course, who came for a few hours a day, three times a week, to keep the house, but when the calendar was marked with an evening soiree, Neda was in their home before Rose had finished putting herself together, before Thomas even woke up. These were deep-clean days of rug beating, dusting, porcelain scrubbing, silver polishing, drape and linen care, and when that was through, Neda cleaned herself at a spigot behind a small partition in the backyard. She wasn't permitted to groom herself in the Winston powder room. It wasn't that Thomas was opposed to Neda using their facilities; it was his paranoid concern for the watchful eyes of others and an aggressive rumor mill that led to this house rule. When the house was clean—and so was Neda— that's when the cooking began. Cucumber-and-watercress finger sandwiches, shrimp cocktail, and fresh fruit were to be served before deviled eggs, which led to the main course of veal loaf and sautéed vegetables, or beef stroganoff, or fresh white fish cooked any number of ways with coleslaw. Thomas's favorite part of these gatherings was the gelatin. Neda had the skill to make a peach cobbler that could have ended the growing conflict in Europe, but that wouldn't have allowed Thomas to show off his new refrigerator with the added icebox compartment option. It's true that anything in a gelatin mold was all the rave, but while Thomas gloated over the appliance that had congealed the jiggling desert, Rose's mouth watered for Neda's cobbler.

When guests arrived, three to four couples at most, including themselves, there were a few minutes of polite greetings, and then, without fail, one party became two—men and women. Men would smoke and sip newly legal whiskey in the back garden while the ladies sat in the living room trading gossip and recipes, neither of which Rose had any need for. She stayed quiet, which gave other women confidence that they could trust her. And the truth is, they could, because she wasn't listening to half the things they said. How could she when her mind was drifting off through the window, daydreaming of sipping something smooth and neat, partaking in conversations that mattered, about politics, social climbing, world events like the Hindenburg catastrophe (who thought traveling in giant balloons of flammable gas was ever a good idea?) and debating where on earth Amelia Earhart had vanished to (Rose's guess was a crash landing in the vast Pacific). Every so often Rose focused back in on the women to catch something trivial, like Angela Jankowski's claim that she'd seen Sam Nelson brush against Wilma Thompson's derriere while his wife wasn't looking, and she was absolutely positive he'd done it on purpose. The women giggled, half wishing they'd been in Wilma's place, the others hoping for the entertainment of watching someone else's marriage fall apart because their own were so ungodly boring. Rose faked her interest with an appropriate "ooh" and then dazed off again. This time to Neda, hard at work with the last of the dinner preparations.

Rose admired Neda, this strong woman who was out in the world earning a living despite nature's assignments of femininity and color. She felt she had more in common with Neda than she did with anyone in her daily life: her own husband, the men he laughed with as they reentered the house for hors d'oeuvres, or the women she sat with who incessantly claimed the moniker of modern women but only dared to say so behind their husbands' backs. Sometimes Rose wondered how it was possible these women didn't understand that she saw right through them, saw through them all. Neda, though? Rose knew that Neda understood her. The two women never spoke of anything more than Neda's duties or passing pleasantries, but Rose felt it. She felt that Neda understood her plight, her prison, her inability to make her true feelings known to those around her. These two women, Rose and Neda, were more similar than their light versus dark skin allowed them to admit.

Over dinner both sexes would turn to conversations neither really wanted to discuss but that each assumed appropriate. Safe. Ultimately, it was a train that always ended up in the same station.

"This house is too big for only two! Why, it's just begging for a little Winston bundle!" Angela Jankowski's broad smile was about to be stolen by her husband, Bradford.

"Darling, I'm sorry I didn't warn you before. Tom and Rose are not . . . They're not . . ."

"It's fine. Please, no worry. So far the good Lord hasn't seen fit to bless my beautiful wife and I, not in that way, anyhow." Thomas did his best not to let his wife be the brunt of embarrassment and gave Rose a sad but caring glance just before Bradford raised his glass to break the tension.

"This is why the good Lord made trying so much fun!"

Chuckles of faux shock splashed onto the group's faces as they all raised their glasses and clinked. Angela's jaw had dropped open, elated by another tidbit to add to the story she'd tell in the women's corner at someone else's home in the near future, and she playfully slapped at Rose's leg under the table as if to say, *You minx, you!*

Rose glanced up to the clock on the wall. Small hand past eleven, big hand on five—it was nearly time to leave for downtown to start her life away from home as the front office secretary at a prestigious firm where a Winston family friend was partner. Her buzzing excitement had slowed her perception while time itself sped forward. She'd sat in her spot on the sofa for nearly four hours with hardly a turn of the head. She needed to leave the house in ten minutes, but that was the torturous thing about time—the movement of the big hand from the five to the seven would take nearly a week, or so she felt. And in that week, she had only two thoughts. The first imagined Thomas's reaction if he ever learned the truth of her life before they'd met. Naturally, this thought led to the second, wondering if Thomas would kill her if he discovered the true reason she could never, and would never, bear him a child.

CHAPTER FOUR

Hank reached into the driver's door of the Caddy to snatch up his educational copy of the *Detroit Free Press*. He tucked it under his arm for a brief second as he closed the door and surveyed the land. Parked across the street from St. Joseph's, next to Rubenstein's cobbler shop and under an unlit neon sign that read CHECKS CASHED, the corner of Gratiot and Orleans didn't look all that different from any other intersection in Black Bottom, but Hank had the car parked on the north side of the street, and that made all the difference in his level of caution.

It wasn't long ago that the Burnstein brothers and their Purple Gang had terrorized Detroit. Rum running, gambling, whoring, and anything in the middle to make a nickel note, and if you got in their way, you got erased. Back in '30 a Black Bottom kid named Arthur was executed up on Hastings and Hendrie Street for letting his ball roll within sight of some Purple heavies in the act of cutting Canadian hooch.

The passing of the Twenty-First Amendment to the United States Constitution, which reversed the Eighteenth and allowed alcohol to flow freely once again, had disturbed a delicate balance in the underworld. Legal booze meant the Purple Gang no longer had a strangle-hold on the supply, and after a series of internal disputes, Detroit's most dangerous gang cannibalized itself and became a shadow of its once foreboding glory. Hank, however, could not shake the stagnant air that currently filled his nose and spilled into his lungs like spoiled milk into fresh black coffee, reminding him that Ben was currently sit-ting inside the building before him, face-to-face with Izzy Gaczynski.

Izzy was a New Yorker through and through, but in 1921, when he heard that Jews were entirely in charge of a major metropolitan un-derground operation, he packed his bags and only looked back to de-fiantly aim his middle finger at the shrinking skyline, then dominated by Downtown's Woolworth Building and now dwarfed by Midtown's Empire State. Yes, things had been relatively quiet since the collapse of his gang, but Izzy's blood still ran Purple, and Hank knew it.

Hank finished his cautious, distrusting survey over the comings and goings of Gratiot Avenue. No do-nothings and nothing doing, so he dropped his attention to the reading lesson awaiting him in the paper. "Detroit Free Press," he sounded out. "Juhn . . . Juhn 11, 1937."

Numbers weren't Hank's problem—letters were—but he was loaded with common sense and a natural gift for reasoning. In this in-stance, the numbers helped with the letters. It was the date, and what better word to be in the current date—"June." A proud grin eased its way onto Hank's face. "June." Ben said he'd get it if he kept after it, and sometimes Hank even believed him.

The dingy back office, somewhere in the belly of the building adorned with the CHECKS CASHED sign, had walls first coated in paint, then nicotine, then wallpaper, then nicotine, then more paint. The bulbous plumes of smoke rising in equally timed orbs from Izzy's Bolivar Coronas Grandes cigar were dutifully working to add the next layer of tinged yellow to the walls. Today's paper, June 11, sat folded open to the stock charts on the very edge of a pile of clutter that took up the vast majority of the room's center, undoubtedly held up by a desk hiding in embarrassment somewhere beneath.

Ben stood just inside the open door. His posture was already better than most, but in here he was at least an inch taller. He stared directly into the face of the slovenly plump dinosaur of a man, the two of them trapped in a game neither would back down from. Would Ben shrink his presence to one of subjugation before Izzy recognized his existence with even the smallest glance in his direction? Knowing a tie in this ridiculous standoff would go to the white man, Ben broke first with a nod to the New York Stock Exchange.

"You're not afraid of another crash?"

"Da only two groups dat lost were da ones who made moronic investments and da ones dat sold. One man's loss is another's gain." Izzy still didn't look up from his paper.

"Some folks lost quite a bit without owning a single share of anything at all."

Izzy leaned back, the wooden chair creaking with stress, and glared up at Ben's face through the wafts of smoke trailing from the Cuban he held close to his cheek. He rolled the cigar slightly back and forth in his fingers, perhaps a tell that he was thinking.

Ben waited just long enough to know that it was still his move, then placed an envelope labeled "Geraldine's" on top of the printed tables of stock prices.

Izzy was a tough thug in his sixties. He'd seen enough in his day that nothing made him jump anymore. Nothing shocked him. Nothing made him move faster than his desired snaillike pace. With a casual lick of the end of his cigar, he said, "Let me know when you have da last ten percent." Then Izzy sucked in another bellyful of smoke, making the lit end glow like a firebrand. His tactic had changed. Now he refused to break the magnetic lock between their two sets of milk chocolate–colored eyes.

Ben's brow furled with his brain's momentary inability to do simple math, and Izzy played his hand. "Don't act confused, genius. When your final payment's a week late, it's no longer your final payment."

"Noted."

In Ben's mind there was almost nothing lower than someone who used another's disadvantage to get ahead. He believed there was a stark difference between using one's own advantage, earned or not, and using someone else's disadvantage to fill one's pockets. The latter was Izzy. He lured colored men and women in with promises of loans, which were no doubt needed, but charged his dark-complexioned customers twice the interest rate. Jasper was somehow on Izzy's side here, arguing that it was "good business" because it was riskier to lend to people who earned less, with less job security, and if the odds of Izzy never getting his investment back at all were higher, then the interest rate needed to reflect that risk. Ben found it infuriatingly difficult to explain something that to him felt so naturally logical. The inability to get cheaper loans helped power the cycle that kept them down, kept Jasper and Ben down, kept the whole Carter family down, kept down all of Black Bottom, all of the South Side of Chicago, all of Harlem, all men and women whose heritage could only be traced back as far as the men who bought their grandfathers. How many more homes could be built, businesses started, debts paid, and families rescued if a man in Black Bottom could borrow money at the same rate as one from Palmer Woods or Grosse Pointe? As backward as it sounds, it might have been easier for Ben to convince Izzy than Jasper. Jasper had a habit of turning off his ears when his own lived experience didn't match up to an idea someone was attempting to enlighten him with. Izzy may actually have agreed with this argument but would still say say it wasn't him that made the rules and there was nothing one man could do to stop it. Ben didn't know which was worse: refusing to hear another person's point of view or understanding and not giving a rat's ass.

The irony was that Ben had already come to terms with the slow tick-tick-tick of progress, and he was ultimately grateful for the loans Izzy supplied to his family. Without Izzy's high interest rates, there would be no flow at all. Ben accepted this . . . for now.

"You need more help dis month?" Izzy asked.

"Even if we did, it sounds like we can't afford you." Ben could smell a gut punch coming.

"See how easy it is to talk like a big shot when you don't need no help? Good for you."

Ben needed to scram. He knew something was on the horizon and didn't want to stick around to deal with it. "Well, I should probably get . . ."

"When you plan to cover Jasper's loss?"

Fuck. There it was. "His loss?"

"He put down a half-a-yard IOU, and none of his numbers came up."

"Half a yard?"

"A frog. General Grant."

Ben ground his teeth to stop his tongue.

This was what put fish flies up Ben's ass. After charging two times the interest plus late fees, Izzy would look those same Black customers in the eyes and ask if they wanted to play the numbers. Ben didn't know if God made man this way to test his will or if man broke the machine once he was in control, but it seemed one thing Black and white folks had in common was that if you offer a desperate man a chance to win a jackpot that could answer all his prayers, solve all this year's problems, this week's woes, even just the shit he stepped in this morning, he will take that chance even when the odds are stacked against him. Even when losing would wrench him further down. Even when the white savior offering this "chance of a lifetime" is the devil himself. In Ben's experience, a human being will for some damned reason always take that shot.

Ben's jaw was clenched so tight, he thought his mouth might never fully open again. "I'll send it by with Hank" were the words pushed through his teeth.

"Don't be mad at me, chump. It was your brother Lance who took Jasper's bet."

With eyes of fire: "Half brother." Sensing a point of no return, Ben forced his eyes to the ground. "If you'll excuse me, I'm running late."

Ben turned and pushed the door open to make his getaway, and Izzy dove back behind his newspaper before firing his final shot. "Yes, massa. Don't wanna keep Massa Jasper waitin' none."

Izzy saw the briefest pause in Ben's movement, and he was proud that his words still had the power to disrupt the internal wiring of the Negroes. He could even fluster Ben, who he considered "one a da good ones." But this was a part of the game Ben was sure he could win. Izzy underestimated the pain and strife Ben had already lived through. In comparison, ignoring a white man's racist quip was nothing. Both men knew that colored people had to do more with less, play smarter since they weren't given the whole deck, but what Ben understood to a finer point was just how much tougher the stacked deck made him. Without another word, Ben stepped out of Izzy's grotesque little office.

Hank was so engrossed in sounding out words in the paper, he didn't hear Ben charging up until the last hasty step.

"Next stop, Hank."

"All right, all right." Hank folded the paper and climbed behind the wheel, and in no time at all, they were shooting down past Trinity Lutheran and turning south on Saint Antoine.

Hank parked with the municipal building to the right and St. Mary's Hospital looming above on the left. Ben hopped out of the car and jogged across Clinton, slowing his pace when a couple white women nearly went catatonic at the sight of a Black man moving that quickly in their direction.

"Pardon me, ladies. I'm just passing through," Ben said with a tip of his hat and a pasted-on smile.

They whispered their concerns to each other as they scurried, click-clacking across Saint Antoine in their two-inch T-straps, toward St. Mary's entrance. When they stole a glance back at Ben, he was caught doing the same back to them. Both sides of the exchange were wild animals keeping track of a potential predator's location.

Ben stopped in front of a two-story building whose first-floor windows had been painted over with white letters and yellow shading that read CARTER FAMILY PRINTING. He looked over his shoulder again as the trailing floral-print, calf-length dresses of the scared white women climbed the sixteen stone-gray stairs of the entrance to the hospital and disappeared inside. Two thoughts hit Ben at nearly the exact same time. First, St. Mary's Hospital was here before Black people. When it opened in 1850, the skin in this area was as white as a fresh January snowfall, but times had changed. Was there any sense in a hospital refusing Black patients in Detroit's Blackest neighborhood? From a white person's perspective, so Ben assumed, it didn't seem like they wanted to come to Black Bottom anyhow. And from the Negro perspective, no assumptions needed, if you were sick or hurt and in need of care, as long as you bled red, shouldn't you go to the closest available help? Black Bottom had some fine and talented doctors, but they were making house calls for most ailments and, for more serious matters, working out of converted homes they called "hospitals." One could only imagine how much that talent would have been amplified by a facility like St. Mary's. No, instead whites came to a place they didn't want to be, and Negroes couldn't use the facilities right next door.

Ben shook his head at the lack of common sense, which brought him to his second thought. Was it really the best idea to put the entrance of a hospital up sixteen concrete steps? How was that convenient for the sick, injured, and infirm?

Inside Carter Family Printing, an old Blue Streak Model 8 Linotype stood next to a casting box and a brass-arm Gordon press, along with all the typesetting, alloy, and inking support equipment. The machines took up the whole back wall of the large room beyond the service counter. Stephen, Ben's sleepy fifteen-year-old nephew who had woken up at his place that morning, was moving an entire wall's worth of cardboard boxes, obviously heavy from the way his skinny frame leaned back to support them. One by one, he stacked them behind the counter, where his brother, Mark, already had grease or ink or both on all his fingers and smeared up his bare forearms from attempting to repair some small piece deep within the nucleus of gears, bolts, and pulleys that made up the Model 8. He could only "see" with the tips of his probing fingers, but Mark knew the machine forward and backward. He didn't necessarily have a mechanical nature about him, but when something broke down that often, you spent profits on hiring someone to fix it, or you got your fingers dirty—quite literally, in this case.

Mark's kid brother, Stephen, had what some called "confidence," which got him in more sticky situations than successful ones. Their older sister, Sharon, who managed both the dry cleaner's and the print shop, required a lot of attention, because she outright demanded it in the way she carried her whole being. This left eighteen-year-old Mark alone with his thoughts. He read everything he could get his inky fingerprints on and desperately wished people would talk, discuss, debate more about the issues he found the most interesting. Unfortunately, Mark was regularly told those were not polite topics for the average conversation. He knew better, though. He knew what people really meant was that talking about real issues could get people boiled up under the collar. These topics could cause division. Certain conversations could trench a chasm between people who otherwise cared for each other. Words had the power to hurt more than belts or baseball bats. That power, that magnetism, is what drew Mark further to the outside, further to the fringe. He wasn't an outcast, but he understood the outcasts.

Ben stepped inside, but this business lacked a bell above the door, and his nephews were too occupied to notice he was there to hear their wisecracking.

"You won't be givin' me shit when I got more dough than you," Mark tossed from under the press.

Stephen dropped the next box in its new stack and attacked his brother, both verbally and physically, all in the same graceful motion. "With all that dough I thought you'd be able to buy more than three damn hairs on your chinny chin chin."

It was no match really. Stephen punched his older brother's ticket every time they scuffled. Mark found himself dragged from under the Model 8, and lickety-split Stephen had him in a headlock, both squirming on the floor but Stephen in control.

"You've read 'The Three Little Pigs'?" Mark squeaked out, never giving up. "I thought that was a big-boy book."

One arm around Mark's neck, Stephen used his free hand to get ahold of a single hair from a thin patch on the peak of his undefined jaw. "Who's got more dough now?" Pluck!

"Get off 'a me, clown!"

"Clown? I'm no clown!" Stephen had to try harder this time, but he got another hair.

"You right. Clowns are funny, and you only funny-looking." Pluck! "Ow!"

"If I sell these face pubes, maybe then I'll have more dough than you." Stephen wouldn't let up and reached for another.

"Until you got more dough than me, you better do as I say and get to school!" Ben made his presence known.

The boys immediately climbed over each other into standing positions, Stephen with a smile he unsuccessfully attempted to hide, and Mark rubbing his chin, even though his pride hurt more than his face.

Stephen grabbed at stacks of printed flyers from the counter and began stuffing them into a canvas delivery bag. "If you telling me you don't want these orders delivered after school, I can just leave 'em here, Uncle Ben."

"Just get what you need and get on out of here." Ben rubbed the top of Stephen's head as the boy scurried by with his delivery bag.

Never knowing when to quit, Stephen stopped with the door open just a few inches. "Hey, Mark, make sure you sweep up real good when you're done, you hear?"

Mark made a threatening jump in his brother's direction, and Stephen yelped with a smile from ear to ear as he made his getaway.

Ben grabbed the closing door before it shut and called out, "Swing by and help your sister after your deliveries."

Stephen was already in the middle of Saint Antoine, nearly getting run over by a Hoover Wagon. "Does anybody else work in this family?" Stephen smacked his lips at two horses pulling an old Dodge Model 30. Ben couldn't tell which was older, the poor horses or the jalopy.

Back inside, Mark was already back at work under and inside the printing press. Ben made his way behind the counter and crouched down to the dial on the black iron box decoratively labeled in a golden scrawl "J. Baum Lock & Safe Co." A twist this way, then that way, then this way again, and Ben turned the lever and pulled. On top of some files and next to a Smith & Wesson hand ejector revolver was the Geraldine's envelope Ben was after, but he found far fewer bills inside than he would have liked. In the back of the safe there was a bowl of change. He picked it up and shook it around to decipher the ratio of silver to copper. Sure, pennies and dimes added up, but it was still short. He put it back down, then momentarily rested his open hand on the pistol. There was that common sense again. If this piece was needed to protect the store, what were the odds Mark or Stephen would be able to spin the dial fast and accurate enough for it to be of any use?

"This it?" Ben asked as he shut the iron door and spun the dial.

"I don't discriminate, Uncle Ben. I take any job that comes in," the boy said as he wiped his hands on his moleskin trousers and grabbed a sheet of tan paper from a small shelf under the counter. "I even wrote up a nice ad and posted it around."

Ben took the flyer from Mark, who simmered with a proud grin. "Looks good, Mark."

The flyer read "Carter Family Printing—Black Bottom's Black-Owned Printing Press," then listed prices and the reasons one might need something printed in the first place.

"What we need is some business from the *Chronicle*."

Ben looked up from admiring his nephew's diligent work to see if he was really suggesting what he was suggesting. The *Chronicle* was a pro-union, Democrat-leaning paper. Sure, it was Black-owned, but the Democrats equaled the South, and the South was everything the Carter brothers had ever tried to escape. He could see the twinkle in Mark's eye but knew the boy wouldn't take any major business without discussing it with Sharon first, and Sharon knew better. "I have to run. I'm meeting your daddy later, and I'm already behind."

Mark's proud simmer cooled, and he turned back to tinkering with the press, but Ben stopped him with a hand on the shoulder and stared at the boy's face until he had good eye contact.

"Copacetic?"

"Copacetic, Uncle Ben. Copacetic."

Ben smiled and got a half-hearted one in return. That would do for now. Nothing else needed to be said. Ben and Mark were like that together. They could somehow synchronize their thoughts with a small glance, leaving everyone else in the dark, including Mark's daddy, Jasper.

The door opened, and Ben was gone. It was time. Mark flipped the power switch next to the Linotype's keyboard, and the machine began to whir. Slightly skeptical of his work, Mark tapped the capital C key on the right-hand side. The machine jumped into action and found the mold for C in the magazine at the top and directed it to the assembly tray. This tray could hold ninety molds, but as this was just a test run, Mark pushed the lever to the right of the keyboard, and the letter C found its way over to the casting area, where the machine would melt an alloy over the mold. Mark hit the power button once again, stopping the machine and finally letting out his held breath. It worked.

Now it was time to get back to the waiting orders.

After Ben had left home that morning, it wasn't but five minutes before the water came back on. Margaret stayed upstairs getting herself "put together," as she would say. She walked a little heavier and made more noise than was necessary to let anyone still sleeping downstairs know she was awake. Any houseguests who stayed at the Carters' were well trained to be up and at 'em, if not already gone, by the time Margaret came down for work. If someone within the Carter ranks was still dragging ass when Margaret came down them stairs, there was no punishment, no screaming, not even a reprimand—no, it was much worse. You got silence and a look that pierced your soul and froze it solid while she put on her hat and stepped out the door. Jasper himself had once been the recipient of one of these looks . . . once. Lying in bed at night, Ben and Margaret would sometimes giggle about this magical authoritarian spell that their houseguests believed could be their demise. The pain and shame of disappointing a respected Black mother had evolved over the course of thousands of years, but Margaret was in a class all her own. Professor? Matriarch? Queen.

Now she was at the counter of the Carter Market, a small general store with fresh fruits and vegetables delivered daily and an assortment of items, from tobacco to Apex beauty products to hardware needed for everyday life in Black Bottom. She wore a blue cotton dress with white buttons from the hem to the neck, a high-waisted woven leather belt, and a shop apron. Her hair was smoothed back with a hint of shine and pulled into an effortless chignon, tied with a silk ribbon to match her dress.

There was no cash register, just a drawer with loosely organized bills and coins where Margaret dropped two quarters and passed Neda back a dime. "How's Keziah doing?"

"Sometimes I think she more trouble than she worth."

"Mm-hmm, I know that age. Sounds like my niece, Sharon. She'll grow out of it."

"Your lips to God's ears, child."

Margaret shook open a paper bag to load Neda's goods: a box of sugar and a can of applesauce. "Cooking up something sweet for the doctor and his wife?"

"Doing up some bread pudding. Don't tell nobody my secrets now." Neda tapped the top of the applesauce can before placing it in the bag. "Replace half the fat with applesauce and give her a splash more sugar."

"Oooh, okay. Your secret's safe with me." The women laughed their knowing goodbyes as Ben came in through the front door and, with a small wink and a nod to his wife, went straight for the back room.

Ben added the cash from the Carter Market safe to another Geraldine's envelope and closed the door, muttering under his breath, "Dammit."

Victor, Ben's youngest at nineteen, manned a wooden table, unpacking new merchandise. Everything about his presence was manufactured to keep attention off him. Dark trousers, tan suspenders over a light gray linen shirt, and a flat cap all added to his bored and dissatisfied demeanor.

"Take off that cap, son. In case you forgot, when you cross over the door's threshold, that's when the outside becomes the inside." Ben's admonishment was meant to be taken seriously but delivered with love.

Victor took off his cap and put it on a shelf under his workstation, then started pulling small yellow tin cans out of a shipping box.

"What do we got here?" Ben picked a can off the table. The label read "Madam C. J. Walker's Glossine and Pressing Oil."

"People be buying it up faster than we can get it in."

"That woman has been dead for probably twenty years, and she's still making money." Ben examined the can more carefully as Victor moved on to the next box of the same contents. "We still selling her hot combs?"

"Not so much lately."

A sly, guilty grin eased onto Ben's face. "Mrs. Denison still got hers, though, huh?"

This got him. This cracked Victor briefly out of his shy façade. "Come on now, Dad. She's a nice lady." He couldn't help but chuckle a little.

"Oh, I agree she's nice, but she had herself a full head of hair before we sold her that heater." Ben guffawed, and Victor let out another shy giggle. Ben was happy to see his son lighten up just a bit, but he leapt back into his shell as soon as Margaret came in from the front.

"What's so funny?" Margaret inquired with a grin.

"We were wondering, do you think maybe the manual was missing from the box when Mrs. Denison bought her hot comb heater?" Ben knowingly asked.

"Watch it now." She knew it was innocent teasing but wasn't sure where the line was. "She's a great woman. Puts you both to shame, that's for sure." Margaret made her way to her husband and put herself in his arms.

"I mean, you say you like the woman but apparently not enough to spend five minutes teaching her not to burn bald patches on her head."

Margaret socked Ben in the arm, but her wide, toothy smile made the punch worth it. "You watch it, Benjamin! I'm gonna be that old someday."

"And I'll love you enough to hide the heater." Ben got what he was after—another laugh from his son.

"You so bad." Margaret saw the joy peeking out from under Victor's eyes as he emptied boxes, and suddenly, making fun of a lovely older woman like Mrs. Denison was worth it. Margaret gave Ben a tiny, tender kiss, instantly making their son uncomfortable. "Victor, baby, go watch the front while I talk to your daddy a minute."

Not knowing whether his mother really needed to talk or if it was a euphemism for wanting some parental privacy, Victor groaned in embarrassment and quickstepped toward the door.

"Hey, I need you to go down and help Sharon after work today. She's a little backed up."

"Sure thing, Dad," he shot back, and then he was gone.

With not a moment wasted, Margaret put another kiss on her man's mouth.

"Good morning." He leaned his forehead against hers.

"Water came back on, just like you said." They shared loving smiles before she continued, "You seeing Jasper at Geraldine's later, right?"

"Yes, ma'am."

"You eating there, then? I don't need to save nothing for when you get home?"

"You don't have to save any food, but don't give anything else away." Ben grabbed her ass with both hands and squeezed tight.

Margaret feigned disgust, but she liked what she playfully pushed away. "You better get on now."

CHAPTER FIVE

Ben slid into the back of his Series 70, Hank took his position behind the wheel, and they merged into traffic. As they made the right-hand turn back onto Hastings, close to where their day started, Hank stole a glimpse of Ben gazing out the window with a happy ease on his face.

"You looking like your day got brighter, boss."

"It's easy to sit around tallying up all our scars, Hank, but we've got to remember our blessings too." His happy ease morphed into an unapologetic smile.

"If I may be so blunt, I don't think it's a coincidence that you all grinning like a schoolboy after seeing Ms. Margaret," Hank called Ben out and topped it off with his trademark laugh of two guttural beats: "He-haa."

"You're not wrong, friend. You're not wrong." Ben slowly faded into a daze, watching the sights go by. Hank felt an emotional connection to the moment as he watched Ben feel his feels in the rearview.

The traffic was made up of cars owned and driven by Black people. Black pedestrians went about their day, not worried about any unspoken societal standards but their own. A bakery that sold sweet potato pone and hot water corn bread without needing to explain to the customers what they were. Natty himself helped you at Natty's Hardware Store. Stanley Moore at Lucky's Drug Store snuck samples of the newest soda flavors to any kid in Black Bottom who knew the magic word: "Banana Bottom." It was the title of a book by Claude McKay. Stanley thought the book was fine, but what he really liked were the giggles of the boys and girls when they said the words together: "Banana Bottom." When white people said, "You're not welcome" or "You can't," the beautiful Black bodies on the Lower East Side did it themselves, and as Ben watched Black Bottom go by, he could feel the spirit and can-do attitude all around him. He was able to glimpse the bright future, as dark as it might sometimes seem.

As they crossed over Gratiot Avenue, officially entering Paradise Valley, everything got just a little more vibrant. Ben was caught off guard when a proud tear dropped from his face. He quickly swiped the streak from his cheek, hoping Hank hadn't caught it, but he had. In Paradise Valley the streets were cleaner, the buildings themselves were somehow more presentable, and the men and women were dressed nicer too. If you worked all day on the line up in Highland Park, came home greasy as a pig and more tired than a sloth, and your wife said, "Let's go out," you'd have to find out where to first. If you were grabbing a beer at the Stagger, then you'd just wash your hands and grab your girl, but if she said you were headed to the Plantation Club or the Brown Bomber Chicken Shack, then it was time to wake up and class it up, because a night was about to be had.

The bars and jazz clubs, some with neon signs that painted the streets orange and green and fiery red, were the star attractions, but you could find anything in Paradise Valley and even more when the sun went down. Drugs, gambling, and skin? Yes, but it was more than that. It was all the drama and ecstasy that made life irresistible and worthwhile. A man could get into enough trouble to lose his girl and find the resources to win her back all in the same evening, on the same intersection. A woman could fall in love three times before midnight and trip over lust in between each one.

And there it was. Geraldine's, the busy and glitzy tavern on the corner of Hastings and Division, the jewel in the crown of the Carter Empire. The brick façade was painted with GERALDINE'S–LET'S MAKE SOME HASTY DECISIONS AT HASTINGS AND DIVISION. Hanging above the sidewalk on the corner was a marquee with a neon green martini glass and a backlit letter board advertising MATINEE PERFORMANCE—HANK JONES and JOE LOUIS DRINK SPECIALS.

There was always a parking spot right out front for Jasper, but Ben knew he wasn't around yet. Hank sprung from the car with excitement and opened the back door as if presenting Ben to his world.

"You heard Hank Jones play? You know he a local boy, right?"

Ben slapped Hank's back. "You don't have to pretend you're more excited by Mr. Jones than two-for-one drinks."

Hank was caught, but it was all fun and games with these two. "I wasn't gonna say nothing, but I do get awful thirsty driving you around."

Ben slipped Hank a coin in a handshake.

"He-haa! Louis gonna be world champion! You wait!" Then Hank sauntered into the joint like he owned the place, and in some fashion, he did. When the Carters had your back, you owned the world.

Ben closed the Caddy door, then brushed his pant leg to get rid of a wrinkle before taking in his surroundings. There wasn't a line to get in, but there were enough people, more Black than white, milling about the club's entrance to make him happy. Jasper held animosity for what he called "white tourists" who felt like being in the same establishment as colored people was exotic and dangerous, but he tolerated them because their money was just as good at the bank. Ben hadn't outwardly argued with his brother on this issue because either way Geraldine's was making money, but he secretly felt the more whites, the merrier. He was so confident in the greatness of the jazz and blues musicians who filled the air of Paradise Valley that he knew any white folks in attendance would take stories back to their neighborhoods, proclaiming the triumphs of Black music and Black life. Was it Jasper's or Ben's responsibility to make white people understand their brilliance, their importance? Absolutely not, but the sooner white people came to their senses, the better off the world would be.

Ben pulled open the door and breathed in the dimly lit, smoky, jazz-filled atmosphere. At the back of the room, Hank already had a drink in hand as he shared a laugh with the bartender. Dragging his fingers across the felt top of the billiards table, Ben made his way through the room and under a doorway blocked by two spring-loaded saloon doors. On the other side sat thirty small tables big enough for two to eat or four to drink, and semicircle booths along the south and east walls. When the tables were pushed to the back in the evenings, there was room for two hundred finely dressed, perspiring bodies to dance till their feet hurt and then keep going. The room was less than half full, but 100 percent of the clientele had a glass in hand. In the northeast corner were a stage veiled in a haze of smoke, an upright Kimball piano, and eighteen-year-old Hank Jones tickling the ivory with enough verve to make the mediocre piano sound like both God and the devil had a hand in tuning the strings.

"Hey, Pops!" Charles Carter, named for Ben's father, swooped in to greet his dad.

Charles was a good-looking kid, twenty-two years old, with dark, mahogany-hued skin and the slightest finger waves across the front of his hairline. His suit was the sharpest one in the room, and his white shoes were close to glow-in-the-dark.

Filled with joy at the sound of his eldest son's voice, Ben grabbed the back of his neck and pulled him in to kiss the side of his head.

"Come on, Pops!" came Charles's half-serious protest. "How are people supposed to take me seriously in this joint if my daddy slobbering all over me?"

"You'll figure a way to live through it, son."

Charles pulled one of the family's standard Geraldine's envelopes from inside the crimson lining of his jacket. "Better than last week."

"That's not all that encouraging."

"We're getting there, Dad. Moving in the right direction."

"Two-for-one 'Joe Louis' specials can't be helping the bottom line."

Margaret's toothy grin splashed onto Charles's face, but his was guilty. "Bottom line don't move much at all when two drinks have the same hooch as one!"

Just then a waitress paused to hand the Carter men their usuals. Old Grand-Dad on the rocks. "Thanks a bushel, Dot." Charles dismissed her casually, but a keen eye could catch something slightly too familiar for the workplace.

Ben sniffed his whiskey with a nervous eye on Charles. "Cutting the drinks?"

"Only the specials, Pops. Uncle Jasper's plan. But don't worry—yours is full price!"

Ben sipped some of the fire, grimacing happily as it went down. "What about my idea?"

Charles motioned to a table near the back, where a woman and a couple men sat in the shadows. "Was waiting for you. I can give the sign anytime."

"I'm ready if you are." Ben took another sip and prepared to be wowed.

Charles removed a silver cigarette case from his pocket and flipped a smoke into his mouth. Then he used the reflective surface of the case to glint some light at Hank Jones on the piano. In an instant the young man's fluid fingers were improvising their way to the song's un-expected ending. He stood up and took center stage to light applause and leaned into the microphone.

"Ladies and gentlemen, it would be rude of me to keep playing these tired tunes and not let it be known that I just spotted none other than Lady Day." The crowd vibrated with shocked anticipation at the announcement. "I think she's acting a little shy, but if you help me give her a hand, I know we can get her up on our little bandstand."

With that, applause broke out, and the woman sitting at the table in the shadows feigned reluctance as she stood and approached the stage.

"Ladies and gents, Billie Holiday!"

Whistles accompanied vigorous applause as she stepped up, briefly took in the room, and then walked the microphone to the back wall, out of her way—she wouldn't be needing it. There was nothing strik-ing about her appearance, but after hearing a single line of melody, every man in this room would drink from her shoe if that was what she requested. A plain black dress with a thin belt just under her bust elicited the suggestion of nonchalance, but her bare shoulders and strong, naked arms defiantly stated that there was nothing accidental about her—not a single crease in her skirt, a casual crack in a note, and certainly not a seemingly random lunchtime performance in a dimly lit Black Bottom bar. At only twenty-two years old she already had the swagger of someone who'd been crooning full houses for two lifetimes. She stepped over to Hank Jones, who was back at the piano, and whispered over his shoulder. He seemed excited by her selection and readied his hands on the keys to wait for her cue. She stood look-ing out at everyone and no one at all until the din of the room faded to silence. When she felt they were prepared for what she had to offer, she closed her eyes and nodded to Mr. Jones, whose fingers began to gracefully pluck out a tune, and together they slayed with the song

"Strange Fruit."

This was one of the first times Billie sang the song that would one day become synonymous with her name. And how apropos that the song be auditioned to the public in Paradise Valley, a place where the histories of Blacks and Jews came to an important intersection. The lyrics were a poem written by Abel Meeropol, the child of Russian Jewish immigrants, who used the pen name Lewis Allan. Sixteen years later, in 1953, Abel, an outspoken communist, and his wife, Anne, would feel a painful sympathy and adopt the orphaned children of Ethel and Julius Rosenberg after the United States made them the only American civilians to be executed for espionage during the Cold War. The successful prosecutor of the Rosenbergs, a twenty-four-year-old Roy Cohn, would go on to work with Senator Joseph McCarthy to accuse and convict people they believed to be communists, whether they were or not. As a final addition to Cohn's resume, he would become the personal attorney and mentor of future president Donald J. Trump. History sometimes has a scary way of tying the world together.

Strange Fruit
Southern trees bear a strange fruit
Blood on the leaves and blood at the root
Black bodies swinging in the Southern breeze
Strange fruit hanging from the poplar trees

As Lady Day's version of the song gained popularity, winning over and angering crowds alike, rules had to be put in place that the song would only be sung last in her set and the room would be darkened more than normal and be filled with club managers and bodyguards, who scanned the crowd for racists as she sang. That day at Geraldine's, however, the impact it had was on the mind of Ben Carter. Standing there, listening with his son who bore his lynched father's name, Ben's resolve hardened to stone. Some fights were more important than personal safety.

Dammit, Ben, stop with your damn self. Two times in one morning? Ben thought as the song ended, and he quickly swatted away the tears from his eyes before the applause died down and Billie stepped off the stage to return to her table.

Charles snapped his fingers toward the bar, catching Dot's and the bartender's ears, and pointed at Billie's table. The man behind the bar quickly poured a whiskey soda, and before the liquids had fully stopped pouring, Dot was on her way to quench Holiday's thirst.

"How much did Miss Holiday require to make this 'unplanned' appearance?" Ben asked to distract his son from his reddened eyes.

"Not so much that the extra drinks these fine people will buy won't double it."

"Good man. Good man."

Just then a voice called out from a nearby table, "The Carter boys are looking gooood!" Thad Jackson was a salesman even when he wasn't at work.

Charles led Ben over to Thad's table, where he was enjoying the company of a white woman at least fifteen years his younger. She was dressed for a ball, not a club. The diamonds around her neck did all they could to distract from the low cut of her gown. On second thought, maybe they served the opposite purpose.

"Thaddeus Jackson! Are you causing trouble?"

"You know!" he shouted back. Oh, Ben knew all right.

Noticing Mr. Jackson's empty glass, Charles showed his father how good he was at his job. "Looks like your tank is empty, Thad!" Another snap toward Dot would rectify the situation.

Not wanting to be rude, Ben stuck out his hand. "Nice to meet you, ma'am."

She stopped swaying to Hank Jones, already back to the piano, just long enough to shake hands with Ben and Charles.

"Millie told me she never been here before, so when Charles gave me the scoop on today's matinee, I convinced her to join me."

"You never know who might drop in at Geraldine's, Miss Millie."

"Strange Fruit" was still weaving its way through Millie's body, but she seemed oblivious to the theme. "She's just phenomenal! Her rough quality and emotive vocals reimagine the rhythm and reveal a whole new dimension! Don't cha think?"

All three men shot curiously confused smiles to one another and watched Millie sway to the current tune with her eyes shut.

Charles saved them with "Ma'am, all I know is, I feel it, and it feels fine."

"It's good seeing you around," Ben said, punching Thad in the arm. "Don't let my boy here run you ragged."

"You planted some good seeds with this one here." Thad laid it on a bit thick, hoping he could get a free drink. Or, at least, one that wasn't cut.

"I'll tell his mother you said so."

Charles, hard at work to keep tabs on the comings and goings of the room, spotted a white man his age at the bar who raised his blood pressure. "Excuse me, gentlemen . . . and lady. I have some business to attend to."

"You good?"

"All good, Pops."

"All right. I'll be back later. I'm meeting your uncle after my drops."

"I'll hold the corner booth for you."

Charles saw his dad to the saloon doors, where Ben signaled for his driver, who quickly downed the last of his drink. When the glass hit the bar top, Hank Malveaux was back in business mode. He buttoned his coat and followed Ben out.

Charles walked to a plain door in the corner by the booths and put his hand on the knob. Eyes on the white man at the bar, he motioned with his head, and the man coldly grabbed his drink and made his way in Charles's direction.

The door was less than two inches thick. The highly polished patron-facing side was a dramatic cover for the reality of the side where Charles now stood with Danny Gaczynski. No lacquer on this side of the door—no time, couldn't be bothered. This side was the real world. The real world, where a once-discarded two-top breakfast table now pretended to be an office desk, holding invoices, receipts, and ledgers, all of which would be carefully tallied if the time could ever be found to cook them in the first place. The real world, where inventory of Seagram's, Schenley, and Hiram Walker moved in and out so fast, it slowly took over any orderly workspace, like maggots cleaning a carcass to the bone.

Danny wanted to be tough, he wanted to mean business, but his father was the reason he was taken seriously. Izzy could giveth, and Izzy could taketh away. At twenty-four, Danny was still holding on to the flushed cheeks and knobby knees of his youth. His desire for physical respect was also not helped by his jaw, which was as fragile as a martini glass. However, Charles had been warned by his father and Uncle Jasper that Danny's weak characteristics, accompanied by a needy ambition to get out from under his father's shadow, were what made Danny a tinderbox.

"There's a new blackie barkeep at the Forest Club been asking questions." Danny leaned his ass on the corner of the table and flicked an ice cube from his glass into his mouth.

Charles didn't flinch. "Talking that vague gives people the need to ask questions, Danny."

"Don't get smart." Danny crunched his cube as the two young men stared each other down, silently jockeying for position.

"If I don't need to know, I don't want to know."

"This bartender knows stuff he shouldn't. About our Polack friend."

All expression fell from Charles's face. "That's got nothing to do with me."

"The Feds might think differently if they find out it happened at Geraldine's. They'd be happy as clams to crack down on the notorious Carter family."

"We legit now, Danny."

"You didn't go legit so much as the repeal of Volstead made you so, and those guys got long memories." Feeling his message was received, Danny reached for the door, attempting to casually brush Charles aside.

"You and your daddy ran with the Purple Gang. Ain't like you're free and clear."

"Didn't say I was." Danny never broke a sweat, a privilege that being Izzy's kid gave him. "But since I'm sure you're more scared of your uncle Jasper finding out than you are the Feds, I figure I can persuade you to help me take care of the problem."

Danny had Charles's number, and he knew it. With a shit-eating grin plastered on his pointy face, Danny turned the doorknob and slid back into the sounds of Hank Jones's piano playing, but all Charles heard was the sound of his own pounding pulse.

CHAPTER SIX

Le Noir Palais was the latest establishment of Minnie Carter—much to the chagrin of Jasper and Ben. It wasn't the whoring that bothered them, no—it was her name. Minnie was the granddaughter of the brother of Jasper and Ben's grandfather. If the family tree was to be drawn out, it would prove that Minnie Carter was a Carter but without the moniker. Their grandfathers were the brothers John "Salty" Carter and the man they had only ever heard called "Trout." Trout was a Carter. His two sons were Carters. His four daughters were Carters, and Minnie's mom was one of those women—Sabina Carter.

Jasper heard that Auntie Sabina made it out to Los Angeles to work in the picture business, but he had a suspicion that meant minding the children of some white person who worked in the picture business. Sadly, Ben agreed with his brother's assumption, but that didn't stop him from paying extra close attention to the Black faces he sometimes saw on the silver screen, usually playing the help under the cloak of some white screenwriter's ignorant mammy stereotype. If Auntie Sabina were as prominent as Fredi Washington or Hattie McDaniel, surely they'd already know it, but Ben couldn't help his hopeful nature that he'd one day see her face larger than life.

But before anyone had left Birmingham for the Motor City or the City of Angels, Sabina married John Wilcox and brought Minnie into the world. That made Minnie a Wilcox, which was the name she had used for years and years, proud to be her daddy's girl. She was shrewd, though, and a businesswoman who understood branding. The Carter brand in Black Bottom was as good as gold, so as insurance after the market crash, Minnie Wilcox took her mother's maiden name. Selling flesh was fine with Jasper and Ben. Hell, it even worked to their advantage when they needed a private place to meet or seduce some wealthy clientele, but running a brothel under the Carter name drew the eyes of people Jasper didn't want peeping around.

Le Noir Palais had grown from being just a building into what was now a community of women helping women in a time when few were lending a hand—and less so the darker your skin got. Minnie had had a hot spot up on Farnsworth Street for nearly a year and a half, a fancy lacquered sign on the front porch and everything. The layout was such that she easily converted the three-bedroom house into six small pleasure suites and one larger, more scandalous room for those with fatter billfolds and a desire to entertain more than one of Minnie's girls at the same time, or perhaps even one of her boys. That incarnation of the Palais was raided last year, and Minnie had done a month's time. The copper who cuffed her made the mistake of saying Minnie was just another example of a "colored girl stepping out of line." She spun on that young man, wrists chained behind her back like so many before her, and said, "That's colored 'madam' to you. Now mind your manners, or I'll tell your daddy. How is he, by the way? Still fighting off that cold?" The jab was worth the extra wrench of the cuffs she received while being shoved into the paddy wagon.

The lacquered sign was missing when Minnie ended her stay at the Detroit House of Correction in Plymouth, but what lingered was the feeling that Jasper had somehow had his hand in the raid. Even though the city of Hamtramck was legally separate from Detroit, Jasper made it perfectly clear that Le Noir Palais was too close to his home in Conant Gardens and too far outside his personal control. *All right, cuz*, she had thought, *you let me know how far you want to travel the next time Valerie uses vodka for hydration and you need to 'relax.'*

Apparently, Jasper felt more comfortable traveling down to Brewster Street, because after a month out of business, that's where Jasper helped Minnie nab another spot. It turned out she was more useful to him than he was willing to say aloud. Jasper and Minnie needed each other. He needed an underground meeting place, and she needed his protection. She'd been in the new place for nearly seven months now, and the unspoken air between cousins was as muddy as ever. Minnie couldn't shake the reality of how hard Jasper had worked to move north to a nicer neighborhood, then found a way to push her south, where a business like hers "belonged." She wasn't sure Jasper even understood how insulting that was to her, let alone their race, but one thing she knew in her heart was that the Hamtramck Le Noir Palais had been raided because he hadn't wanted it there. There was no proof, but she knew.

The new house—this time with no signage, at Jasper's decree—had been decorated by a couple living high on the hog, who had since gone belly up with the rest of the country. It was a bit gaudy for Minnie's personal taste, but when she added a bit of flavor, it gave the place the perfect feel of glamour with a dangerous secret just under the skin. Prohibition hadn't ended all that long ago, but already artifacts from the days of everyone drinking and no one admitting it had become chic: an armoire with a secret half-round rotating shelf of booze that spun out of the side, the oversized molding on the window hinged open to reveal single-bottle shelves from top to bottom, and Minnie even put decorative sliding peepholes in the doors of the eight rooms as a playful allusion that each was its own blind pig.

The antique furnishings of the largest bedroom were more for show than comfort. A lush painting of a shadowy, moonlit Parisian cityscape hung facing the sofa and chairs with their ornately carved handles and pops of upholstered color on the backs and cushions. Golden cream. Muted sapphire. Faded marine. Unobtrusive end tables accompanied each of the two chairs and both ends of the sofa, just big enough to hold a couple rocks glasses and a lamp. Each fringed lamp was assisted by a thin silk that cast gentle shades of red-and-purple light. No sunlight made its way through the permanently drawn window drapes of lavender velvet, standing sentinel to keep the outside out.

The Victrola in the corner played a sexy sax solo as a Black prostitute named Euni seductively rubbed the shoulders of Thomas Schwartz. The man with the pockmarked face was in his late fifties and as round as he was tall. An ivory-handled walking cane leaned on his lap.

"That feels good, doll. I'm relaxing and getting stiff at the same time."

Four other women, three Black and one white, stood side by side in front of him, each dressed in lacy lingerie with garters and stockings. There wasn't a hint of shame on any of them, and if they felt it, it didn't show. It seemed each girl wanted to be picked.

"It's very important to investigate every angle of a business proposition," he lectured. "So I think I need a good look at the undercarriage."

Without losing their smiles, the girls were overcome with expressions of curiosity, wondering what this naughty man was asking for.

"Your asses. I need to see your asses, for Chrissake."

The women giggled and snapped into action, turning and sticking out their bums. Their bodies accentuated by their cute and silky undergarments, they looked over their shoulders with flirtatious smiles back at the rotund man.

Schwartz enjoyed this power over them more than any sexual gratification he may or may not get. The game of feigned indecision was the biggest turn-on. "Now this is a big, big problem. Too many options make for harder decisions!"

The doorknob was heard before the velvet curtain that covered it began to be pulled back. The smiles of each woman melted away. They were not scared enough to scamper off but more so anticipating their next inconvenience—a night of lost wages, or even a full week, or having to move houses again. They weren't afraid of jail because these women had full faith that Minnie would take care of them, protect them any way she could, and she had a lot of ways.

Thomas Schwartz, on the other hand, was simply annoyed, flippantly so, to have his fun interrupted. As a Detroit city councilman, he had a fair level of protection based solely on how much dirt he had access to on others in power, which was exactly why he was important to the Carters. Sure, Schwartz made big blustery shows about "fair practices for all" and being a "white advocate for the colored man," but what actually made him different from other white men in power was that he was willing to trade privileged insider information to the Black community—if they had something he wanted, that is. And what he wanted most were money and women whose job it was to pretend they wanted to fuck the gluttonous, oily crumb that he was.

When the curtain was pulled back to reveal Minnie in her floor-length pleated skirt and standard cashmere shawl dangling from her elbows and loosely hung around her lower back, all five women felt at ease. With a nod from their madam, they dispersed around the room to lean on walls or lounge on furniture until this brief interruption was over.

"Mr. Schwartz, my cousin is here to see you," and with that, she stepped in farther to reveal Ben close at her heels.

"There's the butter-and-egg man!" Schwartz's face exploded with the realization that this wasn't an interruption but rather an addition to the purpose of his afternoon visit.

Ben held his hat in his hand and spoke with his head ever so slightly bowed. "Sorry to interrupt, but I'm already running late, and God only knows how long you'll be when you make up your mind." He glanced at the women around the room, who writhed a little as they hid their put-on innocent smiles in the presence of Mr. Ben.

"You got a gift for me?"

"Yes, sir." Ben stepped forward, pulling a Geraldine's envelope from his coat pocket, and put it in Schwartz's stubby fingers. "Do you have anything for me?"

Schwartz opened the envelope of cash but stopped before getting into the count. He rolled his neck with exaggeration and eyed Euni, who pranced back over to continue his massage.

He started to count the bribe. "There's a rumor going around that Negroes are talking strike. Seems our queer governor and his boy Kemp got 'em too hopeful for their britches when GM organized, and Ford isn't much happy about it. I don't think I have to tell you how bad that would be for our little arrangement."

"Doesn't seem to me that the UAW is asking all that much of Mr. Ford."

Schwartz was less than thrilled with Ben's tone. He stopped counting and stared up at his reluctant benefactor. "Well, if they think they can get better work at Chrysler or GM, they're more than welcome to go looking."

After a momentary silent standoff, Schwartz was confident Ben was back to respecting his lack of melanin. "I know you're trying to do your people right. So just keep the donations coming and I'll be sure to swing by and talk a little too loud about things you're not supposed to hear."

Ben nodded respectfully, but he already knew about the unease at the UAW, so what the hell was he paying for this time? Nothing. Wasted lettuce. It was becoming clear that he'd have to broach the subject with Jasper again, and Ben wasn't looking forward to another session of banging his head against a seized engine block. When Ben turned to make his exit, Schwartz spoke up.

"Hold on there, Benny Boy." Schwartz pointed his thumb up at Euni rubbing his shoulders, then shot his index finger over to the only white hooker in the room. "Show me those titties, ladies."

Euni and Betty Bell, a nineteen-year-old undocumented Russian immigrant, both did as they were told. They lowered their shoulder straps and waited for judgment.

Schwartz didn't look at the women's breasts; he simply stared into Ben's seething eyes. This demoralizing exercise was nothing more than a cheap way to get under Ben's skin, who, no matter how much Minnie told him the girls were willing participants, couldn't get his head around it. Choosing employment at Le Noir Palais was one thing if your other options were lawyer or pharmacist. Yes, women could do these more respectable types of jobs, but the ratios proved the possibility, not the norm. Then add Black skin or a Russian accent, and the odds were about as good as Jasper winning the daily numbers racket. Maybe these ladies were happy to be doing the best they could with what they had, but Ben was filled with hatred and shame that "what they had" was now flopped out naked in front of this infected blister of a man.

"A fine choice, sir."

"That's what I thought. Now be sure to pay your cousin for these fine ladies on your way out."

"Yes, sir."

Ben shot eyes at Minnie, who never flinched or broke decorum. Transaction complete, Ben turned on his heels, and Minnie pulled the drapes back over the door as they left Councilman Thomas Schwartz to his depravity.

When Hank shut Ben into the car on Brewster Street, he could tell his boss's day had taken a turn for the worse. He slid behind the wheel, started the engine, and waited for directions that didn't seem to be coming. Ben simply stared out the window, lost in thought, mind racing somewhere far away.

"Where to, boss?"

Without realizing it, Ben was methodically flipping his 1908 penny between his fingers.

"Boss?"

Snapping to, Ben dropped the penny back into his pocket and took in the time on his wristwatch. A large sigh meant it wasn't getting any earlier in the day, and then Ben was lost once again, gazing thoughtfully out the window toward the back of Le Noir Palais, from where the car was parked.

Ben's eyes narrowed when he caught a glimpse of a shadow saddled up close to the side of the home next door, facing Saint Aubin Street. He knew Hank's eyes were on him in the mirror, but Ben was frozen like a pointer dog trained on his master's kill. The shadow moved when the man who cast it began to pace back and forth, and it became unmistakable even to someone who wasn't his father. The shadow belonged to Charles.

Ben's jaw tightened to stop him from screaming. "Take me to Peck's."

Now fully aware of the line of sight between Ben and the boy set to one day take over the Carter empire, Hank kept silent and rolled the car forward.

From Saint Aubin, a right-hand turn on Gratiot, and downtown Detroit was already visible in the distance, casting afternoon shadows over Black Bottom to its east. Book Tower stood out like a wealthy socialite who wandered into the wrong neighborhood while his nose was stuck in a map. The Fisher Building was trying to be Book Tower but couldn't live up in class or size. The Guardian—now that mama was fine as hell in her smooth rust-colored gown. The Cadillac Hotel had no care in the world, just a giant white box dropped in the city, and the Penobscot was the eighth tallest building in the world. Why anyone cared about the eighth anything was beyond Hank.

Soon enough the Series 70 was rolling in bumper-to-bumper traffic, consumed by thirty- and forty-story shadows, and the skin of almost every human looked as if the warmth of the sun had never touched it. White men and women in white-collar attire walked through city life in a hurry to get to nowhere, no one speaking to no one. Cold. The exact opposite of Black Bottom.

Hank pulled to the curb in front of the First National on Woodward and quickly stepped out to grab the handle of Ben's door, buttoning his coat before it was opened.

"Want me to come up?"

Ben declined with a pat on Hank's shoulder to ease his tension. "I won't be long."

A scan of the area told Hank that no one cared that Ben was marching into the office tower. He was safe. Out of place but safe. Hank retrieved his newspaper and leaned his ass on the quarter panel, but he couldn't help being distracted from his reading lesson.

White. People. Everywhere.

No one was rude, but the sight was eye-catching for both parties in each interaction with every passerby. The white pedestrians could not help watching Hank, and Hank couldn't help but watch right back. He didn't feel any hostility, but within two minutes he felt like an animal at the zoo who'd be more comfortable in its man-made cave, mostly out of view. He folded his paper and slid back behind the wheel to wait.

CHAPTER SEVEN

The law offices of Canfield, Honigman & Peck were churning with the buzz of being close to the end of a day at the end of a week. The attorneys themselves were locked in the offices that lined the inner hallways, the only difference between work and prison being iron bars versus lath and plaster. These prisoners got to start their weekend leaves after they tapped their pencils and shuffled papers through their final calls, or clients, or briefs, which allowed them to announce to their secretaries, "I'll see you on Monday" or "If you need me, ring the cottage in Anchor Bay."

The front office was busy with worker bees buzzing in and out, all pristinely dressed, coifed, and manicured women ranging in age from 21 to 101or, at least, that was the vibe Mrs. Swanson gave off as she shuffled Herb Canfield's final client of the week back to his corner suite. The one person in the office not moving at get-me-out-of-here speed was the woman at the main desk in her navy blouse with the wide white collar and string of pearls. Rose Winston. Her new job consisted of greeting clients, alerting the proper parties of their arrivals, answering calls from the building switchboard operator, and, of course, accepting the delegation of any menial task the attorneys' personal secretaries deemed beneath them: grab dry cleaning curbside, freshen a coffee, dispose of a silk scarf left behind by a mistress. The majority of her first half day on the job was sitting prim and proper at the front desk, staring uneasily between the door and the telephone, terrified that when one of them needed a response, she'd somehow get it wrong. She wanted this job so bad and believed if she could make it through the first day, tomorrow would be easier, as would the next and the next. However, after just over four hours on the job, she had solidified her resolve not to become Mrs. Swanson.

A slight twitch reverberated through Rose's whole body when she heard the door handle unlatch and watched it start to swing in. She straightened her posture, patted a curl, and smoothed her blouse. The first physical object to enter was a tan porkpie hat, followed by the Black hands that carried it and arms sleeved in a khaki herringbone. Rose swallowed. *Hello, welcome to Canfield, Honigman & Peck. May I ask who you're here to see this afternoon?* she thought. The next to enter was the two-tone leather shoe, and then it seemed that all at once Ben Carter was standing in the doorway. This was the last thing she had expected on her first day, and there was no way for her to have prepared. Ben was knocked equally out of his rhythm when his eyes met with those of Rose.

An older Polish man with a cane, a client apparently not too happy with how little movement there had been with his case, was forced to stop dead in his tracks as he tried to make his angry exit. The man froze, looked at Ben standing half in and half out, and made a grand gesture with his body to signify that he wanted to get through. Still nothing.

Lost somewhere in the exciting place between fear and adoration, Rose finally spoke up. "Hello. Welcome to Canfield, Honigman, and Peck." She still hadn't noticed the Polish client trying to flee.

The old man looked back at Rose. Then to Ben. Back to Rose. "Excuse me, friend, but if you don't accept the lady's welcome and get out of my way, I'm going to bludgeon you with my cane and plead insanity." The man turned and yelled his next statement down the hall from which he'd come. "Insanity will hold up! I promise you this, because you make me wacky, Herb, you hear? Fucking wacky!"

A door somewhere down the hallway slammed, presumably in response to the tirade, and with that, the man shuffled by Ben, burrowing and shooing a path to the exit.

"May I ask who you're here to see this afternoon?" Rose asked from her memorized script.

Ben attempted to snap out of his stunned state. He was able to shut the door after the angry old man, but when he looked back to Rose, he got stuck again.

"Hi, um, I'm here to . . . I don't have an appointment, but . . ."

Theatrically acting the part of secretary more than being one, Rose opened the appointment book and flipped some pages. "I see, sir. May I ask who you were hoping to see and what matter this may concern?"

"Peck. I'm here to see Robert Peck. If he'll see me, of course. It concerns a union matter."

"A union matter? Mr. Peck is very busy. Can you be more specific?" Rose was digging for something.

Ben pursed his lips tightly, forcing all the blood out of the wrinkles left behind. This was not the time or place, and he knew it. "Ma'am, if you'll forgive me, it's a Negro issue. A thing I'm certain falls outside your area of expertise."

This stung Rose to the core. She knew the truth, and she knew Ben knew the truth. They both understood that if anyone else knew, there would be hell to pay in every direction. She swallowed her desire to stomp her heels, to scream, or better yet, to march to the door and smack the nerve off his face.

"I'm afraid Mr. Peck's schedule . . ."

"Happens to be free." Neither Ben nor Rose had noticed Mr. Peck's personal secretary, Eileen, peering at them from behind her horn-rimmed glasses and tight red curls. "Right this way, Mr. Carter. I'll show you in." Eileen looked down her nose at Rose as she waited for Ben to follow.

Ben left Rose dizzy from the interaction, flustered and angry, but also hopeful she hadn't spoiled her entrance into the workforce on the very first day on the job.

Eileen led Ben down the narrow hall to a door on the right labeled plainly PECK. She stepped inside, leaving enough room for Ben to skirt by her. "Mr. Peck, Mr. Carter is here to see you." She didn't wait for a response; she simply stepped out and closed the men inside.

Peck was a skinny, angular man. An old fifty-year-old or young sixty—no one knew—with a thin mustache and thinning hair slicked across his brow to cover his receding hairline. A nameplate on his desk in mahogany with brass letters read ROBERT PECK, ESQ., and sitting behind it was the man himself, engrossed in paperwork. Yet another man playing the power game of refusing eye contact.

"I appreciate you seeing me without proper notice."

After a moment of awkward waiting, Ben decided to move toward one of the two highly polished chairs facing Peck's desk.

"White men have to sit in that chair."

Ben gave the man politeness that wasn't being offered to him. He stood and quietly waited until Peck's right hand raised in a request to be handed something. Still no eyes, though, and Ben needed the tiniest win in order to continue with the charade, so he waited. Sooner than he expected, probably due to the power of the item his hand was requesting, Peck's eyes lifted to meet with Ben's. Then and only then did Ben take his cue to reach into his pocket for another of his cash-filled envelopes.

Peck took the envelope, unceremoniously tore off one end, and dumped the cash onto his desk. Eyeing a quick count, Peck's bony fingers reached for a drawer to the left of his desk.

"'Crime doesn't pay.' What a yarn. The salad was a lot greener when the drys ran DC." From the drawer came a silver hip flask. One swipe of his thumb and the cap spun and leapt off to the side, caught by its small hinged arm. He tossed back a biting swig, capped it once again, and dropped it back into the drawer. He leaned back in his chair, folded his arms, and studied Ben's face with motive and intent. Neither man immediately spoke.

"I'm more than happy to bill you for this wonderful conversation, if that's what you came by for." It seemed the intense, studious look was Peck's waiting face.

"No, sir. I came for your legal opinion on a matter concerning the UAW."

Peck's bushy eyebrows raised, and his face lightened. It was possible this was a meeting of interest after all.

Ben continued, "Leon Bates came to see me with a proposal. He inquired about using our connection to Governor Murphy."

"What does Jasper think of this?" The words slid from the corner of a smirk.

"I haven't spoken to him yet. He values your opinion, and I thought . . ."

"You thought if I agreed with you, Jasper would be more easily swayed."

Ben was caught red-handed.

"Murphy's already a fucking Democrat, Ben. You wanna waste the use of your connection to the highest office in Michigan to convince him of something he already supports?"

"I just thought . . ."

"You just thought?" Peck questioned. "Apparently not. A person only gets a couple aces up their sleeve. You wanna waste one on shorter shifts and a measly five cents more an hour?"

Ben put his hat on, a sign of disrespect, while offering a verbal platitude. "I appreciate your time, Mr. Peck."

"I thought you people did whatever your preachers told you to do," quipped the man from behind the safety of his desk.

"Unfortunately, some of us have seen the preachers putting down the good book and getting their sermons from Dearborn. A fine day to you, sir." Ben tipped his hat and walked out cold. His attitude mattered none to Peck; the money he left could still be spent.

Ben escorted himself down the hall, back toward the reception desk. He had momentarily forgotten who sat in the front office, but when he turned to pull the office door closed behind him, there she was, eyes rounded with childlike fear. This woman actually had reason to be scared of eye contact and anyone who may have noticed their connection, but there it was.

He tried to stop the words—in fact, he thought he'd already swallowed them down safely into the pit of his stomach—but Ben had a sensitive gag reflex in certain situations. All it took was the smallest quiver of Rose's chin to bring them back up.

"A white woman should be careful not to make eye contact with a colored man. Or maybe you're special. Are you special?"

Rose's shaking fingers fidgeted with the appointment book, and she sucked a quick burst of air into her lungs, a sob with no tears.

Ben shut the door, careful to make it loud enough that people noticed, but quiet enough that if someone came after him, it would be reasonable that he could apologize, saying he hadn't realized how heavy-handed he'd been with the door.

"Are you okay? How scary." One of the passing legal secretaries had clutched her pearls with one hand and with the other was comforting Rose with a touch of the shoulder. Rose thanked her new colleague for the concern, but there was no way the woman could understand the gravity of the situation. In this moment, Rose questioned the kind and generous character she had once known Ben to possess. Had the state of the world finally gotten to him? Was it possible that he could now somehow understand the drastic decisions she had made in her life? Should she be scared that he'd come back and with a single sentence demolish the skyrise of lies she'd built?

Would that be the end of her life as she knew it?

Would that be the end of her life?

CHAPTER EIGHT

Charles hadn't moved five feet since his father had seen him waiting like a begging cat out back of Le Noir Palais. He hadn't physically gone anywhere, but as he waited, his anxiety grew from a mustard seed into an ungodly burning bush. Every noise he heard from the room on the other side of the exterior wall was almost more than he could take. Grunt, knock, squeak, moan. He was bubbling over with fear and anger. Fear of his own anger and angry that he felt fear, a cycle that sometimes got the best of members of the Carter tribe.

The councilman's muffled voice was barely audible enough to make out. "That's right, open wide, you little whore."

The defenseless milk bottle huddled in the litter of the alley had no chance. Charles grabbed it by the neck and threw it as hard and as far as he could. The shattering glass was distant enough that it wouldn't draw attention to Charles in his place of desperation. Something crashed to the floor within, a lamp maybe, as the bed began to rhythmically bang against the wall, accompanied by the quivering grunts of pleasure from deep in Schwartz's loins. The women moaned in pleasure, but their motives were hard to decipher. Charles certainly didn't think they could be enjoying his sweaty thrusts, so he chose to believe the courtesans put on their best purrs and squeals in hopes that they could push him more quickly over the cliff of ecstasy. This belief didn't make it any easier on his eardrums or his heartstrings, so he sat on the bottom step of the stoop with his palms suctioned to his ears and pinned between his cowering knees, rocking back and forth, begging for the man to give up his load.

*Sharon held the door open for Victor and Stephen, who were just ar-*riving at Carter Dry Cleaning. She looked up at the sky, which was beginning to show the slightest tinge of orange, and wondered if she'd ever have free time in the sunlit hours again. Then she closed herself, her brother, and her cousin behind the door that she had locked to customers an hour ago. It was after seven, and she was calculating whether or not the three of them could beat the darkness that would fully cast itself over the city around nine. None of her calculations had taken into account Stephen leaping on Victor's back and covering his eyes.

"Giddyup, my blind and buxom stallion!"

Even though he had a shy and muted personality, Victor's extra four years of teenage growth easily matched Stephen's fifteen-year-old vigor. It didn't take much to shake the rowdy rascal off his back and send him tumbling into a rolling rack of freshly plastic-draped clothes. Hung over his shoulder and across his chest, Stephen's elbow got stuck in his canvas delivery bag. Had he not gotten tangled, he may have had one more shot before . . .

"Stop it now! Stephen, you're on slacks. Victor, you doing shirts. Is Mark coming?" One thing Sharon knew how to do was take charge.

Both boys hopped to it and headed behind the service counter.

Victor repeated the nicety that had been fed to him. "My mama told me Aunt Valerie wasn't feeling good and so she needed Mark's help."

All Stephen needed was the length of time it took Sharon to roll her eyes to decide he could squeeze in another jab. Like lightning he had one of Victor's arms wrenched behind his back. Victor snatched up a clothes hanger with his free arm and began swatting at his cousin's head somewhere around his back. To evade his wire beatings, Stephen yanked Victor's arm further around with each swipe while continuously screaming, "Hi-yo, Silver! Away!" as they spun in dizzying circles.

The unadulterated glee in Stephen's mischievous shouts could sometimes crack Sharon, but not tonight. "Come on now! We work fast, we only need to be here an hour or two!"

Stephen let go of Victor's arm and immediately dodged a retaliatory blow but slipped and fell to his butt, spilling papers from his bag. Better than getting hit.

"You didn't finish your deliveries? Oh, your daddy gonna have your hide!" Victor was smart enough to know Jasper was Stephen's Achilles' heel.

Stephen lunged back into the fray, but Victor escaped behind his shirt-ironing station.

"No. Uh-uh. Slacks. Now," Sharon demanded when Stephen attempted to pick up his spilled flyers. She'd rather he be pressing so she picked up the flyers herself.

Stephen complained as he threw some pants onto the ironing board. "School! Printing deliveries! Helping out here! May as well be a slave!"

Sharon slammed the spilled leaflets she'd collected onto the counter next to Victor and stormed Stephen with fire and brimstone. "Shut your damn mouth! Talking about things you know nothing about! You're lucky Daddy ain't heard you say some ignorant shit like that! He liable to show you what being a slave was really like!"

Stephen fully accepted his tongue-lashing. He knew he was wrong. He put his head down and got to business on his first pair of pants, ratty ones that probably should have been tossed long ago.

There was tension in the silent air as Sharon went to the register to start work on the day's receipts, but tension or not, silent was how Victor preferred his surroundings. He paused for a moment as if he weren't in the world but merely a bystander watching it happen, and no one was aware he was paying attention. He watched Stephen—doing his work, but a boiling inner geyser within him building pressure from all that he believed the world expected from him. He watched Sharon—more than capable, possibly even the best Carter of the bunch, but if something didn't go her way soon, she'd force her hand. He could see it. He could see the weight on his family, on his race. Then, just when it was time to reenter the world and become one of its players once again by ironing a shirt, it hit him. A sign. A sign from his cousin Sharon, who slammed it down next to him. But it was bigger than that. It was a message from the Messenger of Allah. Victor hadn't seen the flyers that Carter Family Printing had been hired to reproduce, the ones Stephen was supposed to have delivered after school that day. But there it was. However the message got to him, there it was, right there for him to receive. He picked it up and read the large, bold black ink:

ALLAH TEMPLE OF ISLAM
**Focusing on the advancement of the Black race
in today's social and economic reality.**

She hardly looked up from her bookkeeping, but Sharon had eyes in every direction. "I don't know about you, Victor, but I want to go home sometime tonight."

Victor folded the paper and slid it into the pocket of his dark twill trousers. His body fell into the well-rehearsed muscle memory of pressing shirts, but his mind had cracked open.

The sun was barely hanging on to its daily life. With no clouds in the sky, it was a perfect gradient from feather-boa pink to midnight blue, and not too far to the east, the sky was surely black. The air was finally absent of the poisonous sounds of paid-for passion. Charles had his ear pressed against the back door of Minnie's pleasure palace to make sure. No sounds. None.

He slowly brought his finger up to his head and ever so gently tapped his fingernail on the door. He couldn't afford to get caught, so he hoped she was listening for his fragile mating call.

The bolt on the door flipped over, and Charles jumped back. A second of fear in which his body refused to move. The bolt slid to the side, and the doorknob rubbed a bit as it turned. If it was Minnie, he'd be front-page Carter family gossip by sundown. What would his father say? *Good God, what would Uncle Jasper do?*

The door opened just enough for Betty to slink out into the shadows and quietly pull the door closed behind her. Before she could fully turn around, Charles's body was there, and his lips were on hers. She pulled away, looking back at the door, looking all around.

"Did he hurt you?"

"Shhh!" Betty's pale blue eyes pleaded from under her platinum bob. If her skin didn't already make her stand out in the night, the white silk robe wasn't helping their cover. She glowed. "You can't be here," she whispered in her thick Saint Petersburg accent.

With a soft touch, Charles took her face in his hands and delivered a firm look. "Did he hurt you?"

"No. Please, you have to go."

"My day ain't going that smooth, and I needed to see you." His soft touch turned into a deep and passionate kiss that made her knees buckle. For Charles, the kiss also acted as a bucket of soapy water to clean the touch of the last man who paid, and it scratched his ever-present itch to be the last man on her lips.

Breaking away only for individual words to escape: "Minnie would not be happy."

Who is kissing who is no longer decipherable. Neither is capable of anything more than the faintest protest.

"I don't want you to get in trouble," she muttered, hoping to be ignored.

Their hands began to explore each other's bodies, and she instinctually lifted her leg over his hip and began to undo his belt.

"I could be deported."

He stopped her mouth with another kiss. At this point it would seem all punishments were worth the intensity of the occasion. She looked around over his shoulder and saw no one—not that it mattered. She reached down between their bodies as a guide until her eyes rolled into the back of her head.

"I love you."

"I need you."

Maybe it was a quirk in the translation, but to Charles, the word "need" didn't carry the weight of the word he'd used. He pushed her against the door; they could talk about linguistics later.

On the other side of the door, halfway down the hall, Euni giggled with a Vietnamese working girl about the sound of the door softly rocking in and out like a slow-moving metronome. A third woman, Black as night, stepped out of her room, annoyed.

"You know she pitching woo with a Black man," she snapped.

Euni smiled wider and took on the challenge. "Oh, it's fine for her to fuck Black guys in here all day and all night, but keep it Jim Crow on her own time?"

It was a hard disagree for the annoyed woman, but before she turned on her heels and marched to her next john: "It's different in here. In here they paying."

Euni's sidekick hollered after the woman, "Baby, they paying out there too, trust it." Not a lick of accent on any word. She saved that Asian game for her clueless clients.

"Ladies."

The women failed to notice their madam standing in one of the doorways. One word from her said plenty, and the girls quickly slipped away to find more gentleman callers, leaving Minnie alone with the gentle squeak of the back door each time the bodies on the outside pushed against it. Minnie wasn't deaf, and she hadn't been blind to this forbidden relationship, not for a second. She hadn't decided yet whether she was keeping this secret to look after an employee, to protect her nephew, or to have a token of power in her pocket for the next time she may need it. Whenever that might be.

CHAPTER NINE

Traffic was heavy heading north toward the neon of Paradise Valley, and Ben's deadpan face stared out the window, watching context personified. Hastings Street in Black Bottom was a different place at night. Most shops were closed, locked up tight. The sporadic pub was open, and the light that spilled from those joints became meeting places for streetwalkers, pimps, and pushers who were out to play. He'd been in Black Bottom long enough to know these people, and if he didn't know them personally, he knew their daddy or their cousin, or sold groceries to their sister. Sure, he'd climbed himself out, but Ben had once lived poor in Black Bottom, which was why he didn't judge these people. He'd been there. He'd been them. Thinking back on some of the things he and Jasper had done on these very streets brought him shame and, at the same time, made him proud of what they had achieved. They'd "gotten out," but Ben would never really leave.

The unfair part was that all societies partook in these activities, but the world judged them based on how they were marketed. Ben got an opportunity to go to France for a month during college, and while in Paris, he visited the site of the famed Moulin Rouge, which had burned down the year before he arrived. He went because the fire had made international news. The world-famous club was a mecca for artists and thinkers. When he got there, he stood in the middle of the Boulevard de Clichy, mouth agape. He was in the center of a sex district. The Moulin Rouge had been a glamourous, elite, socially acceptable whorehouse, but a whorehouse nonetheless. Take away the famous posters, the extravagant costumes, make all the ladies descendants of the Middle Passage, and the press would have deemed it a slum. A ghetto. A blight on the land. And the people inside would be heathens, and scoundrels, and diseased, and troublesome. Add a little money, paint already white skin whiter, scrounge up some dancers, and show them that the intersection between art and commerce is sex, and there you have it, the Moulin Rouge. Ben wanted to scream at all the French people passing by, "C'est une maison de pute!" His French was fairly good, a byproduct of living so close to Canada, but the Parisians would never understand without knowing the intimate details of Black Bottom. The context of Black Bottom.

The world Black folks live in is a product of hypocrisy. A Black woman sells her body? Stay away! Make a law! Set up boundaries! Put her in a cage! A white woman sells her body? New opportunities must be created to give this woman a better life! She needs assistance! She's providing a service in a free market! Thus, the Black sex worker is delegated to "streetwalker," and the white one is a "courtesan." And at the streetwalker level, a woman has less respect, less money, more danger, and is closer to drugs, theft, and brokenness. The same goes for Black pickpockets, con men, pimps, and gangsters. What options do they have, really? If a life vest is never thrown into the deep end, you either drown, or you learn to do business with sharks.

Ben got out, so maybe these men and women could too. He was, at the very least, proof that there was light on the other side. Or was he? Things got bad during Prohibition. Lines were crossed—Ben's lines, Carter family lines, human lines. When Volstead was lifted, they made a conscious effort to choose the straight and narrow—Jasper because he didn't want to lose what they had gained, and Ben because he saw how far they could get with how far they'd come—but that didn't mean it was easy.

As the car rolled north, the lights shined brighter and the reflections in the window grew livelier. Ben sat up straighter in his seat. Black and white revel-makers happily pranced and strutted to their first destination of this glorious Friday night on the town. Soon jazz could be heard spilling into the street from all directions. For a brief moment, Ben even recognized his own hypocrisy. Seeing the nice duds, the sleek cars, the neon lights? Damn. It brought Ben back to Paris, and it felt good.

When Hank pulled to the curb, the window covering Ben's face reflected the glory of Geraldine's. The club was already going hard, easily the most popular spot on the strip this fine evening. After a day dealing with Leon Bates, Thomas Schwartz, Robert Peck, and *Goddamnit, Charles, why are you sniffing around Minnie's place*, it felt nice, safe, to be in his own domain.

Hank opened his door, and Ben stepped into the party that was Paradise Valley.

"Looks like it's gonna be a good night tonight, boss."

"Thank the Lord." Ben slipped Hank a buck. "You worked long enough today. Drink one for me too. I'll drive her home myself."

"All right, all right! He-haa!"

"Don't party too hard! I still need you in the morning."

As Hank slipped through the crowded doorway, Ben spotted Charles excusing himself from a patron he'd been schmoozing. He walked toward his father with a grin that seemed to extend beyond the confines of his face. The turnout tonight, no doubt due to word of mouth from Ben and Charles's lunchtime stunt with Lady Day, was plenty to earn a smile that wide, but Ben knew there was something else that filled boys with that much glee.

Charles went in for a hug—"Hey, Pops!"—but was met with a surprisingly hard fist check to his chest. Charles immediately surveyed the crowd to see which of his patrons may have witnessed this disrespect.

"You think I'm a twit? You think I don't got the lowdown on you?"

"What!" Charles was fully blind to what was going down.

"This family doesn't need your shit gumming up the works!"

Ben went for another chest jab, but Charles was ready this time and flinched back. "Pops! Stop! What's going on? Did Danny talk to you?"

Ben was instantly irate. His smile was long gone, perhaps inside, having a drink with Hank. "Danny?! What the hell does Danny have to do with that face I know you've been seeing?"

There it was. Charles knew he was caught, and like center stage at amateur hour, he had also spilled intel that was supposed to have remained up his sleeve.

New thoughts, none of them good, streamed into Ben's consciousness. "Shit, boy! Danny? Don't you even let me catch you having dealings with Danny."

"Your daddy's right." The voice of Jasper ended their hushed conversation, both father and son wondering what exactly he had heard.

Caught up in their own little world and camouflaged by the city lights and sounds, Ben and Charles hadn't seen Jasper's 1936 Lincoln Model K LeBaron coupe slide into its designated spot. Been there for less than thirty seconds and the car already had an audience of drooling onlookers who knew better than to touch the polished baby blue steel. Majestic chrome accents, gleaming white walls, lines like the perfect lover—there was nothing more luxuriously sophisticated as this tin can. It was also a sly way to stay neutral, because everything about this car was Ford, Edsel Ford. Jasper liked Edsel. A daddy's boy, sure, but he wasn't willing to follow the same blueprint. Edsel was willing to use the advantage he was born with and run for the hills, creating something altogether his own. Jasper's ride was just enough Ford to keep Henry's heavy-handed fixer, Harry Bennett, at bay, and just enough not Ford that if you squinted your eyes in just the right light, one could read the faint fuck-you to the man.

Jasper stood bathed in the green neon of the Geraldine's marquee. Even with his face freshly shaven, it looked rough. He was decked in a shining white zoot suit with the thinnest widely spaced black pin-stripes. On his head, a black-and-white fedora with a weaved leather band, and peeking out at his neck from under his coat was the black on black of his shirt and tie. Holding a small wooden box under his arm, he lifted the sole of one of his black-and-white leather shoes to knock the ash off the end of his Cinco cigar, then snapped it, half-finished, into a gold case that he casually dropped inside his left breast pocket. Without a doubt, Jasper was king of his wolf pack.

Was the Cinco also a political statement? Ben wondered. The cigar was far too cheap to go with Jasper's ensemble, but any cigar from Eisenlohr was currently in fashion to support the Polish women in the cigar plants all over Detroit who went on strike earlier that year, eventually winning each and every one of their demands. *Is Jasper more open to the labor movement than I give him credit?*

"The joint is hopping tonight." Jasper kissed the side of Ben's head and patted his back. Charles got the same greeting.

"Holiday agreed to play all week," Charles proudly proclaimed.

"Aces." Then Jasper's focus changed to Ben. "I changed our meeting to the Palais."

Slightly annoyed: "I was just there, Jasper."

"And now we going back."

There was no arguing. It was time to change the game plan.

"Charles, grab Hank before he gets hammered. I let him go 'cause I thought we were done."

Jasper touched Charles's forearm to stop him from running off but kept his gaze on his brother. "You know which one's the gas, don't you?" he said as he motioned for Charles to open the passenger door of Ben's Caddy.

"And if our meeting gets rough?"

"It won't."

Charles pulled the door handle, and his uncle lowered himself in and rolled down the window, pretending to mind his own business.

Charles knew there was still air to clear with his dad. He stepped to Ben with his most apologetic expression. "Hey, Pops."

"That's enough out of you. We'll deal with this later."

Jasper giggled and shouted from the car, "Don't act like you ain't never been attracted to no white tomato."

A passerby used the distraction to grab Charles's attention, "Yo, Chuck! I thought Geraldine's was sunk when I seen Fats Waller playing BJs. Now you got Holiday? *The* Billie Holiday?!"

Instantly, he was "on" like the professional club manager he was. "Don't you forget it, Joe. And don't pretend like BJs ain't cutting their hooch."

The man entered the club, all smiles, with Charles's hand on his back, and as soon as he disappeared inside, Charles once again became the pouting boy who had to answer to his father. Ben stared him down. Charles knew this could go both ways but was happy when Ben reached out his arm and pulled him in for a hug.

A pat on one side of the face while he kissed the other, Ben offered a praiseful warning. "Me and Jasper are proud of you. Real proud. I just don't want to see you crash and burn. We'll talk more later."

"Yes, sir."

No more time. Jasper was waiting, and everyone knew better than to keep Jasper waiting. Ben rounded the car and hopped in next to his brother, behind the wheel. Jasper winked at his nephew as the car pulled away, headed back into the fray, toward Le Noir Palais.

Charles's mind was in a flurry. Did the reason they were heading to Minnie's have anything to do with Betty? Why the hell had he mentioned Danny's name?

"Charles! My fella! I'd like you to meet Lisa . . ."

"Leeza," she corrected the man.

The club manager switch was flipped back on. "Well, hello, Leeza. How nice to meet cha."

The door to Geraldine's swung open, and Charles led his guests into the hypnotic vibrations of Holiday's siren song.

The Carter brothers drove in silence. Jasper was quietly confident with the small box resting in his lap, but Ben had the world on his mind. Like a carnival game at the Michigan State Fair where revelers squirt water into a scary clown's mouth until a balloon pops, Ben had no idea when the burst would happen or which thought would tumble out first.

Money is light this week. . . . I saw Rose today. She got a job working in Peck's office. . . . Sharon is drowning at the dry cleaner's; the girl has so much promise. . . . Are you proud of me for landing Billie Holiday? Charles doesn't know what he's getting into with one of Minnie's girls, let alone a white one. . . . Dammit, Jasper, Izzy says you lost fifty on the numbers. Do we really want to owe that man . . . ? And why do you insist on having any dealings with Lance at all? How's Valerie doing? Can you see that she's getting worse, or are you numb to it? I paid Schwartz, and he only told me stuff I already knew. . . .

"I got a visit from Leon Bates" was the first to slip from his mind into his mouth.

"United Auto Workers." Jasper let Ben know he was aware.

It was never easy for Ben to ask Jasper for favors. On one hand, he'd done so much. Ben owed him everything. On the other, Jasper wasn't known for his even temperament.

"He wants us to help open the lines of communication to the governor."

"Ain't that why you were screaming at everyone to vote Charles Diggs last November? That's what you preach all the time, right? Vote Black and all our problems'll be solved? Well, we did that, so I believe that's Diggs's job now." Jasper had a point.

But so did Ben. "If Bradby or any other preacher Ford has in his pocket finds out Diggs is talking to UAW officials, they'll see to it that every God-fearing Black man in Detroit votes him out the second they get a chance."

"Why is that our problem?"

"Because we're Black, Jasper."

Jasper calmly turned his head to Ben and smiled. "Thanks. I almost forgot."

"At some point we have to stand up for ourselves."

"We doing just fine."

"No, brother, I mean the whole Black race!"

Jasper had been dealing with Ben's pushy need for advancement his whole life, but the man never seemed to fully comprehend just how far they'd come since Birmingham. Was there further to climb? Sure, but *take a look around*!

"Name me a white man that done more for the Black man than Ford."

"Lincoln."

"All right, smart-ass. Both men Republicans, but you saying Lincoln was a savior and Ford wants us back in chains?"

"The party changed, Jasper! FDR! The New Deal! You were there!

You were there when the First Lady came to the ghetto and started building Black people homes!"

Jasper scoffed. "Seven hundred and one apartments. And two years later they ain't even done."

"You have to start somewhere." This was where they always came to the crossroads. Ben believed Jasper made perfect the enemy of the good, and Ben was willing to pull on any thread he could if it meant moving in the right direction.

Jasper would settle for nothing less than immediate equality in the eyes of the law, and if that wasn't going to happen, then he'd continue to play by his own rules.

"There's a hundred and forty thousand Negroes living on the east side, Ben. Most of them in Black Bottom. How many you think we can stuff in them seven hundred and one apartments?"

"It's progress."

"No, it ain't." Jasper raised his voice above calm, which at least made Ben feel like he cared. "It's the white man givin' us just enough to make us *think* it's progress."

"You just made my point, Jasper. That's why we need to consider what Bates is asking."

Jasper's face contorted with frustration. Ben had him on the ropes, and not even Joe Louis could box his way out of this valid point. He waited for his calm to come back before: "You wanna be responsible?"

"For what?"

"We call in a favor to Murphy, and the UAW gains some ground. Maybe even strikes. Ford don't want that. Overnight the Black churches lose hiring privileges at the plants. Then tomorrow you wake up to wishing unemployment could go back to what it was today."

"Sounds pretty Uncle Tom to me."

Jasper pounded his door with the side of his fist hard enough to rattle the dashboard. "Excuse me?"

Ben couldn't settle for a TKO; he needed a knockout. "Yes! Ford has done good for Black Detroit. But we don't owe him anything. We're even, Jasper! The way the employee-employer relationship works is, we give them labor, and they give us money. Fair trade. Neither side owes anything more until the next day, when we trade work for money all over again!"

"I think you need to remember who you're talking to." Jasper stared straight on, trying to hold it together.

"What, are you a Mafia boss now? Are you going to break my legs?"

Jasper turned his head and watched his brother squirm in his desire to make him understand. When Ben's wave of brash was over, Jasper spoke. "You done? What I meant was, remember that you're talking to your big brother. So there ain't no need to be rude. We're family."

"I'm sorry."

Jasper broke the tension with a grin. "You too damn smart for your own good. Sometimes I regret putting you through university."

"Sometimes I do too, because you remind me of it every chance you get."

They shared a laugh, which brought them back to neutral, but then the air filled with quiet again, which was always how the tension between them began to bubble.

"So you'll think about it?" Ben finally asked.

"No. I won't."

Ben's eyes rolled over. He thought he'd made some headway, but Jasper was done, and silence ruled once more.

Soon Ben depressed the clutch, released the accelerator, and coasted to the curb on Brewster a few doors down from Le Noir Palais. Jasper turned the box over in his lap, not really looking at it, just fidgeting for time until he spoke.

"I know you saw Peck. What did he say?"

Ben didn't bother answering. They both already knew what Peck had said. Word always got back to Jasper.

"Family sticks together, Benny. Let's stick together on this. We done lost one sister. It would kill me to lose a brother." Then Jasper changed the tired subject. "How was payday?"

"The pickups were light, and the drops were heavy." Ben waited for Jasper to digest the information, then added, "We're beat, Jasper. We don't have what this young crumb, Valentino, is trying to bleed."

Jasper answered his brother by opening the box in his lap. He removed some light packing straw, tossed it to the floor, and slid out the finely sculpted bottle of hooch. The sight of the bottle injected a shot of fear into Ben that slowly pulsed through his veins.

Jasper pulled the door latch and exited into a night of unknown consequences for which he saw no other option.

CHAPTER TEN

illie Holiday was on the Geraldine's stage singing "One Never Knows, Does One?" with a quartet that included Hank Jones on the piano. Charles Burrell, another young man who Hank knew from Cass Tech High School, was in bliss while he plucked at the bass. The master Lester Young was on sax, and Cozy Cole happened to be passing though Detroit just long enough to bang on the buckets, at Day's request. Sure, there were people known for playing together, but one of the greatest things about live jazz is that on a random night, the audience could be treated to any mix of stand-ins, substitutes, or a musician who happened to be in the club for a drink. The lineups were sometimes as improvisational as the jazz itself, and that was part of the beauty. The artists all knew one another, and they all loved to play jazz. That night at Geraldine's with Miss Day might have been the only time any ears ever heard this magnificent group play together. The same reasoning was also a travesty of jazz—it might have been the only time any ears ever heard this magnificent group play together.

With all the work put in to get Billie to play his family's club, it was a shame the noise in Charles's head blocked him from hearing her. It was normal for people to stop and want to shoot the breeze as he wandered the club. Schmoozing was one of the most important parts of club managing, but tonight he was distracted as he tried to push through the crowd. His destination, the back door to the alley, seemed to get farther away with every step he took.

"There he is! Ladies, meet Charles, the man in charge. I told you I had friends in high places!" the man said from behind his glazed eyes.

Charles wasn't sure he'd ever seen this Joe's face, but he threw up a jovial, familiar front. "If he's gonna be bothering you ladies, make sure he's buying your drinks!"

The women ate it up, and the man was happy to oblige Charles's order.

He needed to get to the back alley. Charles sped his charge, but he made it less than ten steps.

"Charles!"

"Well, well, if it ain't Jimmy Larson!"

Jimmy dove right in with his yarn. "I was talking about this . . ."

But a pat on the back and a slick side step got Charles away without insulting the man completely. He reached the back room, darted through to the door leading outside, and pushed into the night.

Leaned against the wall, smoking some hand-rolled tobacco, was Danny Gaczynski. "About time." Danny's cadence was far too soft-spoken for the weight of the evening.

Charles paused long enough to take the man in: unnatural, trying too hard, with a manufactured lean, as if posed for a picture. The drag on his cigarette was timed like he was delivering dialogue for a Gary Cooper cowboy flick. No offense to Mr. Cooper, but he was made to look tough with makeup and costumes, and the guns he carried onscreen were for show. Danny looked like a chump, but firsthand experience told Charles not to underestimate his crazy.

Charles strutted off down the alley with purpose. "If we're doing this, let's do it."

Danny snuffed his cigarette and abandoned his cool cat pose to prance after Charles.

The Forest Club's advantage was its size. The stage was big, the main ballroom was big, and the big crowds made big noise, which attracted the names of big artists. You could fit four Geraldine's in one Forest Club, but—tonight, anyway—the ratio of booze-buying patrons per square foot was far better at Geraldine's.

In his current predicament, Charles weighed the pros and cons of such a large place. Pros: You could get lost in the crowd and become a fly on the wall. Secret meetings. Overhear information. Do business. Cons: It wasn't possible to keep track of everyone in there, or who might be watching you, or what they may be packing. As they got within half a block of Forest Avenue, a third man attached himself to Charles and Danny's stride toward the club. Charles did a double take and stopped dead.

"No, Danny. Not happening." Charles spun on his heels to head back in the direction they came from, but Danny caught his shoulder.

"Lance works for my father."

Lance Edwards was a lumbering man who never said much, and tonight was no exception. He rarely wore any expression at all on his face. Angry, sad, jovial—they were all equal on Lance. The name Edwards was a Jasper-Ben compromise. Most of the time Ben went along with or was forced to follow Jasper's lead when they disagreed. Lance, however, had been a sticking point. Jasper refused to disobey his father's dying wish to take care of his brothers. Their mother had been pregnant with Jasper at the same time that Lance's mother had carried him. They were born nine days apart, and for reasons their father took to his fiery cross, he chose Jasper and Ben's mother instead of Lance's. Years later, when Ben hardened his heart against Lance, he had one condition for Jasper—Lance could not use the Carter name.

And in the very moment that Ben put his foot down, literally and figuratively, they were standing within sight of the signage for Edwards Paint and Mortar store.

In one of those horrible acts of cruelty that life sometimes lays in your lap, a tornado ripped through the greater Birmingham area in the early hours of March 25, 1901. In Pratt City, Charles had already gone to the mine. A neighbor had been asked to watch ten-year-old Jasper, five-year-old Ben, and an infant sister less than two months old while Mrs. Carter visited the church to pick up a few charitable items to help with her new baby daughter. Ten-year-old Lance was home alone while his mother worked at the high school, where she cleaned for an hour or two each morning. The *Pratt City Herald* only counted four among the dead, and neither mother was listed, but it was common practice to give less attention to a natural disaster's Negro death toll. The paper did, however, say that in the storm's two-hundred-foot path of destruction, both the Southern Methodist Church and Pratt City High School were leveled. The women, the mothers, were never seen or heard from again.

Charles had tried to take Lance in, but the trauma was too much for Lance's young brain. He ran away and lived as a beggar for years in and around Birmingham, only occasionally showing his face in Pratt City. The week their father was lynched just happened to be one of those occasions, and with his father's dying words ringing in his head, Jasper all but forced Lance against his will to travel north with them.

"I ain't got nothing against him, but I'm already risking being seen with you. It's family stuff, Danny."

Lance glued his eyes to the sidewalk beneath his feet. He assumed his nephew was incapable of comprehending the negativity it stirred inside him to be standing in front of the second man named Charles Carter to reject him.

"My father wants him on this, Charles." Danny turned to Lance.

"Tell him. Tell him my father wants you on this."

Lance was uncomfortable being put on the spot, especially when the purpose was to be obviously redundant. "Izzy wants me on this."

How could Charles be sure? How could he trust this wasn't a setup? He couldn't, but he also didn't have much of a choice.

Then Danny sealed the deal. "If we go down for this, we're taking you with us."

The heat in Charles's eyes in that instant was proof he could handle whatever waited for them inside the Forest Club. What he couldn't handle was looking at Danny's smug face any longer, so he trudged forward, nudging the little twerp as he entered the club to find his fate.

Off the main hall was a smoky back-room bar for more intimate performances. Sitting on a stool on a small corner stage was a beautifully large woman making love to her microphone, flanked by a clarinet player and a piano man. Hunched over the microphone, sweat beading on her forehead, this canary, known only as Mama Do, was getting her guests hot under the collar with her rendition of "A Good Man Is Hard to Find." The crowd was lost in the sexy groove and took advantage of the excuse to get closer to the person they hoped to go home with when the lights eventually came up.

Charles, Danny, and Lance emerged from a doorway slung with beads, moving slow and talking low to blend in with the room's current vibe, but they had no interest in the songbird or whose hands were where at table three. Their eyes were all on the small bar in the opposite corner from the stage, where a Black bartender was mixing whiskey and egg whites.

"That him?" Charles asked.

Danny nodded affirmation, and the three men sauntered to the bar, where Charles tossed up his hand to signal for a drink.

The clean-cut and confident man they'd come to see answered the call. "She got pipes, don't she?"

"Yeah, she sounds good," Charles responded, studying the man intently.

"What can I get you?"

"Three whiskeys." Danny knew Charles would pay.

"Coming right up." The bartender flipped over three rocks glasses from behind the bar and grabbed a bottle of Old Hermit. "I don't think I seen you cats before. New in town?"

Danny tossed a glance from the sides of his eyes, as if the man had somehow just given himself away. Maybe he didn't know Danny or Lance, but not knowing Jasper's nephew, who ran another Paradise Valley hot spot?

"We usually hit Geraldine's," Charles explained, hoping Danny would sit tight with his lips buttoned.

"Geraldine's? What y'all doing here tonight, then? Ain't you see the marquee right now at Geraldine's?"

"You asking a lot of questions, don't you think?" Danny came in hot.

"I didn't mean any harm. I saw Billie Holiday's name, and . . ."

"Yeah? Well, careful. Questions can get you in trouble."

So much for buttoned lips. Charles placed his hand on Danny's chest in an attempt to de-escalate the matter, but it had the opposite effect.

"Get your hand off me." He swiped Charles away and went right back at the barkeep. "You know what? I know a lot of people, and somehow I don't know you. Why is that?"

"I just moved from Chicago last month," he responded as he casually tapped a panic button under the bar top.

Danny was getting more irate at the speed of light. "Pretty suspicious, if you ask me. Only just got here from Chi-Town and he tries to interrogate *us* about why he never seen *our* mugs before?"

"Danny!"

Before Danny could respond to Charles's plea, an expensive suit approached with the swagger of an important man. Charles hunched his shoulders and folded his arms, wishing he could melt into the floorboards. The man in the suit was Jameson Tillman. He owned the place. Ben had just told Charles not to have dealings with Danny, and here they stood, not an hour later, with enough eyeballs to get word back to his father before he had time to shoot his whiskey.

"These gentlemen causing trouble, Jon Jon?" Jameson asked his barkeep.

"Trouble? This fucking grifter is the one causing trouble. Ain't that right, Jon Jon?" Danny clumsily swung his hand and knocked over one of the drinks, drawing in even more of the spotlight. "You wanna keep asking people about my comings and goings? Go on! Ask me!"

"It's time to go, Danny."

Charles was more afraid of his father and uncle than he was of Danny and Izzy, so it was time he took matters into his own hands. He pushed Danny toward the door, but they hadn't escaped yet.

"I'm glad your daddy taught you manners, Charles," Jameson called after them.

Charles looked back, in utter disbelief that their outing had gone this bad, this fast. There was nothing he could do now but own it. "I'm sorry, Mr. Tillman. I'll see him out. Must'a had one too many."

Danny straightened his jacket and marched out, still aiming the evil eye at the bartender. Lance followed. Then went Charles with his tail between his legs.

Mama Do's room was annoyed to have been interrupted, but in less than sixteen bars, she had her crowd right back into the heat of foreplay.

CHAPTER ELEVEN

As Ben stepped from the car up to Le Noir Palais, his watch said it was two minutes past nine, and his face said he hated being late. The front door and both windows on the porch were open, and raucous jazz slipped into the night to alert passing ears that they were open for business. That was enough for her regulars, but what about potential first-timers? Minnie had learned in her time that the majority of new customers were men who happened to walk by and decided to lead with curiosity. This was why on any given night there were three or four attractive women sitting on the porch, directed to giggle just so as men walked by. Once the men were in the door, away from eyes on the street, it was a forgone conclusion that cash would be spent. The women were trained in the art of getting the highest price a client could afford, which always started when a price was asked for and the woman bit her lip, winked, and said, "How much you got, honey?" For him it was playful banter, but for her it was a business move to get him to throw out the first number, a number close to everything in his billfold, which of course he'd never agree to, but that was the starting place. From there they'd work backward until the arrival of the slightest pause or stutter of a "maybe." That's when all negotiations stopped, and the woman would stand her ground and push booze until the "maybe" was a "yes."

Drinks were served full proof for the client and either water or iced tea for the working girl. The more the man drank, the more lettuce he'd be willing to part with, and the woman whose attention he was renting would stay sober and in control of the entire show. If a bloke came in with a fat stack but a rancid smell or was over eighty or was grotesque beyond some invisible line that was always apparent the moment the man stepped into the parlor, Minnie would whisper in the bartender's ear, and drinks would arrive, ordered or not, and both would be alcohol. Sometimes a shot was needed to get through the job. Depending on the kind of "job," a girl might be given two.

Minnie made the men feel like kings. Yes, she was after money, but she also had a reputation for being "honest enough." She knew there was a line between a john wishing he hadn't spent so much and one reporting a robbery to the authorities. She was all about upselling an energetic Joe who wanted to do things he'd never be brave enough to ask his wife, but no one ever claimed they were rolled at Le Noir Palais. The girls felt safe too, taken care of. They were allowed to say no for any reason, no questions asked, and if a man refused that no, the bartender, who the women all had different nicknames for—Mouse, the General, Trim—would escort the disrespectful man from the premises. Most of the time, it only took a stern "The lady would prefer if you left now, sir," but on one occasion a broken arm and ruptured kidney were required before the client understood the definition of the word "no." Finally, whether Minnie loved her girls as her own or it was simply good business, anyone selling sin under Minnie's roof was supplied with condoms and weekly house calls from a doctor. A clean bill of health was a benefit for the girls, and a check mark in the column for client recidivism.

Minnie stood in the doorway as Jasper came up the walk with Ben in tow. The women on the porch all knew Jasper personally, and their flirtatious catcalls made him smile. For all his gruff machismo, Jasper was shy with these women, and Minnie's girls loved it. As he climbed the porch steps, Euni dragged her fingers up the arm of his suit, and he got a loud purr from the woman who disliked Betty giving it away to Charles for free. Jasper liked the attention; even Minnie chuckled, well aware of the games being played from every direction. That's when Jasper was stopped by the youngest and newest of Minnie's ebony beauties. She slid in, wrapping a hand around the back of his head like falling silk, and kissed his mouth. The eyes of everyone in the receiving party widened in disbelief.

Hard enough to be a jolt but not hurt the poor girl who was only trying to make an impression, Jasper shoved her off. "A little forward, don't you think?"

The girl looked to Minnie for help but quickly learned from her eyes that no help was coming, because she had been in the wrong. Jasper put his sculpted booze bottle in his left hand so he could grab the pocket square at his chest with his right and wipe his mouth.

"Don't do that again," he said as he dropped the cloth into his pant pocket and stepped up to Minnie. He forgot the incident as quickly as it had happened, but if the new girl disrespected his wife, Valerie, in the sight of others again, she'd be out on her ass.

"Cousin," Minnie said with a stern face.

"Cousin," Jasper matched her.

Tension was thick, onlookers watching and waiting with anticipation. Were they angry with each other? Was a gossip-worthy event about to occur? Then Minnie cracked a smile, freeing Jasper to laugh full-out. Just a game between fun-loving cousins. He kissed her hand like she was a queen, and she bowed with a graceful, swooping gesture, welcoming them to her Palais.

"Right this way, gentlemen."

Inside the grand salon, with its freestanding balcony around the entire perimeter of the second floor and the one-of-a-kind highly polished sixteen-foot oak-slab bar that Minnie looted when Jethro's pub foreclosed, the evening's potential customers loitered in the company of Minnie's women. The place did its job perfectly. The Palais made a man feel loose, unrestricted, independent, desired.

It felt like freedom.

Being desired felt like freedom.

Jasper didn't add up the exact count of the men, but he did note where each of the three white customers was sitting. The women were less and more diverse at the same time. All the girls were Black except for two Asians—one "Indian" and one "Chinese"—and one white, Betty Bell. Each of the non-Black employees leaned hard into their corresponding stereotypes. The woman known as Liling wore a traditional Chinese hanfu even though her real name was Bian and she was Vietnamese. The one with the bindi on her forehead was called Ramya, Tanvi, or Padmavati, but both her parents were Muslims from Bangladesh who called her Nasrin. Betty Bell was the American name chosen by Galina Sokolova. She regularly dressed like silver screen starlets, but her lederhosen and pigtails had become a favorite of her standing 6:15 on Tuesdays and Fridays.

Minnie herself was looking damn good as she slinked through the room, leading Jasper and Ben to the back hallway, where the sounds of adult-themed good times spilled from the doors on either side.

"Be nice. He spends." Minnie rapped her knuckle on the door to her cousins' regular meeting room and opened it without stepping in, allowing a path for them to enter.

Inside, a young, flat-chested Black woman with zero percent body fat was making up for her lack of curves with writhing and sass as she finished up a lap dance for a twenty-six-year-old white man in a flashy burgundy pin-striped suit—Valentino Locurto.

"Don't you leave without saying goodbye now, Valentino." She slid his red silk tie through her fingers as she slipped away.

Minnie held the door open from the hallway, actively not looking into the room but waiting for Skinny's seductive exit. The girl gave a final, sexy flick of her tongue back at Valentino before Minnie pulled the door closed, leaving the three men alone together at last.

Jasper presented the sculpted bottle to Valentino like he was a hand model, then moved toward the wet bar, where he flipped three waiting glasses right side up. "I get this shipped from the Savoy in New York. For special occasions."

"So what you're saying is, it cost more than it should," Valentino quipped.

Jasper glanced over his shoulder with a smirk at the man before reaching into the Westinghouse freezer next to the bar to retrieve the aluminum ice tray.

Ben busied himself by sliding over an armchair and its ottoman so he and Jasper could sit near their guest, then he stood, staring at the painting of nighttime in Paris while Jasper played bartender.

A slight twist of the tray cracked the cubes loose, and Jasper dropped two in each glass. Then he pulled the decorative stopper out with a satisfying pop and poured the caramel-colored beverage into the glasses. The ice crackled and split with the splash of the room temperature fluid. Jasper handed a glass to Ben as he took his seat on the ottoman and passed another to Valentino before grabbing his own off the bar.

The room was quiet except for the tinny sound of the Victrola softly spinning King Oliver's 1926 "Someday Sweetheart" in the corner. Jasper sat in the armchair, leaned back, and crossed his legs with his drink-holding hand in his lap. Business could now begin.

Valentino sipped his drink, swishing the burn to the back of his throat and swallowing with a surprised grimace. "A little better than I gave you credit for."

"I guess you underestimated me." Jasper spoke with airy contemplation.

Both Carter men stared at Valentino, allowing the room to fill with an awkward, almost scary, silence. Valentino felt the pressure, but he understood the tactic. He was on their turf. As far as he was concerned, they could put on any show they liked, because he knew he held all the cards. This was about to be his territory, whether the Carter boys liked it or not.

Valentino took another sip of his drink and sat forward in his chair to lay out his rude and condescending pitch. "You gotta look at the big picture, fellas. Sure, some months my delivery fees will seem extreme. I mean, after all, it's the same fee no matter how much you need. But on big weeks? Like this week? You know the customers are gonna need a lot of hooch when they cram in to hear that floozy quiff Holiday."

Ben's face was a rock, not a twitch, but Jasper couldn't wipe the knowing grin off his face. Valentino thought it was their turn to talk, but all he got was more intimidating silence from his unwilling business partners while King Oliver was accompanied by the rocks Jasper swirled in his glass.

The young man took another sip, this time out of nervousness. Beads of sweat began to form on his forehead. He wiped them away with a hanky and went back to it.

"I'm attentive enough to know your silence means you ain't got my scratch, so I'm gonna do you a favor and let you double up next time. Don't worry. My driver will still make the drop. You won't be short. Just have it next month, because it would be a sad day if deliveries to Geraldine's dried up altogether."

"That a threat?" Jasper asked, as if Valentino had just told a joke.

He wiped more sweat from his brow. "No need for threats, my

brother."

"You ain't my brother." Jasper's grin was gone.

Valentino shifted in his chair and took another drink, this time for the courage he needed to strengthen his approach. "Listen, pal, I know you think you're some sort of hotshot, gin-running Black Al Capone, but even Al Capone had to pay the delivery drivers." Feeling out of his element, he loosened his tie. *Would it kill someone to open a window around here?*

Ben knew there was nothing he could do to stay Jasper's hand when someone crossed one of his lines. This poor kid was only a few years older than his boy Charles and stepping in more shit than he was capable of scraping off the bottom of his overpriced shoes. Not wanting to watch as Valentino slipped further down the rabbit hole, Ben kept his eyes on the ice slowly melting in his glass.

Jasper juggled a thought or two in his head before deciding on: "Booze is legal these days, Valentino. After living through Prohibition, the racket you trying to run on delivery trucks seems like child's play."

"A businessman always seizes on opportunity." Valentino proudly delivered the line he had picked up from someone in his life who had been trying to teach him right.

"Ain't that so? I was just talking with Benny here about how we could use another revenue stream."

"If you're making me a proposition, I'm listening." Valentino wiped his head again. He was really sweating bad now. He downed the last bit of his drink, hoping the cooled beverage would rescue him.

"Sure. A proposition." Jasper pulled himself forward and planted his elbows on his knees, drink dangling from his fingertips by the rim of the glass, eyes burrowing into Valentino's soul. "How about this for a proposition? I take your trucks, your drivers, and your Chicago contacts off your hands. Then I don't have to pay you, *and* I got more bread coming in. Now that right there sounds like seizing opportunity."

Valentino was feeling the pressure now. Lightheaded, his left eyelid started to droop, and then he saw it. How had he missed the obvious? His father would be so ashamed. His two young girls, Joan and Lizzy, would be too young to even remember his face. They hadn't even been trying to hide it from him, no. Jasper and Ben hadn't so much as sipped their drinks. Not a single drop.

The glass slipped from Valentino's manicured fingers and tumbled to the floor, sending the partially melted ice cubes halfway across the room. The young father tried to stand, but he didn't realize he was on a boat in choppy seas, and his legs failed him. He fell to his knees, reaching back to the chair to keep him upright.

Jasper stood and casually reached for Ben's glass, then took both full drinks back to the wet bar, poured them in the sink, and put the glasses in the basin before turning to address Valentino one last time.

"Black Al Capone? Nah, it's just Jasper Carter. Don't forget it."

On cue, Valentino's eyes rolled into the back of his head, and he collapsed to the floor with a hollow thump that was surely heard in the room below. Minnie, who'd stood guard outside the door, came in with a world of worry washed over her face.

"We're good, cousin. We're good." Jasper gently pushed her out and closed the door.

Ben was still in the same position, staring at his fidgeting fingers that recently held a cocktail of hydrogen cyanide. "He dead?"

"He's still breathing."

"Will it kill him?" Ben asked.

"I'm not a chemist." Jasper put his shoe on the armrest of the chair he'd sat in and started untying the laces.

Ben lifted his eyes, concerned with his brother's actions. "We've done enough, Jas."

Shoe untied, Jasper began to pull the laces out completely.

"What's the point here? He may already be doomed, but if we're lucky, he'll wake up in his own piss, and we'll never hear from him again. This is a step backward from going straight, Jasper." Ben made no attempt to stop his brother physically.

Jasper lowered himself to one knee over Valentino's unconscious body, slid one end of his shoelace under his neck, and pulled up on both ends. The veins in the man's neck began to bulge blue against his pale white skin.

"Jasper."

But Jasper was steadfast. He didn't release any tension, and there wouldn't be another protest out of Ben.

Valentino convulsed slightly, and a little spittle escaped his mouth. His body went limp. Still, Jasper held tight to the laces for another thirty horrifying seconds. When he finally let go, the Carters no longer needed to pay for booze delivery.

Jasper looked up to make sure his kid brother understood. "Going straight can be a dirty business."

PART
TWO

PART
TWO

CHAPTER TWELVE

Taft had been in the White House for going on three years, bathing in a specially built "Taft-sized" tub that the newspapers found worthy of ink. Orville Wright flew a glider for over nine and a half minutes, a record that wouldn't be broken for a decade. Chevrolet officially started giving Henry Ford a run for his money, and board game magnate Milton Bradley left the world, making room for the birth of future actor turned president of the United States Ronald Reagan, but for Jasper Carter, 1911 was unappreciated, backbreaking labor in the Barnsley mine in rural western Kentucky.

Two coal veins were discovered under that part of the state, numbers nine and eleven, so the St. Bernard Mining Company founded and built the town of Earlington, but it became apparent right away that there simply weren't enough people to get the fuel out of the ground. Luckily, there was a tried-and-true, age-old plan of action—poor people—and in America the poorest people were Black. Recruiters were dispatched to the poor neighborhoods of cities and towns near and far. The pitch was made with a ticket to Earlington and some cash to ease the cost of relocation, and slowly Black men filled the mines. So many came that a free and public school for colored children was built, and a column in the weekly *Earlington Bee* was dedicated to "Colored News."

When the Carter kids made it to Nashville, Jasper set his brothers and sister up with some rags and shoe polish on a street corner, then went off to do the harder work of begging white men in suits for pennies. That's when Jasper met the smiling white man who offered him "a future in Kentucky." That night, with four train tickets in Jasper's pocket, the Carters had full bellies and slept in an actual bed in a rundown boardinghouse. Maybe they could make it after all.

After Jasper had been working two years for the St. Bernard Mining Company, Ben and Rosalind were enrolled in school, Lance was running numbers out of a blacksmith storefront while discovering Kentucky bourbon to excess, and the coal dust Jasper breathed every single day graveled the sound of his voice for good.

Twenty years old and he already felt like his life was over. When Ben asked how his day was, Jasper felt anger, not at his brother but at the fact that every day was so hard, so monotonous, so exactly the same. Answering the question felt like failure. He wanted to say something exciting had happened. He wanted to tell his brother that he saw a path toward a promotion, maybe a shot at owning their own house someday, a chance for Ben to go to college, but every evening the same words came out of his mouth. "Same shit, different day," he'd say, as if he were an old-timer who'd already given up on life.

Jasper woke up before the sun with the aid of a gentle nudge from Ben, and before his eyes could even focus, his kid brother was out the door to start his first job. Lance's bed, as usual, hadn't been slept in. Only ten-year-old Rosalind remained in slumber, and Jasper was fine to let her stay that way as long as possible, in her dreams, in her childhood, away from reality. He shimmied into his clothes and snuck out of the room, knowing full well that Ben would help get their sister off to school when he got home. Jasper was as quiet as possible coming down the stairs, but Miss Virgie always beat him to the kitchen, where she'd offer him a cup of sludge-like coffee sweetened with molasses. Everything else about their relationship was the business between a landlady and tenant, but he suspected something in this act of kindness was in memory of her late husband, who'd worked mine number eleven until the evening of April 30, 1901, when he went to bed and never woke. Now Jasper and his kin lived in the second bedroom of the house Miss Virgie's husband had built for her with the money he saved working the mines.

It was about a quarter mile to the main road, where a handful of company trucks would pass by as the sky started to lighten, picking up coal men along the way. Dressed in boots, overalls, a long-sleeve shirt buttoned to his neck, and thick work gloves, all still dirty from the days before, Jasper led his two assigned mules and empty coal cart down the slanting shaft. Within fifteen feet of the entrance, men needed to light the carbide lamps strapped to their soft caps, which produced a white flame in front of a small reflective disk to light the way.

"By the end of the day, I'll be as black as you, boys," Jasper heard an Irishman everyone called Mic say to anyone willing to listen.

"You'll still have your little prick, though, Mic."

A couple chuckles echoed in the shaft but not one from Jasper. He knew the man only wanted to breed some common ground with his colleagues, and, let's face it, the Irish had it pretty bad too, but when Mic washed the artificial blackness from his skin that evening, he would be allowed to eat dinner at any table in any of the nine restaurants in Earlington.

On a good day, Jasper would wait his turn to pull his cart next to a heap of black rocks at the end of the tunnel, and the delirious sounds of the pneumatic pick, operated by another Irishman, would rattle Jasper's eardrums as he loaded up. Then, as he accompanied the mules back to the top, his mind would wander. The only thing worse than hard physical labor was hard physical labor that didn't require your brain. Jasper was jealous of simpler folks who somehow accepted their lot, some even finding joy hidden under the black dust. "I tell you what. Nothin' better than a bottle a suds after a long day a work." "Coal keeps me honest. No time for idle hands, and enough coin to put grub on the table." "At least we free and livin', not like them poor bastards down in Bama."

In April of that year, 128 men died in the Banner Mine near Birmingham. Banner was a Pratt mine. Jasper's daddy had worked that mine once or twice. No exact reason was given in the paper for what went wrong, but Jasper was intensely aware of the dangers. A blast had been reported, but not one big enough to kill that many men. The rest was left to the imagination. Cave-in. Flood. Black damp suffocation. The talk among his fellow workers was all about those "poor souls" or "heaven help them," but Jasper secretly thought they'd been delivered from their misery. Of the 128 men, 90 percent were Black, and all but five were convicts leased to Pratt Consolidated Coal Company. When the mines needed filling, the jails in Alabama would be stocked with Negroes on trumped-up misdemeanors of parole violation or "vagrancy," because there were mandated state quotas for convict labor. What if there weren't enough people locked up to meet those quotas? The answer was simple—arrest more Black people.

Jasper scoffed, and one of his mules brayed. *These twits down here thinking they're somehow better than those boys buried under Banner. Better how? Better 'cause you chose to come down here? Down here being thankful to be free. Free? Hell, at least those Banner boys had the excuse that they was forced underground.* Jasper hung his head and kicked a pebble. *This ain't free. Ain't none of us free.*

Back in the daylight, Jasper and his mules climbed to the upper level of the tipple, and the carts were dumped into giant sifters that separated the larger blocks from the lump and nut coal and the slack. Then he hitched up another cart and got back in line to fetch more rocks. On the way down, his mind drifted again, this time to the other big mining news no one would shut the hell up about. Up in Westmoreland County, Pennsylvania, thousands of minors went on strike to protest working conditions. They were after an eight-hour workday, pay equal to other coal operations close by, and standardized coal cart sizes since they were paid by the ton. They also demanded to be paid for "dead work." The only way to get paid was to dump coal, so when a man spent his time shoring up mine walls with timber—no pay. When cart tracks needed to be laid, or floodwater had to be pumped out, or worthless slate and clay needed to be hauled away before they could even get to the black gold—no pay.

What did these Westmoreland County fools achieve? What exactly did they win? Nothing. They lost. Strikers stopped production in over sixty mines between March and June, but in the end, the United Mine Workers of America ran out of money to fight the coal companies and voted to end the strike. To make matters worse, the coal companies banded together. They evicted the families of thousands of coal workers from company housing. Men, women, and children lived in tents through a brutal Pennsylvania winter. Wages were dropped by 16 percent, down to fifty-eight cents per ton and a half of coal. And to top it off, a private force known as the Coal and Iron Police, along with the Pennsylvania State Police, beat and murdered protestors.

Tell me again how being a union man pays, Jasper thought, trudging up and down the shaft, blisters on his feet, coughing up black mucus. Jasper's bitterness hardened along with his resolve to get out of this godforsaken hole in the ground. The rocks that paid his shit wages never got the chance to become diamonds, but the pressure this filthy black life continuously dumped on Jasper Carter would make him unbreakable. At the end of the day, the only things that gave him the slightest relief were a bath, a drink, and a fuck. On a good night, he'd get all three before the cycle began again the next morning.

On his walk back to the main road, Jasper was faced with the same dilemma every day. Stop off at Auntie's place and spend some of his weekly wages to get a shower and release some tension, or continue on home with money still in his pocket and use the creek that ran out back of Miss Virgie's house to bathe. He and his family would be better off if he went straight home every night, but the thing about instant gratification is its immediacy. He could feel the anxiety of the choice building inside him from the moment the house came into view until he either went inside or passed it by. Auntie was twice his age and looked every day of it, but she was soft and kind. Never more than a few sentences passed between them, but that was plenty. She put him in the shower while she undressed herself and "freshened up." Jasper didn't know what that entailed and didn't care, because the warm running water was his only thought until Auntie quietly joined him and lifted her leg onto the side of the basin, arched her back, and pulled him closer.

At home that night on the porch, with a bottle of moonshine he bought off a fellow miner for half the price of a bottle at the company store, Jasper could tell something was on Ben's mind.

"Out with it."

Ben's face was scrunched like he was figuring calculus in his head. "There's this girl. . . ."

"Damn, boy! You fifteen already. I was wondering when you were gonna get some pussy."

"What?! No! God! I just really like this girl! That's all!"

Ben wanted to crawl under a rock, but Jasper couldn't help having a laugh. He had guessed wrong but still felt the relief of knowing his brother at least liked women.

"Obviously you know about pussy, or you wouldn't be so embarrassed. What are you worried about? Tell me about this lucky lady."

Ben laid down in a grassy patch and stared up at the sky, imagining Emma. "She's . . . She's . . ." He went silent as his thoughts rounded the curve of her neck. "She's . . ."

"Boy, you in trouble!" Jasper croaked with a smile. He slung his bottle back for a swig and dove in. "Listen up, buck. I'll give you three rules, and then you on your own to figure out the rest. And if you figure out the rest, you let me know, you hear?"

Ben sat up, legs crossed, putting his best attention forward for his lesson.

"Rule one: a filly is a filly, but family is family. Don't get the two mixed up. And someday, not today, not tomorrow, but someday, when you meet a woman and you want to sign a contract to make her family? You check with me first."

Ben didn't know good advice from bad, so he took it all in. He'd have to sort it out later.

"Rule two: if you pay for it, the transaction is over. You're even. If you don't pay for it, the price is higher. Neither way is wrong, but you gotta know the difference."

This one was harder for Ben to comprehend. He knew Jasper sometimes stopped at Auntie's but had no idea why that was relevant to Emma.

Jasper took another swig and stood up, ready to go inside. "Rule three: when it feels like your dick 'bout to explode in, like, a good way, you take it out and put your shit on her leg, or the bed, or in the grass, but never let that shit inside her."

Horrified: "Shit?"

"Not like *shit* shit, but, like, your shit. Know what I mean?"

He knew what Jasper meant but hadn't even considered going to bed with Emma. "I just want her to come over for supper, Jas."

"You run it by Miss Virgie?"

"Yes, sir."

"What she say?"

"She said if it was all right with you, she'd be happy to have her over tomorrow night for stew."

Jasper corked his bottle and smiled at his brother. This kid had something. "Well, all right, then. I look forward to meeting . . ."

"Emma."

"Emma. All right, then." With that, Jasper opened the screen door and disappeared inside, letting the door's spring slam it shut behind him.

Ben's experience in Kentucky was worlds away from Jaspers. He was thriving in structure. He succeeded when he had a schedule or a deadline to meet. His first job of the day was as a callboy for the St. Bernard Mining Company. He ran to the homes of the ten men on his list to make sure they were awake and on their way to work. He took this job seriously. If he was late, then the men were late, and if the men were late, then the company lost money, and that was bad business. From his earliest days, bad business weighed heavily on Ben. He hated his overdeveloped feeling of disappointment for letting others down, but it kept him honest.

After the men were off to the mines, Ben returned to accompany Rosalind to school and always made a mental note as to whether or not Lance had been home yet. A full day at school, where he was grade levels smarter than any colored boy his age and had more capacity for critical thinking than the teacher herself, was followed by getting his sister home and then off to Mr. Hoffeman's zinnia field to cut the crop. This was the best part of his day. Emma was the best part of his day.

Ben's young mind couldn't fathom a better feeling than the clammy hot flash that washed over his goose-pimpled flesh when he watched Emma in the field under her soft-brimmed felt hat, flower basket on her hip, with the strap slung over her shoulder as she cut the pink-

and-yellow blooms. He couldn't help the extra attention his gaze gave to the valley between her breasts, forged by the basket's strap. After a momentary slip, he remembered the gentlemanly qualities he was being taught in school, and he lowered his eyes. After a deep, centering breath, he raised them again and was able to take in the bigger picture. The afternoon sun cascading across the field of gently blowing reds and lavenders. The delicate elegance that Emma used to cut the stem of each flower and gently place it in the basket, with care for those that had been placed before it. Her cream-colored blouse buttoned to the neck and tucked into her navy skirt, which she had tied between her legs to create loose-fitting britches. The only visible skin, the only pieces of the actual Emma that could be seen, were her graceful hands and exquisite face. He needed to see her face—he needed it like nutrients to keep him alive—and the only way to get more than a passing glance was to speak.

"Hi, Emma." Her face. Her cheeks. Her eyebrows. Holy hellfire, her smile. One front tooth pushed ever so slightly forward was somehow the most attractive tooth Ben had ever seen.

"Hello, Ben." She smiled wider when Ben's response was just delayed enough to be noticeable.

"Miss Virgie said it would be lovely having you for dinner. Plenty of food to go around."

"That sounds good."

Ben was frozen and didn't know if he'd ever come back to life.

"Should I bring anything?"

"Oh, no, we've got it. . . . I'm sure Miss Virgie has everything she needs. My sister and at least one of my brothers will be there too." He was suddenly nervous. "He works the Barnsley mine, so sometimes he can be pretty mucked up when he gets home. Sorry about that."

"My daddy works the mines. He says the muck is proof he been working hard."

Ben was all of a sudden highly conscious of just how clean he was. Did she think he didn't work hard? Panic consumed him and stole the spit from his mouth and throat when he noticed Emma had twice as many flowers in her basket than he had in his. He choked down a dry swallow and shifted his weight from foot to foot.

"You a cute one, Ben." Then she went right back to cutting stems, face hidden under her hat. "I'll see you at quitting time."

"Yes, ma'am . . . I mean, Emma. Yes, Emma."

Ben shuffled off to another section of waiting zinnias before he could embarrass himself any further.

When the whistle blew and the flower pickers dropped their last baskets, Ben led Emma on the path next to the creek, back to Miss Virgie's. It was prettier than the main road, but he hadn't taken into consideration the mosquitoes. The conversation was slow to develop until Emma realized the problem and picked up the reins.

"You ever been with a girl before?"

"Well, my mom passed on when I was real young, but I spend a lot of time with my sister." He was shocked to find her looking at him funny and tried to correct whatever his mistake had been. "I help Miss Virgie cook and tend the yard. I been around her a lot, I guess."

She didn't want to embarrass him, but she was becoming aware of their differences.

"How old are you, Ben?"

"Fifteen . . . You're sixteen, right?"

"Yeah."

"I guess you don't hang around with too many fifteen-year-olds, then."

"No. Not too many."

"I'm sorry."

"You ain't got nothing to be sorry about."

She smiled and took his hand, which lit dynamite in his chest. As he concentrated on his breathing and became aware of how sweaty his palms were, she was gathering the courage to ask the next question. This question made her look as young as she was.

"Would a boy like you be interested in a girl if she had a boyfriend before?"

They walked a few paces before: "What do you mean, exactly?" Now Ben was older.

"I mean, I've had boyfriends, and sometimes nice boys don't really . . . understand."

"You mean, you've had boyfriends, like you've . . ." Ben didn't know how to finish the sentence like a gentleman, so he froze. Luckily Emma didn't let him hang out to dry.

"Yeah. Like that."

Ben no longer thought about perspiration, mosquitoes, or the thumping in his chest. He felt the weight of her question, and it calmed him. He wanted her to feel safe, but he still wasn't sure how to answer, and they walked along quite a ways in silence.

Then she stopped cold. "Ben," she whispered.

"What? What's wrong?"

She motioned up ahead about fifty yards, where a bend in the creek cut in front of them. There, standing in all his buck-naked glory, was Jasper rinsing the coal dust off his body, with his already rinsed clothes laid out over nearby bushes.

Suppressed laughter bursting through, Ben grabbed Emma's hand tighter, and they took off before Jasper could make heads or tails of the rustle in the distant bushes.

Minutes later Emma and Ben were chatting on the porch about school. She'd never gone before and had a bunch of questions. Fielding her questions made Ben certain she would have been a good student if she had ever gone.

Miss Virgie leaned out the screen door. "Benjamin, I need you to run down to Parkers and grab a can a them OXO bouillon cubes."

"Yes, ma'am." He jumped up and hoped to be racing along quicker than Emma could put two and two together but no such luck.

"You told me Miss Virgie didn't need nothing." Then she hollered toward the door Miss Virgie had just appeared in, "Sorry, Miss Virgie, we'll hurry. Thank you so much for having me."

She swatted at Ben as they rounded the house to head out on their errand and found Jasper coming up the path. He was wearing his damp overalls but carrying the rest of his clothing, shirt included, hung over one arm and holding his boots in his opposite hand.

"Heya, Jasper. Um. This is Emma, who I told you about. Emma, this is my brother Jasper."

Jasper nodded his head politely. "Nice to meet you, Miss Emma. Pardon my appearance, but I promise you it's better than how I looked after work today."

"I understand. Ben told me you were a miner. My daddy's a miner too."

"Sometimes I stop"—Jasper motioned up the road—"For a hot shower, but I didn't want to miss our dinner guest tonight, so I opted for the creek instead."

Ben hated how masculine Jasper looked in that moment and couldn't wait to get on their way. "We gotta run. We'll be back real quick."

"Where y'all running off to?"

"Miss Virgie needs some OXO for the stew," Emma replied.

"She loves those bouillon cubes." Jasper turned on his brother. "I thought she asked you to grab more on Tuesday?"

"I forgot. We'll be back quick." Ben pulled Emma's hand, but Jasper wasn't done.

"Both y'all going? If Miss Virgie don't got the bouillon, I bet that means she's behind. That woman does an awful lot for us." Jasper

looked at his brother, who he hoped would make it to the next conclusion on his own but apparently not. "Emma, you think you could
give her a hand while I get some dry things on and Benny runs to
Parkers and back?"

"Oh, I'd be more than happy to help. That okay with you, Ben?"
The question wasn't really a question because she said it as she let go
of his hand. A sure sign the decision had already been made.

"Absolutely. I'll be quick. I'll be right back!" Not wanting to be out
of Emma's presence a second longer than he had to, Ben took off in a
full sprint.

The slight awkwardness between two people who barely knew
each other was broken by Emma. "You pointed up toward Auntie's
house. That where you sometimes shower?"

"You know Auntie?" The question was loaded with unspoken context.

Twelve minutes later, small brown paper bag in hand, Ben sprinted
back up toward Miss Virgie's place. He was already thinking about
how he was going to excuse himself and change his clothes, which
were now as wet with sweat as Jasper's were from the creek, but as he
rounded the house, his whole world shattered. Suddenly his lungs,
which only moments before were gasping for air, now couldn't take
a breath. Jasper's overalls were unclasped and around his ankles.
Emma's legs were wrapped tightly around his waist as he repeatedly
thrust her against the side of the house with his face buried in her
neck. Ben had never experienced them personally but knew the complicated sounds that could be mistaken for pain were actually those
of pleasure. He dropped the bag of bouillon and screamed at the top
of his lungs.

Emma leapt off Jasper, mortified, pulling down her skirt as he
pulled up his overalls. Jasper was already angry at himself but knew
there was nothing he could do to take it back now.

Miss Virgie came around the corner to find out what the yelling was all about. "Oh Lord, have mercy."

Emma started to sob from deep in her chest. She barely got out her apology. "I'm so sorry, Miss Virgie. I'm so sorry." Then she sprinted off in the direction from which Ben had just come. She didn't even glance at him. She couldn't.

Ben collapsed to his knees, not understanding this new world he now lived in.

Jasper should have just gone inside, but like he sometimes did, he spoke up when he shouldn't have. "If she was willing to do that with me . . . ? I did you a favor. Someday you'll see that." Jasper maybe even believed this excuse to be true, but there was a psychological reason that he would never understand. Ben was all Jasper had, an invest-ment in time, money, backbreaking labor, and he knew there was a single force powerful enough to steal it all away if he wasn't careful— the love of a woman.

As Jasper walked by Miss Virgie, he was met with a two-fisted as-sault on his shoulder and back. "Are you out of your mind? You sup-posed to be the man of the family, and you acting this stupid?"

Ben didn't move from that spot for nearly half an hour. He slept on the porch that night, and in the morning, he didn't have it in him to go inside and nudge Jasper awake before he left to start his day of structured responsibility.

CHAPTER THIRTEEN

Nine days had passed since anyone had seen Chicago's boy wonder, Valentino. Nine days that made Jasper and Ben feel like squirrels hopped up on Benzedrine inhalers trying to cross Gratiot Avenue at quitting time. Life was moving faster than the Carter brothers liked, hardly enough time to think, but for the Carter children, the days still rolled along at a normal pace, sixty minutes to the hour, twenty-four hours to the day, because that's what parents do for their children—lie that the world is peaceful for as long as possible.

The clock had ticked over to June 22 less than five hours ago. The night before had been a late one at Geraldine's, so Charles crashed in the back office rather than going home. He needed to be uncomfortable to avoid falling into a deep slumber and missing his window. Sleeping at the club also meant there was no chance his busybody parents, Ben and Margaret, would hear him leaving the house before dawn. The hour and a half between four and five thirty, when the black sky dawned into the slightest shade of blue, was magic. At that time of day, nothing was expected but peace and quiet. Responsibilities were politely on hold. There was no traffic, no appointments, and mostly no worry. This was a time for dreaming, and though he was awake, Charles did what the moment asked. Lying in the twin bed, in the closet-sized room, on the second floor of Le Noir Palais, wrapped in his sleeping Betty's arms—he dreamed.

Every night this week, he'd silently hoisted himself onto the roof over the back porch with the aid of a rain barrel that had seen better days and snuck in through Betty's window. Sex was too dangerous because the bed was creaky and the silence was deafening, but Charles would crawl under Betty's sheets, and she would nestle in and drape her arm over his chest and her knee over his thigh. He wasn't sure if she was fully conscious during this transition, but as they settled together, for a brief flash, Charles understood the existence of man and the size of the universe.

If his presence was known by any of the other girls or, God forbid, Minnie herself, there would be repercussions. Falling asleep would be disastrous, so he stared at the ceiling while playing with Betty's hair and tried to keep his mind active to avoid the sandman.

Today was a big day, the day that the Brown Bomber, Joe Louis, would attempt to take the honor of heavyweight boxing champion away from Jim "Cinderella Man" Braddock. Charles was no fighter, but fighting was not why Detroit worshipped Joe Louis. Joe Louis represented something intangible. Kids from Black Bottom worked hard; many never even got to go to school, because every able-bodied person in a household needed to have a job to keep the family alive. But Joe? He rose above one boy's dream and became personified proof that dreams could be captured. Housewives and grannies loved Joe Louis. Blue-collar men, white and Black, loved Joe Louis. Little boys wanted to be Joe Louis. Women wanted Joe Louis. When Joe lost to the German last year, Charles saw grown men, hard men, openly weep on Hastings Street. *If Joe wins tonight, he'll be the second Black heavyweight champion in history. If he wins tonight, he'll mend bro-*

ken hearts and reclaim his record. If he wins tonight, he'll lift an entire race to a higher rung on the ladder.

If he loses, Charles thought, we all lose. . . .

When a white man loses, he falls down a peg, maybe two. Hell, he may even fall back to level earth. But when a Black man loses, he hits the ground, his ladder is stolen, and he's kicked in the teeth. Charles was no different than those men crying in the streets. He needed Joe Louis just as much as they did.

Look at how beautiful she is.

He swore to his father that he'd stop seeing Betty, but he was addicted to her. Charles was sure that after getting his fix in the morning, a clearer mind would prevail. He'd understand why Ben was against this love affair, and he'd agree. But around lunchtime, he'd find himself in the stage of questioning. Why is it bad? People treated her white until she spoke, then Betty became an immigrant in their eyes. Didn't they both understand the fight? Don't they both deserve better? Then, sometime between five fifteen and six o'clock, as he prepped for the after-work crowd at Geraldine's, all of Charles's thoughts would become annoyed, flustered, and defiant. Why shouldn't we be together? It's people's minds, the country, the laws, that are wrong, not our love. Since when did Carters not fight for what was right?

Doubt followed like heartburn. His family had already dealt with so much, and there was always a storm brewing just over the horizon. The biggest, and oddly least spoken about, was just how sick Aunt Valerie seemed to be. People could complain about her high jinks all they wanted, but remove Aunt Valerie from the Carters, and half the family's love, spontaneity, and joy would go with her. Sharon worried him too. She was struggling at the dry cleaner's. It was hard for that little shop to keep up with the larger factory-style cleaners, but that wasn't the problem. It was the emptiness in her eyes, the missing twinkle. Sharon was known for her fight. She fought Charles all the damn time, about everything: the layout of the tables at Geraldine's, women's suffrage, how far the moon was from the Earth. Lately, something was missing in her eyes, and though he'd never say it to her face, Charles cared about Sharon. And he wasn't blind to his own privileged place in the family ranks either. Ben had handed him the opportunity to go to college when he hadn't even been interested. Charles knew Sharon wanted his degree, but he wasn't sure Jasper had ever even offered her the chance.

The list of the people he worried about kept going. The Carters were a large and complicated family. Stephen just wouldn't quit, and it was only a matter of time before he opened his wiseass mouth to the wrong person. Mark was a genius but got forgotten because everyone was so sure he could take care of himself. How was that fair? Then there was his little brother, Victor. Their three-year age difference should have meant they were peers growing up, but they were so different. Charles was outgoing and charismatic. Victor was introverted and shy, bordering on antisocial. The boy was never rude, but he also never made much of an effort to belong—at least, that's how Charles saw it. His brother never had a real hobby, or a girlfriend, or a crew of kids he felt was worthy enough for his attention. Charles's big-brother instinct told him that if Victor didn't make more of an effort, he'd be a loner for life.

By the end of the night, Charles was so deep in Betty withdrawal that nothing could shake the image of her face, her belly button, her quivering moan, from his mind. He'd tried to beat the disease of her. He'd tried erasing Betty with the attention of all the women who fancied him for free drinks. He buried himself in work, pressing shirts for Sharon, making deliveries for his family's various businesses, helping Mark fix the printer with spare parts from an old lawn mower. One night he even attempted to cure his Betty addiction with morphine. That one hadn't ended well. Vomit everywhere.

The only fix was Betty. Her face. Her smell. Being next to her. Making love to her. She was the only thing that made him well.

She's risking as much as I am. More. Please don't let my idiotic actions bring her harm.

Last week Betty told Charles some men had come to the Palais swinging badges around, asking questions about a missing person. When he asked who, all she could remember was "Polish. Ski-something. A local politician." This was enough to let Charles know she was nervous for all the wrong reasons. He knew full well the authorities weren't poking around because of her immigration status or profession. They were looking for him. They were looking for Danny Gaczynski, but Danny wasn't the "ski" that turned this whole mess into a federal investigation; it was Joseph Frolovski. The men with badges had the "local politician" thing wrong too. Frolovski was a political hopeful at best who had announced he was challenging Charles Diggs for a seat in the Michigan state senate, but he disappeared before Election Day. Betty didn't understand that her appropriate reaction should have been crippling fear and running away in the middle of the night, because Charles kept his cool. Sure, he was afraid of the police, and he was afraid of Joseph Frolovski, and he was even afraid of that twerp Danny, but nothing topped the terror of losing Betty.

"Are you awake?" Charles asked, quietly enough to ensure she'd stay asleep.

A heavy sigh and a slight readjustment of her arm on his chest were the only response. This meant Charles was free to whisper the words on his mind.

"I'm gonna take you away from here. I don't know when, but I will. I'm gonna take you somewhere far away, where there ain't any G-men. And there ain't any immigration officers, and no racists either. Even if I gotta take you on a rocket ship to Mars, we're gonna have a little cottage in the middle of nowhere. We'll grow our own food. Raise a family. Three boys. We can have girls too, but at least three boys. I'll never have to bow my head and walk in the gutter when a soda cracker wants the whole sidewalk. No one will ever ask you for your papers, and there certainly won't be any goddamned Le Noir Palais. I'll be your only man. And I'll take care of you. I swear to God, I'll take care of you."

Half a snore escaped from her slightly parted lips, and he loved her even more for it.

"I'm glad you agree."

The sandman was catching up to him. *Don't fall asleep. Don't fall asleep. Just get up now. It's best if you just get . . .*

The glow from the window was bright. Betty slammed her way back into the room in an alarmed frenzy.

"Go! You have to go!"

Instantly up on his elbows and more confused than he'd ever been: "What time is it?"

She thrust his clothes into his chest and threw open the window. "They have guns!"

The stomping of boots slamming their way up the stairs entered the soundscape of his fresh consciousness, and he leapt to follow Betty's orders. He pulled her face in for a kiss, which she reluctantly gave before shoving him out onto the roof over the back porch. Before he could think, the window was closed and the drapes were drawn. He heard the door to Betty's room crash open, and she screamed. She also heard Minnie yelling and fighting back. According to her screams, they had "no right," but she was quickly reminded that she had "no rights." The *S* made all the difference in this situation.

Charles peered around the corner from his rooftop perch, and the street was full of black-and-white Lincolns—coppers. But the men barricaded behind the open car doors aiming their weapons at the Palais were suited, not uniformed—Hoover's boys. Jumping to ground level would mean a foot chase. Charles certainly knew Black Bottom better than any of these drips, but bullets ran faster than Jesse Owens.

His eyes darted for another option as he fumbled into his pants. Up seemed like the only option. He tossed his shirt and shoes to the second-floor roof. Without the burst of adrenaline, there was no way Charles could have pulled off the feat, but two steps and a bare foot planted into the wooden clapboard were all he needed to propel himself high and away enough to get his left hand and right forearm up and over the eave. With another burst of energy, fired in the furnace of not wanting to get shot, Charles got himself to the upper roof in a single snatch and hid himself in a valley behind a chimney.

CHAPTER FOURTEEN

The pounding was incessant and vigorous enough to wake even sleeping teenagers. Everyone, including Ben and Margaret, was stirring with varied levels of alarm, but it was Stephen who got to the door first. Shirtless, wearing yesterday's trousers, the kid angrily swung the door open to find his father staring back at him. Jasper was also angry, but both their expressions flipped to surprise on sight.

"Boy! What you doing here? You're supposed to be uptown in your own damn bed!" Jasper snapped at his son.

"My deliveries are all in Paradise Valley and Black Bottom. Uncle Ben's place is closer."

"Your mama know? Or you just making decision on your own like you a man now?"

"If I'm still such a little boy, then I guess I'm too young to work. Someone else'll just have to be the Carter family slave."

As if Jasper already had it in the chamber, a slap ran across Stephen's face that made his ears ring, but he took it without so much as a flinch and glared on. One hundred percent Jasper's boy.

"Get your ass home. Where's your uncle?"

Ben was trotting down the stairs, tying a robe at the waist. "What the hell's going on, Jasper?"

"Tell me you know, Ben. Tell me you got the courtesy that I did not, and it just slipped your mind to let me know."

Ben stepped between Jasper and Stephen. He didn't know where to begin. "Get your things together. You heard your daddy."

Stephen gathered his shirt, shoes, and delivery bag as Ben ushered his brother out onto the porch and closed the door. Over Jasper's shoulder, Ben saw the blue LeBaron, complete with the shape of Valerie in the passenger seat, dead asleep against the window.

"She all right?" Ben asked.

Jasper ignored him and moved right in. "Did you know? I need to know if I got issues with Detroit's finest or my baby brother. And if I'm honest, I think it's gonna be easier if it's you."

"Well, I'm lost, so I guess we're leaning the hard way."

The door opened, and Stephen slipped out. He hopped off the porch, grabbed his bike, and pedaled off. Before Ben could pull the door closed again, Margaret was there. She declined Ben's desire to keep the conversation private and stood with stern patience, head covered in a silk nightcap, arms folded over her robe, to hear what was worth Jasper's dramatic entrance.

"Blake and the Feds raided Minnie's."

"What?"

"You heard me!"

Ben turned to Margaret. "Charles home? Get Charles."

Margaret raised her eyebrows at Ben, silently declaring that Charles better not have anything to do with whatever was going down, before turning to go back inside.

A bicycle bell turned Jasper and Ben's heads toward Lance, pedaling up as fast as he could. Fully out of breath, he dropped his bike in the yard and jogged closer to his half brothers.

"I see this is a family affair," Ben said, incapable of hiding his disdain for Lance.

"Coppers all over Minnie's place." Lance stood in the yard, looking up at his brothers on the porch. Catching his breath, he glanced over and saw Valerie's head leaning on the glass. "She good?"

"You made the drops, right? You paid Schwartz?" Jasper asked Ben, essentially ignoring Lance.

"I did. You know I did. He was who told me the rumors about the UAW wanting to move on Ford."

"Rumors ain't all we pay him for. He knows what we got, right? He knows we got him?"

Neighbors were starting to appear on porches. It was hard to keep a secret in Black Bottom, but some things still needed to be more quiet than others.

Ben put his hand on his brother's shoulder and spoke in a much softer voice, hoping Jasper would follow suit. "Do you know why? What they were after?"

Jasper shrugged Ben's hand away and spoke even louder. "All I know is that when we pay his fat ass and shower him with pussy, we ain't supposed to worry about the PD."

Margaret reappeared on the porch, shaking her head. Charles was not inside. Ben was lost. He needed half a moment to think. He looked to the sky, to his feet, back into Jasper's angry eyes. The answers were nowhere visible, but another question hit him in the teeth. "I thought you were on the Motor City Special. You should be arriving in Chicago about now."

"I'm sure that's what Blake thought too."

"Why you still here?"

Jasper spied his wife in the car, motionless. "We had a bit of a night. Missed the midnight train. We're catching the Wolverine at seven forty."

Margaret interjected, "You gonna miss that one too if you don't hurry."

It was then that the car pulled up. A black-and-white Lincoln.

"Jasper." Ben watched his brother's heart turn to stone through the window of his eyes. "Jasper, I can handle this. I got this."

At the sight of Michael Blake getting out of his ride, Jasper oozed exasperated displeasure. He chewed on his own cheeks and forced buckets of air through his nose to try and keep his cool. He didn't love house calls from the police, especially not assistant police chiefs who were on the Carter payroll.

Michael Blake was a good-looking man, everything a white woman could want. Six foot two. Blue eyes. Broad shoulders. Thick, wavy brown hair shorn close over the ears and around the back. He was always in the same dapper suit, and he had the legal right to carry a bean shooter. Unfortunately, when he smiled, he revealed a set of snaggled chompers that only a mother could love, and it didn't help that one of his front uppers had gone dark after getting it knocked in a fight. Jasper was ready and willing to box the dead tooth out and use his fists to straighten the rest.

Blake only made it a few steps before Ben casually stepped off his porch to meet the man in the yard. "What can I do for you, Mr. Blake?"

"I came to give you a courtesy call, but I'm guessing from our audience, someone beat me to the honor."

Jasper was a lion charging a bull, and as much as everyone wanted to see who'd win the match, Ben physically put himself between the animals. It didn't stop the charge, though. Blake pushed aside his coat and laid his hand on the grip of his weapon.

Jasper slammed his chest into Ben's shoulder, leaning his head as close to Blake as Ben would allow. Seething through gritted teeth, he raged, "Surprised to see me, Blake? Thought I'd be gone on the midnight train, so you felt safe? Thought the ass whooping would be lighter if only the sane Carter brother was in town?"

Ben was successfully holding Jasper back, but they both knew it was only because somewhere deep inside, Jasper understood it was best to be held back.

"It was the Feds, Jasper. You think I can stop the Feds? And Jesus, Mary, and Joseph, if you're caught up in this, I'll take you down myself."

Jasper almost burst through Ben's defensive line, but the play was interrupted when the door to Ben's house slammed open and Victor, fully dressed, burst out, making a mad dash to go north on Hastings.

"Victor!" Margaret called out, but didn't go after him.

"Son!" Ben shoved Jasper back but kept his hand on his chest.

Victor turned, walking backward as he explained himself through tears at a level of passion only possible when you bottle it up for a good long while, "I can't, Dad! I can't!"

"You can't what? Come on back now."

Come back? Open your eyes, Dad! Open them! He wished he could say how he felt, but all he managed was a bitter, resentful exhale and a swipe of the hand to clear all the invisible drama off his dinner table. Then he turned back around and charged into the world alone.

Coincidentally, watching Victor go was when Charles came into view up the road. He screamed from too far-off for conversation, so all he really did was get more neighbors' attention. "Pops! Hey, Pops!"

"Ben?" Margaret's one-word question said all it needed to.

He looked at his wife to absorb some of her qualities and then put both his hands on Jasper's chest. "Go to Chicago. I can take care of the homestead."

Jasper wasn't so sure, so Ben reaffirmed, "I. Got. This."

"Pops, they busted up Minnie's." Charles took in his surroundings. *What's Lance doing here?* "Where's Victor going? He was crying."

"Hanging around Minnie's, are you?" Blake needled.

Ben had to physically bear-hug Jasper to stop his fury. "Did I say you could speak to my nephew, you Okie wheat?"

"Ever heard the name Joseph Frolovski?" Blake didn't take his eyes off Charles, and Ben took note.

"Does it look like . . ."

Ben shut Jasper up with an interruption. "We've never heard of him. But if you want to enlighten us as to the reasons you think we might have any information, I can assure you, we're willing to cooperate."

"Polish fella. Was gonna run against Mr. Diggs for the state senate seat. Announced his campaign, then vanished, and now he ain't been seen for a few months," Blake explained.

"The Carters and politics don't really mix," Jasper hissed.

"I hate to break it to you, Mr. Carter, but bribes on both sides? The law and the mob? That's politics, friend."

"I ain't your friend, Dick."

"Right, but according to Mr. Schwartz, we are partners. Correct? So if you happen to hear anything about Frolovski, why don't you give a holler? Seems like top dogs such as yourselves might know an ear or two to pull back. Find out why and how a white man going missing gave a Black man a seat at the political table." Blake slowly moved toward his car.

"Mr. Diggs won because he got more votes. That's how the system works, Blake," Ben shouted from his position of temporary human barricade.

"I apologize for the intrusion at your cousin's . . . place of repute . . . but the last known sighting of our Polack friend was the Forest Club, and we're told he was with a Negro gentleman who frequents Minnie's and only eats white meat." Blake opened his car door and connected with Charles one more time.

Jasper let out a snort, a small pressure-release valve on his temper.

The yard got even more crowded when Sharon and Mark arrived. It couldn't be said that the Carters didn't show up for one another.

"This your oldest, Jasper?" Blake settled his gaze on Sharon.

Ben raised his second hand to Jasper's chest. He didn't know where this was headed, but he knew there were limits to his control over the situation.

"Damn." Blake smacked his lips. "Hey, Charles, if you convince your cousin here to get in the rotation at the Palais, we could compare notes on what's tastier, light meat or dark."

Ben dropped his arms. He knew it was over. He couldn't hold back the power of a tsunami. Jasper charged the Lincoln. Assistant police chief Michael Blake smartly hopped in and slammed the door.

"If you so much as think about my daughter!" Jasper was already at the car door with Blake smirking on the other side of the window.

Ben and Charles were on Jasper's heels, but they didn't fully intervene because the man was already safe inside his black-and-white. It was usually best to let Jasper get it out and calm down on his own terms, but when Blake turned the key to make his getaway, Jasper snapped.

"If you're gonna harass my family, it's best I give you probable cause." Jasper put an exclamation point on his statement with a fist into the window, shattering it into ten thousand shards raining in on Blake's shocked and terrified mug.

Luckily, Ben and Charles united in time to stop Jasper from pulling him through the window and stomping him into ground beef. A nephew on one arm and a brother on the other were just barely enough. Not able to relieve the pressure with violence, Jasper needed another way.

"You know we got insurance, right? Minnie's place is a family joint, so we like to keep it homey by taking lots a photographs."

"Jasper! Shut your damn mouth!" Ben struggled with all his physical might. He was sure now that the lion could devour the bull.

"Got pictures of all our top clients. Very important people. So maybe next time you'll think twice about marching into Carter territory!" Finally, Jasper realized his brother and nephew were probably correct. Getting in the car would be bad. But getting in his head was too tempting. "Be warned, Blake. Glass houses an' rock throwing an' all."

As the Lincoln pulled away, Jasper shook off his human restraints and smoothed his coat. Looking through the window of his own wheels, he could see that Valerie hadn't so much as moved. Margaret and Sharon looked on like poker players without tells. Mark watched the whole scene with his mouth agape, stunned whenever he glimpsed the feared side of his family that he knew kept them in Black society's high regards.

Ben went to his brother, trying to corral him into his line of vision. "Jasper." First he tried by the shoulders, but it was no use; he was too wily. "Jasper, listen." Ben grabbed the back of Jasper's head, then slid both his hands onto his face and pulled their foreheads together. Jasper closed his eyes and tried breathing through it.

Ben spoke like a trained hypnotist. Even-toned. Easy. "Jas. Listen to me, Jas. Get your ass to Chicago. You're gonna miss your train. Go." Jasper tried to wriggle away, but Ben held on. "Go show those Chicago goons what a Carter looks like. We don't hide. We don't scare. I can handle things here. I'll check on Minnie, but most of the town will be consumed with the Shriners Parade and won't remember any of this tomorrow. You know what they will remember? They'll remember Joe Louis knocking the living hell out of Cinderella."

Jasper wasn't what a normal man would call calm, but he'd come down enough to hear his brother out. "My bacon says Joe gets him in the first round."

"You're the betting man, but on this one, I'm with you."

The two men hugged before Jasper went back to his car, but it was too hard to face his children and nephews. He kept his head down, got behind the wheel next to his comatose wife, and pulled away, leaving the wreckage behind for Ben to take care of.

Ben watched as the blue car turned west and disappeared. *He built this city. He made me everything I am. Even if that means sometimes I have to clean up his shit.*

Hank had the day off for multiple reasons. Not only was it a day of possible jubilation or commiseration—the day Joe Louis would fight Jim Braddock for the championship at Comiskey Park in Chicago, an event that was sure to captivate all of Black Detroit and stir it into a frenzy—but it was also going to be a nightmare driving anywhere in Detroit due to the seventy-five thousand Shriners who had shown up in the previous days to prepare for the first national Shriner convention to be held in Detroit in forty years. The festivities kicked off with a parade this very morning. What no one could have predicted was that by the end of the first of three days of Shriner festivities and the biggest boxing match the world had ever seen, every member of the Carter family would be on new and unexpected individual paths. The only thing Hank needed to accomplish before figuring out his plans to listen to the fight was to swing by Checks Cashed and pay Jasper's debt to Izzy.

Much to Ben's dismay, the fifty spot Jasper originally lost on the numbers had been doubled, plus interest, for late payment. One hundred twenty greenbacks in ten-dollar bills would make them even. Hank stood nervously in Izzy's office at 9:05 a.m., hands folded, holding a Geraldine's envelope, eyes on the floor as he listened to Izzy scream into his office telephone. In front of him was the stock section that Hank was familiar with from regularly setting it aside for Ben.

Izzy jabbed his finger at the numbers to stress his words even though whoever received his abuse on the other end of the wire obviously couldn't see him.

"You listen ta me, you son of a mongrel bitch. Take dat dog shit outta your ears and listen to me again. It says 'Jan. 1 to date.' Do you see dat, you Oriental clown? 'Jan. 1 to date.' Not total of the day, not 'week ago,' not 'year ago'—the numbers are 'Jan. 1 to date.' You pay out on any other fucking numbers and I'll open those chinky eyes of yours by cuttin' off da lids, you understand?"

Izzy slammed the mouthpiece onto its hook and the entire unit onto his desk. "To what do I owe da pleasure of Mr. Hank Malveaux?" Like magic, all the rage of the phone call was gone from Izzy's personage.

"I come to pay ya what Jasper owes. Mr. Ben told me to tell ya he's sorry it's late." Hank took half a step closer and placed the envelope of cash on the edge of Izzy's desk.

"Debt's been paid. Jasper came and saw me a few days ago."

"He paid you?"

"Not wit one of those little envelopes he didn't, but he came by wit a gracious apology for his tardiness and signed over half of da Carter Dry Cleaning."

Hank was obviously shocked by this. He couldn't find the words in his throat.

Izzy eyed the envelope. "You're welcome to take dat back to Ben." The man's steely gaze turned on Hank. "Unless you know something I don't, and the cleaners ain't worth da cheddar in dat envelope."

"No, sir. Sharon does a fine job. So much business, it's hard to keep up."

"Well, den, I suggest you take dat back and leave before I get itchy and change my mind."

Hank took the envelope as instructed and turned to the door, but

Izzy wasn't quite done.

"For your troubles, take a tenner. Treat all your blackie comrades when Braddock lays Louis out. On me."

Hank knew better than to answer. He turned on his heels and stepped out, cash in hand.

When he got back to the Series 70 parked on Gratiot, he opened the back door and leaned in to find the last stock section he'd given Ben still on the seat where his boss had left it. They were Friday's stocks listed in Saturday's paper. He closed himself in behind the wheel and spread the paper in front of him. On the top of the page, in bold black letters that Hank didn't even attempt to read: "Detroit's Complete Page of Transactions on the New York Stock Exchange." In the middle of the page, on the far right-hand side, was a small section for totals. Not all the letters made sense to him, but this was mostly numbers. He traced his finger over them. The words were a blur, but he knew what he was looking for.

"Jan. 1. Jan. 1. Jan. 1."

He passed over "Total Sales, June 19"—that wasn't it. Then "Previous Day," "Week Ago," "Year Ago," "Two Years Ago"—all a blur of letters. He got "June." He knew that one, but he didn't have time to sound out all the others right now.

Then he saw it. The number one was easy to spot. This line he could sound out because he'd just heard Izzy do it. "Jan. 1." He traced the line of dots leading to the right and found a number with nine digits—223,759,792.

As he walked north on Saint Antoine, Victor's tears were long dried, and his resolve grew stronger with each step. As he turned right on Livingstone Street, he pulled the folded flyer from his pocket. "Allah Temple of Islam." At the bottom of the page was the address: "Ma-son's Hall—632 Livingstone." The next meeting time listed on the paper wasn't until 8:00 p.m. the next day, but Victor couldn't wait any longer. He felt alone in the world, alone in his family, alone in his skin. His family was proud, but somehow their experience was not his. While they put on the airs of rising above, Victor felt the foreboding, crippling weight of his Blackness in every waking moment. He didn't know if this flyer had the answers, and he didn't know if the Black man and woman standing on the stoop of 632 Livingstone had them either, but he needed to find out before he shattered into a million pieces.

The morning light bathed the couple. The man, dressed in a crisp dark blue suit, and the woman, clad in an elegant Sunday dress that gave the command of an Egyptian pharaoh but that was also somehow still appropriate for the modern era, were entranced in the kind of deep conversation that felt wrong to interrupt. However, ignoring the trembling nineteen-year-old boy standing on the sidewalk staring up at them was impossible.

The man spoke. "Assalamu alaikum, young brother. You look lost."

"I . . . I feel lost." Victor was surprised by his own voice. Not knowing what to do next, he held the paper up in the couple's direction.

The man and woman, who Victor assumed were close in age to Sharon and Charles, briefly acknowledged each other before slowly strolling to meet Victor where he stood. The man continued, "My name is John."

"I'm Victor. Victor Carter."

Usually people, especially Black people, had some kind of reaction to hearing the Carter name, not always good, not always bad, but it didn't faze these two at all.

"I didn't know if anyone would be here. The flyer says Wednesday at eight."

"We're meeting with some of our brothers and sisters to go to the parade this morning." The woman's voice was strong and sure like his mother, Margaret.

"You're marching?"

The man smiled, and a chuckle slipped out. "No, we're not marching. We just want our presence to be known."

They stood quietly for a few moments. They'd never met, but their connection was palpable.

"How would you like to be found, Brother Victor?" the woman asked.

"I'd like that very much."

CHAPTER FIFTEEN

I n the week prior, the city of Detroit had given more attention to Black Bottom than Ben had ever seen. The Shriners Parade route was to march west on Jefferson, from Elmwood to Woodward, where the Arabian-dressed masses would turn north toward Grand Circus Park. This meant that tens of thousands of Shriners from all over the country and an estimated half million spectators would be visiting Black Bottom. The city couldn't take any chances. All up and down Jefferson, buildings and signage had been repaired, potholes filled, businesses and homes along the route got fresh coats of paint, and hordes of white church ladies had picked up trash with police- men on their flanks—as if the Negro population was going to raise arms against getting their streets cleaned. Detroit wanted to put its best foot forward for the press, but Black Bottom residents felt like Detroit sprucing up Jefferson was akin to tidying up the house or the club before guests arrived to listen to the Louis-Braddock fight.

A stage was erected at Elmwood and Jefferson the night before, and now it was shoulder-to-shoulder madness in all directions. Farther to the west, marching bands were getting in one last practice while they waited for those who needed their faces seen in the papers to organize themselves and kick off the event. Ben stood patiently with Mark while Stephen ran around getting into God only knows what kind of trouble. Every so often he'd appear out of nowhere, eating popcorn or wearing a Shriner's fez, showing off his impression of one of the camels he'd seen, then he'd vanish again, and Ben would just hope for the best.

"I'm glad you finally got that thing working." Ben motioned to the camera hung around Mark's neck with twine in place of the missing strap. "Your daddy got you some film?"

"Actually, the *Chronicle* is looking for a photographer. I went over and made a deal that if they gave me a roll of film, they could take it off the price of whatever they pay for the photos I take."

"Okay, now. That sounds good. . . . What happens if they don't buy any pictures?"

"I'll owe 'em eighty cents."

Ben chuckled and patted his nephew on the back. "Guess you better get some shots, then, huh?"

"The lens has a small scratch, but if I frame it up just right, I can hide it in the composition, so it's not right in the middle of someone's face or something." Mark's excitement was a spark of wonder.

"Framing? Composition? I didn't know you were all that interested in photography."

"I like it fine, but . . ." He shot his eyes up at his uncle, nervous he had said one word too many.

"Oh, I see. You got a plan. Carters always have a plan. Let's hear it."

The boy knew there was no getting out of this. Besides, it might be good to have Uncle Ben on his side before telling Jasper. "I wanna write. The *Chronicle* doesn't have any openings for a journalist right now, but I figure if I can build a relationship with them now, I'll have my foot in the door when the time is right."

"Look at you, Mark. Look at you!" Ben took off his hat to wipe his brow, admiring his nephew. The sun wasn't hot yet, but rain was expected later, and that meant the humidity was out with a vengeance. "I keep my ear to the ground, Mark. I know the parties are changing, and I'm glad we got Governor Murphy, but politics can be tricky. A Black newspaper leaning democratic is an odd thing to some people, especially those of us who escaped the South."

"I know, Uncle Ben," Mark said, with the tone that humankind reserved only for responding to elders who thought they knew better.

Just then, Stephen proudly stepped up, licking an ice-cream cone.

"It's nine thirty in the morning! Where on earth did you get an ice-cream cone?" Before Ben even finished the question, Stephen was gone again.

Mark had his eye smashed against the back of the camera, scanning the crowd around the stage. Ben watched with pride and jealousy all tangled into one ball of yarn. How hard had he and Jasper worked to give these kids even the smallest opportunities in life? How many situations had they been in where life or freedom was at risk? So then why was he here, warning his nephew not to chase a job, not to chase a dream? In college Ben had learned about the Supreme Court's case over the Spanish ship *La Amistad*. Kidnapped men from Sierra Leone had been put on the ship bound for Cuba to be sold into slavery. The men escaped their shackles and took control of the boat with the intent to sail back home. Unfortunately, the navigators they took prisoner tricked them into sailing north rather than east, and they were caught off the coast of Long Island. The court case, which was argued by ex-president John Quincy Adams, ultimately decided that since the men had been obtained illegally in Sierra Leone, they were free. And as freemen, they were within their right to do all in their power to escape captivity, including the use of force. Jasper and Ben were captives of a nation of laws that saw them as less than fully human. Harder to prove, sure, but every time Ben found himself in one of

Jasper's plans, usually packed full of illegal activities, many of which Ben still had regular nightmares about, it was the *Amistad* that justified their actions in Ben's mind. After learning about the *Amistad*, Ben found a quote from John Quincy Adams, which had been on his mind more and more in the last few years. Not everyone believed the quote came from John Quincy Adams, but once the words were in Ben's head, he didn't care who had said them or why. He just knew he needed to live by them.

I am a warrior, so that my son may be a merchant, so that his son may be a poet.

Jasper was a warrior. Ben was a warrior. Now their children wanted to be merchants, and Ben hoped to one day read the poems of his grandchildren.

"You know what, Mark? You learn that camera forward and backward. You take the best photographs the world has ever seen, and you work that magic into whatever future you desire. If journalism is the dream you dream, then dream it."

Mark pulled his eye away from the camera for half a second. "Thanks, Uncle Ben." Then he went right back to scanning the crowd.

Almost embarrassed by the cliché of his next words, Ben knew it was his duty to say them. "One thing, though. You need to bury your peers in hard work. You can't settle for the best colored journalist. You need to be the best journalist."

This time Mark didn't bother taking his eye off the camera. "People say 'Negro' now, Uncle Ben. You shouldn't say 'colored' anymore."

Yes, sir, the next generation was waiting on the sidelines to take their place, but Ben wasn't ready to pass the torch yet. He still had some fight. And that's when Governor Murphy took to the stage and began to address the crowd. There wasn't anything important to hear, only mandatory ass-kissing thank-yous, but even if Murphy had been speaking in tongues, declaring beyond definitive proof the earth's one true religion, Ben wouldn't have heard any of it.

Hand in his pocket, Ben slid his thumb back and forth over the grain of wheat on the back of his special penny as he beat himself up for not following his own advice. It was standard "do as I say, not as I do" but directed at himself. Jasper hadn't been the only one on their journey from Alabama to Kentucky to Ohio to Michigan. Ben had learned things along the way; he'd seen things. There's a big difference between twelve and seventeen, but not forty-one and forty-six. If Ben believed in an idea, in a pursuit, in a future, he should stand by it, with or without Jasper Carter.

Ben was snapped out of his inner pep talk by the crowd jostling into position for the start of the parade. He'd stood there for nearly twenty minutes of speeches, not hearing a word, and now Murphy was leaving the stage as a drum major and his band from London, Ontario, honored Michigan with "Victor's Song." On his way toward the car that would take him away, the governor was going to pass right. . . .

"Governor Murphy, if you don't mind, sir, I'd like a minute of your time to pick your brain." Ben spoke loud enough to be heard, but the brass band blaring nearby gave them just enough privacy.

Mark was shocked that his uncle had gone right up to the governor of the entire state, and even more shocked that the politician knew who he was and granted Ben a chat on the way to his motorcade. He watched it all develop through the lens of his camera, occasionally clicking the shutter button.

"I heard there was a bit of a scene this morning between Jasper and Assistant Chief Blake. Anything I need to be nervous about?"

"With all due respect, sir, I'm not my brother's keeper, nor do I control my cousin Minnie's business, but I was under the impression that your special relationship with our family came with more respect than an unannounced raid."

The governor liked Ben, but being spoken to like that was enough to freeze the man midstep. He looked Ben up and down, attempting to decide if he should be upset by his tone or not. "A man is missing, Ben. His family isn't going to let up until we have some answers."

"My brother and I had nothing to do with it."

"You and Jasper are not the only Carters."

"Who exactly are you accusing, Governor?"

One of Murphy's assistants opened the back door of his Ford. "We know your people will vote for whoever you and Jasper tell them to. We also know the Polish are a voting constituency the Negroes have been able to rely on in the past."

"What are you getting at?"

"Mr. Frolovski was throwing his hat in the ring for state senator, Ben. Do you think his people were going to vote for Charles Diggs?"

"I have no idea what happened to Mr. Frolovski, and I don't think Jasper would be very happy with what you seem to be insinuating."

The governor leaned in real close to Ben's ear. "It wouldn't be the first time that a person who threatened your standing in the community went missing, would it?"

Jasper and Ben had been in Black Bottom for coming on twenty years. That history was long, it was dirty, and it was almost never legal. It didn't mean that each and every action they took wasn't absolutely necessary for their family's survival, but the Carters were no longer desperate. Those times were in the past. They could now reap the benefits of the hard road they'd taken, and Ben was determined to make up for as many of the wrongs as possible. At that moment, for Ben, it meant changing the subject.

"As you've stated, the respect for our family name gives us some sway over an ever-growing and active voting bloc. And I know you're aware of how many of us are employed by Mr. Ford."

Murphy was intrigued, not only by the obvious dance around the topic of unionizing but also what appeared to be a crack in the Carter family façade. "I don't see it, Ben. You'd go against Jasper on this?"

"It's not about going against my brother. It's about doing right by our fellow man. White men at Ford aren't too happy these days, and colored folks have got it far worse. If you publicly support the UAW at Ford and I energize my base, we could do a lot of good for a lot of people, yours and mine."

Murphy searched Ben's eyes for his level of seriousness. "People say 'Negro' now, Ben."

That stung, but Ben couldn't let one little quip distract him from his goal.

Murphy stuck out his hand, and Ben shook it firmly. That was it. That was the shot Mark had been waiting for, but what he couldn't hear from his vantage point were Murphy's final words to his uncle Ben.

"I can't say I fully believe you'd move without Jasper's blessing, but . . ." Murphy let go of Ben's hand and made his first move to get into the waiting car. Was he ready to make a commitment? Was this the right move? Then he spoke. "I'll do it if you do it."

Valerie and Jasper were halfway to Chicago on the train christened "Wolverine." They sat facing each other in a car that was half coach, half baggage. Valerie stared out the large window as a blur of green trees rushed by while Jasper kept his eyes trained on her. He watched her scratch one of her increasingly swollen ankles, then settle, then scratch her neck, settle, scratch her arm, settle, scratch, settle, scratch, settle. She was probably aware of his attention but would never let him know, a skill she perfected long ago, before Jasper rescued her from the abusive, downward spiral of her life in Kentucky. There was no anger in Jasper's eyes but no pleasure either. When it came to Valerie, he felt paralyzed. Black physicians had prescribed everything from home-cooked elixirs to a strict kosher diet, none of which worked, and white doctors hid behind rules of segregated hospitals and licenses they needed to keep.

The good life Jasper carved out for her hadn't cured the pain of a childhood scarred by sexual violence, but the volume of hootch that passed through their lives dulled it a bit. Being the man who took her away from all of it also hadn't come with any grace. He wanted to save her, but after all Jasper had done, he hadn't learned that simply listening was the needle and thread needed to sew her back together. Even if his ears suddenly became capable this many years later, it may already have been too late. Never breaking her glossy stare out the window, Valerie reached inside her black wool coat with the reddish-brown fox-fur collar and pulled out a small, half-empty bottle of Canadian Club. Jasper didn't stop her. His expression didn't even twitch. These days it was the only medicine that helped, the only potion that made her whole again and allowed the world to see the twinkle of her magic. Jasper lived for those glimpses of her spellbinding former self. Now, sitting on the train, all he could do was continue to stare through the space between them, but no one could be sure anymore if he actually saw her.

As Mark and Ben walked along, Mark carried on an active, one-sided conversation with his uncle while randomly clicking photos of the parade. Ben's mind only checked in periodically to hear a question like "Is Joe Louis really gonna whoop him?" or to take in the oddity of camels walking down Jefferson Avenue or a band of Shriner pipers whose bagpipes could also be used as portable chairs. He couldn't hold his concentration to the present moment, because the words he had just spoken to Governor Murphy tugged at his every synapse. Would Murphy really back him? Could he make a move without Jasper?

Ben momentarily snapped to attention for Mark's next questions: "Where do you think Victor ran off to this morning?" and "Should we be nervous that we haven't seen Stephen for a few minutes?" Not fully aware of the autopilot answers he gave, Ben looked up and saw that they had already walked the sidelines of the parade route to Woodward, where marching bands from all over the country were turning north.

At the corner there was a tight group of seven or eight smiling Black women shaking hands and making small talk with everyone who came by. Ben could recognize a politician's smile from a klick. These women wanted something. Their friendly faces and warm conversations were tools to woo targets close enough to hit them with an agenda. When he saw the face of Mrs. Rosa Gragg, he knew the product being sold was women's liberation. Jasper had once been offered one of Mrs. Gragg's warm handshakes, along with a proposal to sit down and talk about the role of women in Black Bottom, and he bluntly told her that getting the vote had gone to women's heads. Ben understood that Gragg's legion of lady followers only wanted a proverbial seat at the table, but he also knew Jasper meant no harm. Jasper thought women's liberation was a silly place for a Black woman to put her energy, because this was one area in which they were already ahead in the race. Black women were not sitting at home worrying about which ambrosia recipe made them better than the neighbor wives or gossiping about who sat next to who at the May Day luncheon. No, Black women were the lifeblood of Black civilization in America. Without Black women, Black society would have fallen flat on its ass a long time ago.

It was the second woman Ben noticed in the group of street-corner proselytizers who concerned him. Not that it would have been the end of the world, but adding even the smallest annoyance to the kettle right now could make it boil over.

"Sharon!"

When Sharon turned toward Ben's call, her smile faded, and her teeth fell back behind her lips. Mark snapped a picture of his sister's disdain, which pleased him and distracted her just enough for Ben to throw another jab.

"The parade doesn't go anywhere near the cleaner's, so why in heaven's name . . ."

She cut him off. "Talk to your damn brother. I ain't a part of it. I'm out."

"Girl, what do you think your daddy knows that I don't? Does he know your work is completed and that all the fine folks in Black Bottom have fresh slacks, shirts, and skirts ready for the morning? Is that why you're here and not there?"

The speed at which her hand hit her thrusting hip could have broken the sound barrier. "First of all, I ain't no girl. I'm a woman. Second of all, I meant Lance, not Daddy."

"Uncle Ben." Mark wanted his attention.

"What the hell does Lance have anything to do with you out here shaking hands with suffragettes when we're so far behind?"

"Hey, Uncle Ben," Mark insisted.

"Like I said, take it up with Lance. . . . Mrs. Campbell, hi! Did you know Ms. Rosa is giving a fireside tonight at the Current Topic Study Club? Oh my goodness, we'd just love to have you out." Her recruitment smile was right back on her face but a little more forced this time.

"Uncle Ben, I really think you . . ."

"What in the hell has gotten into you, Sharon?"

"Did you know Ms. Rosa is the reason the First Lady came to the ribbon cutting of the Brewster Homes? She is fighting for Black families, fighting for Black women. If you're against Rosa Gragg, then you're against Sharon Carter."

"You really need to see this, Uncle Ben." Mark wasn't letting up.

Fully stunned by Sharon's dismissive tone, Ben needed a good jolt to the system to shake him free. That jolt came in the form of two clowns marching by in the parade who'd traded in their rainbow-colored Barnum suits and painted-on sad faces of blues, reds, and yellows for a tired blackface act. A derogatory minstrel show married with the generous theft of a poor Charlie Chaplin impression. One of the clowns pranced right up to Ben and fell into a string of stereotyped pantomimes, from a trumpet player, to a jockey, to an ignorant farmhand.

The man's greased-black face and large white-painted smile was close enough that Ben didn't even need to raise his voice. "I'm about ready to beat your ass, clown."

The blackface act simply went off to spread its racism to the next happy parade watchers, but Mark was tired of being ignored and finally jerked Ben's arm to force his attention.

"Uncle Ben! Look!"

An all-white crowd had gathered just to the north. Made of both marching Shriners and paradegoers alike, the people were joyously clapping their hands and stomping their feet like they were smack-dab in the middle of a Southern hoedown. Ben raised an eyebrow at Mark, not fully understanding why the jovial white marauders were of concern to him, but the expression plastered on his nephew's face put his feet into motion. Ben couldn't see what exactly the crowd was provoking, but next to them, on the west side of the route, standing shoulder to shoulder, twelve men and women long and three deep, were straight-faced Black folks with their hands folded in peace. Defiant, a tad threatening, a few gave side-eye to the celebration that had broken out just to their right.

These were Black Muslims from the Allah Temple of Islam. Though they hadn't specifically affected the Carters, their group started making appearances in the *Detroit Free Press* in '32. A Black Bottom man had erected a makeshift sacrificial altar and murdered a Black man he rented a room to. When he was captured, the papers printed that Mr. Harris was a member of the Allah Temple of Islam, and that, as such, he was required to kill devils. Then, in '34, when large numbers of Negro children stopped attending public school, leaders of the temple were arrested on truancy charges. The district attorney failed to make the charges stick, so the sheriff ran the temple leadership out of town to Chicago. The Carters steered clear of the group's spotlight because they had enough attention to navigate on their own, but one of the many unfair things about being Black in America is that individuals are never blamed alone. If a Negro committed a crime, the stigma landed square at the feet of every Black man, woman, and child. For that reason and that reason alone, Ben held resentment for the group. Aside from that, from what Ben had heard, they taught their followers Black excellence, Black power, Black entitlement. They taught that the Negro race was the first man and that the whites were devils. These were messages Ben could quietly get behind. Jasper was a different story. Every mention of the temple or Allah or the sight of Black Muslim evangelists angered him on the spot. All Jasper ever saw were the unflattering and relentless news stories. Every time a newspaper printed the words "voodoo" or "Negro cult" or "murder" or "sacrifice" in the same story as "Black Bottom," it made it a little harder for any Black Detroiter to rise above their already marginalized status.

The current parade situation had nothing to do with this group of well-dressed, peaceful members of the Allah Temple of Islam, but one thing Ben could be sure of was that a group of white people energetically celebrating next to a group of stone-faced, mortified Black people meant something terrible was going down. Ben hurried toward the backs of the revelers, hoping that whatever it was they were celebrating was something he could justify ignoring.

Ben shouldered into the crowd, careful not to touch any of the whites in a way that could possibly be misconstrued, and when his eyes fell upon the performance before him, the pilot light in the pit of his gut erupted into a ferocious fireball.

Encouraged by cheers that he was too young to understand were insulting, Stephen and a monkey dressed in a fez were haplessly dancing to the mixed melodic tones of an organ-grinder, applause, and the camouflaged condescending cheers of their white audience. The monkey danced, and then Stephen followed with his best dancing monkey impression. While Stephen unknowingly performed stereotypes back to the stereotypers, the monkey circled the crowd, collecting coins in a little cup. Then it would dance again, Stephen would imitate again, and the crowd would cheer again. It was the perfect circle of collective reward that would only fail to function if the white men ran out of coins for the monkey's cup. The monkey got money, the most important trick he'd been taught by the organ-grinder. Stephen had an audience, which had been the reason for most of his troublemaking. The whites got a real-life example to "prove" the jungle-based racism toward the "inferior" Negro. It would not have been so amusing to the festive crowd if they believed what the members of the Allah Temple of Islam held to be true—a clan of savage white men in ancient Europe had attempted to graft themselves back into the likeness of the earth's original, superior Black civilization but failed miserably, and they only got as far as evolving into monkeys and apes.

Ben shoved into the action and grabbed Stephen's arm, physically yanking him out of his ignorance. The crowd hissed with boos as a patrolling officer happened by to move along the action that was interfering with the parade's progress. In no time at all, a band from Rochester, led by a three-hundred-pound drum major with all the swagger of a peacock in mating season, was leading his flashy band's version of "It's a Sin to Tell a Lie."

Sharon witnessed Ben dragging Stephen from the fray and Mark pulling on their uncle's arm. Nervous her brothers were in some kind of trouble, she abandoned her post at Rosa Gragg's side to intervene.

Stephen didn't understand exactly why he was in trouble, because the feeling in his gut felt like life. A smile still plastered to his face, he bragged to his uncle, who tightly gripped his arm, "Did you hear them? They loved me!"

"You tryna rip his arm out his socket? Let him go!" Sharon yelled at Ben.

"Boy, would you stop pulling on me?" Ben shot at Mark tugging on his free arm.

"I wasn't talking about Stephen making an ass of himself! Look!" Mark pointed at the stern-faced, cross-armed Black Muslims who were witnessing their every move.

How had Ben missed it? His own son, Victor, was standing in their midst.

Ben stomped toward his son, still gripping Stephen's arm, with Mark and Sharon close on his heels. "What in the hell kind of drugs is my family on today?" He stopped ten feet from Victor. "Get your ass over here right now."

Victor looked to his right, where John stood, the man he'd met at the address on the flyer Stephen had failed to deliver. John didn't acknowledge Victor's silent request for help but kept his disapproving look on Ben. Victor turned back to face his father and defied the man for the first time that either of them could remember.

"No."

Before Ben could demand his son's fealty, he was being screamed at from the west side of Woodward Avenue.

"Boss!"

It was only just audible over the applause that accompanied a giant elephant float and its attendants tossing handfuls of candy to the eager masses lining the streets.

"Boss!" Louder and closer this time. Soon the only man who called Ben "boss" appeared, sweating and out of breath.

Hank smashed the cash that Izzy had refused into Ben's hand. "He wouldn't take the money. He wouldn't take it. He said . . . he said . . ." Hank could barely breathe through his heart-attack-level enthusiasm.

"Calm down, Hank. What's going on? Izzy wouldn't take the money?" Ben released his grip on Stephen to put a gentle hand on Hank's shoulder.

"He said Jasper done paid in full with the cleaner's."

Ben shot a panicked look at Sharon, who instantly responded with deflection, "I told you. Talk to Lance."

Hank swung an arm up to the east. "Lance is there. He already there." He still couldn't capture enough oxygen.

Every head, even those of John and the other members of the Allah Temple of Islam, turned toward Hank's gesturing. Maybe five blocks away, ten at the most, black smoke was starting to rise into the sky. Stephen was the first to bolt; he'd always been the kind of kid who ran toward fire. Ben, Sharon, and Mark followed in full sprints, and the already exhausted Hank lumbered after them.

Concern filled Victor's face, and he started to move slowly in the direction of his family, but John's compassionate hand stopped him.

"There's nothing you can do, brother. Whatever drama your daddy finds under that smoke is insignificant to the problems facing our people. Come stand with us in the Grand Circus and bear witness to the white devils celebrating themselves and all their wicked ways. There are other lost brothers and sisters like yourself who need to see us proudly standing together."

John had faith in the power of his words, so he turned away from his budding convert to join his brethren walking north toward the festivities at the end of the parade route. Victor watched Hank walking in the direction of his family, who had already disappeared, then made his decision. He would follow after John and his new family.

Stephen got to Carter Dry Cleaning first and found Lance standing in the street, entranced by the flames climbing out of the broken windows and licking the roofline. Mark jogged up, then came Sharon, each falling victim to the hypnosis of the growing fire. Ben sprinted onto the scene, landing closer to the inferno, hands on his head, mouth hanging wide, fire dancing in the reflection of his moist black eyes.

"What are you doing?" Ben screamed at the fire, fully needing it to answer. Flustered and grasping for any dreamlike possibility to wake up from a nightmare, he spun on his family and zeroed in on Lance. "What have you done? Why?"

Lance hung his head. Ben already held a grudge, and there was no reasoning he could offer that would be good enough for the brother whose acceptance he so yearned for. Sharon was forced to answer for her temporarily mute half uncle.

"Daddy signed half ownership to Izzy. He said they had a plan."

"This? This is a plan?" A tear ran down Ben's cheek.

An explosion of ignited chemicals boomed from inside the fully engulfed structure, sending out new and darker clouds of smoke from the windows and roof. Bells from the fire brigade could be heard in the distance, and Ben couldn't help speaking words out loud to his brother, who sat silently across from Valerie on a train hundreds of miles away.

"Insurance, Jas? Do you really think they won't find some godforsaken justification to not give us a single cent?"

Ben got dizzy. Lightheaded. He needed to sit. Lance instinctively grabbed his arm to make sure he didn't stumble, then helped Ben to the ground. And that was where he sat, elbows on his knees, head in his hands, until the firemen had thoroughly soaked every charred ember.

CHAPTER SIXTEEN

fter witnessing the fight between Jasper and Assistant Chief Blake, Charles went back to the Palais to see Betty, but he was met by Minnie and her knowing game of doublespeak.

"I have to see her, Minnie."

"I'm surprised by you, Charles. A young'un like you needs to pay for it?"

"Pay? No. I just . . . I just need to see her."

"When you were little, I understood your daddy keeping what went on here a little hush-hush, but you a man now. Honey, my girls cost. If you want to 'see' Betty, you got to pay. And after our little visit from the authorities this morning, the prices have gone up. Way up."

"Minnie, please! You don't understand!"

"You right. I don't understand, but I can't argue with the math. That little white ass of hers brings in good business."

Frustrated, Charles scampered down the back steps and screamed up at the window with the drawn curtains, "Betty!"

"What do you think your uncle gonna say if I tell him you here making a scene? I think we got all the eyeballs we want right now, so keep your damn voice down."

Charles was flustered, and that was the point. She was so much better at the game than he was. Not only was he inexperienced but love made people foolish. It was a truism that kept Madam Minnie in business.

"I'm coming back for her, Minnie. I'm coming back."

"Okay, honey. You go crack open your piggy bank and let me know when you got enough."

Charles looked up at the window again. Was she in there listening to the entire exchange? There may be no getting past Minnie, but he could attempt to cover whatever scent the Feds were sniffing out. He skipped the Shriners Parade and spent the next couple hours scoping out the Forest Club for the perfect moment to strike.

When the Model A panel truck pulled up to the loading dock, Danny and Charles were watching from the shadows of Saint Antoine and Hancock. Jon Jon hopped out of the truck without a care in the world. He unlocked and swung open the hinged cargo doors, grabbed the first crate of inventory, and slid it onto the loading platform. Danny saw this as his cue to snuff his hand-rolled smoke and slide into a pair of gloves he pulled from his back pocket.

Charles's eyes were drawn away from the unsuspecting bartender, who apparently did more around the club than serve drinks.

"Gloves? We don't need gloves, Danny. . . . You know what? This was a mistake."

Danny kept his snakelike eyes on Jon Jon. "You're already a part of this. If you'd done your job properly, no one would be nosing around."

"My job? My job!"

"Keep your goddamn voice down."

Charles lowered the volume of his argument. "My job was literally to clean up your mess! If anyone's nosing around, it's because of the mess, not the cleanup. We don't even know if this brother knows anything."

"This 'brother' had a full-on conversation with a friend of mine about how suspicious it was that Chuck Diggs's competition disappeared."

Charles couldn't hide his irritation with Danny's daft deductive reasoning. "Everyone was talking about it, Danny! Everyone! And why the hell would this 'friend of yours' even know to bring you this information? Who did *you* tell?"

"I think maybe you should mind your business. We got work to do."

Does everything he says have to sound like he's trying to be some hot-shot dick from True Detective *magazine?* Charles thought. "What work, Danny? What if he doesn't know anything?"

"We'll just rough him up a bit to find out."

Danny was on the move across Hancock Street toward the loading dock, and Charles had no option but to follow. Jon Jon was totally unaware of the coming storm, his mind and body concentrating on getting the truck emptied.

"Danny, the guy is obviously working for a buck here. How does tending bar and unloading trucks . . ."

Danny reached back a hand to shut Charles up, and his pace quickened. Jon Jon put another crate on the dock. Danny hugged the side of the truck, hidden by the open hinged door as Jon Jon dragged the next crate out. Charles was right behind Danny, and Danny was right behind the door. Jon Jon dropped the crate and spun back for the next, but he froze solid at the sight before him—legs visible under the open cargo door.

He was frightened, but why jump to conclusions? "That you, Mr. Tillman?"

Jon Jon reached for the door to reveal the face above the legs, but Danny heard his feet shuffle closer and, without another thought, all of Danny's weight slammed into the door as hard as he could. It swung fiercely for a foot before making solid contact with Jon Jon's face. His head arched back, and a wide, vertical split instantly opened in his forehead, releasing a river of blood. He stumbled back a step, then two, but that's where his balance failed him completely, and he fell as if the swing of a lumberjack's ax had just taken the final wedge from his ankles. Slow motion at first, then picking up speed in free fall until the back of his head crushed against the unforgiving corner of the concrete loading dock. His chin slammed into his chest, and Jon Jon's body hit the ground with a dull thud.

Charles grabbed Danny and threw him against the side of the truck, forearm pressed into his neck. Charles's eyes were already wet with the tears he inherited from his father.

"You call that roughing him up?!"

Charles's right fist reared back and delivered a rib-cracking blow to Danny's body. "I don't think he knew anything!" Charles screamed.

Unable to breathe or even grunt, Danny frantically smacked at Charles's arm, his only way to communicate. That's when an untapped darkness rose from Charles's gut and took over his mind.

"I could kill you right now, and no one would miss you. I'd be doing the Lord's work by removing you from His domain."

Danny swatted more ferociously, and finally Charles's grasp on reality successfully choked back his inner demon and whispered sense into his heart. It would be easy to physically kill this deserving creep, but then he would be sentenced to looking over his shoulder for Gaczynski goons the rest of his life. The pressure on Danny's throat eased. This could put Charles's family in danger. Or Betty.

Charles's forearm dropped, and Danny gasped for air. Of course his first words were enough to deserve another choking.

"I knew you'd see it my way."

Danny crouched over Jon Jon's body and dug into his pockets, searching.

"Killing him wasn't enough, so you're going to rob him too?" Self-pity now made Charles feel he deserved whatever consequences came his way.

"I'm looking for the keys, ya twit. . . . Found 'em. Now help me get him in the truck."

Danny pocketed the keys and positioned himself under the man's legs, waiting for Charles to lift the bloody half of the body. He would have refused if Jon Jon hadn't coughed at that precise moment and tried to speak. He only gave a faint mumble, but he definitely tried to speak.

Charles rushed to Jon Jon's side. The man's eyes fluttered open and then closed again. Charles slapped his cheek, desperate for another response. Nothing. He put his ear to Jon Jon's blood-soaked chest, and Charles's face lit up.

"He's alive!"

Danny took advantage of the situation to get Charles on the move. "Then do what I said and pick him up! My family knows a doctor. Come on!"

Danny grabbed a leg under each of his arms, and Charles cradled Jon Jon's limp torso. Together they lifted him into the back of the truck. Charles removed his shirt, tore it in half, and used it to tie an ugly but effective bandage around Jon Jon's head, covering the gashes on both the front and back of his skull. When Charles was satisfied, Danny slammed the cargo doors and raced for the driver's seat. Shirt-less and painted in blood, Charles joined on the passenger side like a lost lemming.

*Valerie and Jasper were in Chicago, taking their seats for the Braddock-*Louis fight.

Sharon was greeting guests who came to the Current Topic Study

Club to hear Rosa Gragg moderate a discussion on "buying Black."

God only knew where Stephen was, but Mark was certain that if his younger brother were anywhere in the house, his presence would be known by the volume of his existence.

This meant Mark was alone at home in Conant Gardens, doing something he'd never have dared before now—snooping in his father's den. The room was exquisitely designed and built but sparsely decorated. One outcome of Jasper's poor early years was that the clothes, the cars, and the house he bought had to be of the finest craftsmanship. He needed the world to know he was valuable. But never having had "things" growing up was the reason this den felt so bare. The room's single personal touch came from an intense Carter family trait that both Jasper and Ben believed should be as common as humans with heads but sadly was not—an iron family bond. They would kill for anyone with Carter blood, and they'd kill an entire family for a Carter child. Whether or not that was literal or figurative was up to the offender to dare. The children were represented in the room by projects they'd done together. A stack of charcoal sketches they made of one another. Sharon's picture of Stephen was surprisingly good for someone who had never studied art. Individual Erector Set contraptions they built last Christmas. A family picture of Jasper's and Ben's families outside Hamtramck Stadium was framed next to a baseball, encased in glass, that was signed by the great Turkey Stearnes. Other than the handful of family mementos, the room was uninviting.

There was a sitting area with two sofas but no throw pillows. Between them was a coffee table but no doilies, table runner, centerpiece statue, or decorative bowl holding potpourri. Three walls had oil paintings of jazz scenes: a Mardi Gras street band, Ma Rainey belting into a microphone, and a white-tuxedoed big-band horn section playing behind two tap dancers in midstep. A highly polished oak desk dominated the southern wall with a high-backed, green velvet upholstered chair but no calendar, writing utensils, or stationery, and the five finely carved drawers with their decorative-knocker-style handles stored nothing.

Or did they?

When Mark was seven years old, all of Detroit buzzed with the shock that the world-renowned Houdini had collapsed onstage at the Garrick Theatre on Griswold Street and later died at Grace Hospital. Annoyed by the worship of a white man who famously got out of handcuffs and took punches to the gut for entertainment, Jasper would joke that Black men performed these feats every day and got no credit. A couple years later, the papers announced that the "Colored Houdini" was coming to town. Mark was old enough at the time to understand that his father was only taking him to see "Hooper! The World's Favorite Colored Magician!" because he was Black, but not quite mature enough to know why this was important.

The show was incredible. Hooper escaped from a straitjacket, he performed a puppet show, his assistant was a mind-reading princess, he swallowed and coughed up a baby chick, he made the hat of a boy in the audience disappear in a magic box, and on and on it went. Laughter and amazement abounded by adults and children alike. Mark's friend Sammy had instantly wanted to learn magic and become a performer, but Mark only had the desire to know how it was done. His inner investigator was born. He learned that the straitjacket escape was accomplished by keeping enough room inside the jacket while it was being put on. The illusion was making people think it was tight, not the escape. He didn't know the specifics of the baby chick trick, but he did know it was about distraction and sleight of hand. He just didn't know exactly where the distraction came from. The one he couldn't figure out at all was the disappearing hat trick. Jasper assured him there was a hidden compartment in the box, but how was there enough room to show the box empty while also hiding the hat?

A fire was lit in Mark, sending him on a quest to understand the "how" of even the most common things. For example, people simply accepted that newspapers showed up in the morning, but Mark needed to know how. How did reporters learn what they learned? How were the articles typed? How did they get it all done and printed in time to put them on the newsstands and in the arms of paperboys before the sun came up the next day? While other kids mused about the impossibility of Santa Claus, Mark was amazed by the implausibility of news distribution . . . transatlantic telephone calls . . . the digging of the Lincoln Tunnel . . . movie production . . .

Standing in his father's study, Mark was hit with his itch to solve a mystery. That morning, when his father screamed at a policeman in a suit, Mark had learned about the existence of compromising pictures of important men at Minnie's place. On a number of occasions, he'd also witnessed Minnie or one of her girls come to the house to give Jasper envelopes. Each time his father would take the delivery into the study and close the door. There should be dozens of envelopes, maybe hundreds, but the den was bare. No safe, no bookshelf, no stacks on the table, no fireplace.

Mark sat at the desk. He deduced this must be the place his father reviewed the contents of the envelopes. Three metal Tinkertoy contraptions lined the back of the desk, each made by one of Jasper's kids: an airplane by Sharon, a car by Mark, and a crane by Stephen. Mark opened the top middle drawer. Empty. Nothing out of the ordinary. He twisted his body to let his eyes wander around the room. Surely a room with so little clutter would be harder to hide things in. The rug! An area rug, fifteen feet by fifteen feet, covered the floor under the coffee table, with one side under the front legs of a sofa. Mark got up with a jolt and lifted every edge, checking for some sort of trapdoor in the floorboards. He moved the sofa to look under the pinned edge, but there was nothing. He slid the sofa back onto the rug, careful to put the carved wooden feet back in the same carpet indentations.

The desk. It had to be the desk.

He sat back down and opened the left and right top drawers at the same time. Empty, clean wooden boxes. He closed them and moved to the two lower drawers, also clean and empty. A magnetic force seemed to hold his attention. Was something off? He pulled the right drawer open as far as it would go and examined it. He pulled open the drawer above it to compare. The wood grain of the drawer bottoms ran in opposite directions. This didn't have to mean anything, but it was different. He checked the other drawers. The wood grain of the top drawers all ran side to side while the bottom two drawers ran front to back. There was another difference. On the front edge of the bottom of each lower drawer were two silver-colored screwheads, perfectly flush with the surface, about an inch apart. The top three drawers with the side-to-side wood grain had no screws.

Due to the fine craftsmanship of this piece of furniture, it took a much closer examination of the top three drawers to know for sure that the drawer bottoms were set inside a routed-out groove in the drawer sides, meaning the drawer bottoms could not be lifted or lowered without taking the whole drawer apart. The bottom drawers were also well made, but there was a shadow of a gap, only the width of a sheet of paper, around the entire edge. Mark attempted to get a fingernail into the gap to see if it could be lifted. Too narrow. He reached under the drawer and pushed up on the bottom. Solid.

He leaned back and let his gaze circle his surroundings again. If not in this room, then where were the photos hidden? Was Jasper bluffing, and there were no photos? Possible.

Stephen's Erector Set crane.

Mark studied the mechanics of the mini machine: dual-hinged arm with pulleys and a handle just big enough to pinch between a thumb and forefinger. Spin to the left and it wound a string through the pulleys, raising a horseshoe magnet dangling from the crane's arm. Spin the handle to the right and the magnet lowered. Mark drew the toy closer and slowly pulled the crane's magnet until the wound spool reached its final knot. He touched the magnet to the toy's hole-punched steel frame. Surprisingly strong for a little magnet. The north and south poles of the curved iron were about an inch apart.

Mark held Stephen's crane over the bottom drawer so that the string hung inside. There was no need to reach in and guide the magnet, because like a bloodhound on the scent, the string went rigid and stopped swinging even before the magnet made contact with the two mysterious, perfectly spaced screws. Using the crane like a fishing pole, Mark lifted the false bottom out of the drawer, uncovering the hidden envelopes that held enough blackmail to keep the Carter family in power for at least another generation.

Sixty-five thousand people were crammed into Chicago's Comiskey Park with Jasper and Valerie Carter to watch Joe Louis and James "Cinderella Man" Braddock battle it out for the title of heavyweight boxing world champion. Nearly sixty million more were gathered around radios all over America to hear if Detroit's golden boy would become the second Black man to hold the title, after Jack Johnson, who had given it up twenty-two years before.

Less than a minute after the starting bell, a right hook from Braddock put Louis on his ass, but that was the last time Jimmy had a chance. In the eighth round, Joe delivered a left jab–right hook combo that laid Jim out cold. Knockout. Later, Braddock said, "It's like someone jammed an electric lightbulb in your face and busted it. I thought my head was blown off. When he knocked me down, I could've stayed there for three weeks." In the coming days, newspapers abounded with racist jabs at Joe Louis, but nothing could stop the celebration of Black Americans from coast to coast. It was even reported that two men in Detroit, George Crinshaw and James Wilkerson, literally died from excitement within minutes of Braddock hitting the mat.

Braddock's reign as champ was over, but the night was not. Jasper and Valerie had tickets to one of the many after-parties, and word on the street was that Joe Louis might make an appearance. Joe and Jasper didn't run in the same circles, but Jasper knew the kid from the neighborhood, so seeing him wasn't the draw. The purpose of the night, the whole reason to come to Chicago, was not to see anyone but to be seen. Valentino's delivery racket was a small-time operation of the Chicago Outfit, and Jasper knew that hiding in the shadows would get him nowhere. He needed to be seen, and Valerie's magic would help turn on the spotlight.

Once Danny pulled away from the Forest Club's loading dock, any thought of getting help from a doctor friend of the family went out the window, along with the cigarette he flicked onto Grand River Avenue at sixty miles an hour. Somewhere just past Brighton, Danny took a random dirt road to the south. The plan was to bury Jon Jon in the middle of nowhere, putting an end to any discussions he was having about Frolovski with the merrymakers at the Forest Club. Charles was furious, but what option did he have? He could jump out of the speeding truck covered in another man's blood and try to figure out how to get home without arousing any suspicions, or he could stick as close to Danny as possible, because Charles knew Danny would do everything in his power to save his own hide.

Danny picked a desolate location and lit a small area with the truck's headlamps to aid the setting sun. When they got out, Danny retrieved a shovel from behind a nearby tree, proving that this had been his plan for Jon Jon all along and that Charles had once again become his gullible accomplice. When the cargo doors were opened, to Charles and Danny's shock, Jon Jon was sitting up, huddled in the back corner with his eyes wide.

"Good mother of God, you people just won't die!"

Jon Jon saw the shovel in Danny's hand and then moved his eyes to Charles. Surely the other Black man would do something to help. Right?

"Come here," Danny ordered.

The poor man stayed huddled in the back corner. Speechless. Overwhelmed.

Danny waited a moment and seemed to breathe through a wave of anxiety. Then he asked again, nicer this time. "Come on now. Don't make this harder than it has to be."

Silent. Motionless. Charles and Jon Jon clung to each other with their eyes.

Another long exhale through the nose. Then Danny bared his teeth and chomped them together three times, like a fast countdown to becoming unhinged.

"Goddamnit! Did you hear what I said?" Shovel in hand, Danny grabbed the side of the truck and pulled himself up. "Get your Black ass . . ."

Two steps in, Danny's foot slid out from under him on Jon Jon's blood, putting him flat on his white ass that was now stained scarlet. There would be no more facial tics or calming breaths to hold back the flash flood of Danny's rage. He half screamed, half grunted as he scurried to get up but fell again, this time onto his hands and knees. Had the moment not been so gory, those pratfalls could have taught Buster Keaton a thing or two, but all they did was enrage the privileged monster within. When Danny got to his feet, he grabbed ahold of one of Jon Jon's feet and began dragging him out, screaming at the man the whole way.

"When I talk, you fucking listen! You fucking listen!"

At first Jon Jon simply muttered, "No. No."

"Now I gotta burn my clothes because of you! Goddamnit!"

At the open end of the truck, Danny hopped down, never letting go of the pant leg at Jon Jon's ankle.

Charles's torn, blood-soaked shirt around Jon Jon's head was probably the only thing that had kept him alive. Now Charles wished he hadn't helped. Already being dead was certainly better than continued torture.

Danny transferred his grip to the man's ankle and yanked.

As Jon Jon's body slid toward the short free fall, he screamed through blood and spittle, "I didn't do anyth—"

His torso hit the earth with a thump, knocking the oxygen from his lungs.

"Danny! Enough! He learned his lesson! He won't talk about shit anymore!"

But Danny was already dragging Jon Jon around to the front end of the truck. Charles followed helplessly as the screamed interrogation began.

"Who do you work for, the Feds? You an informant? You undercover?"

Jon Jon reconnected with Charles, pleading for help with his eyes.

"Asking questions to anyone who would sit at your bar? You know what asking questions gets you?!"

A smashing kick to the lower back slammed Jon Jon's eyes closed in splitting pain. Danny rounded his body and tossed the shovel to Charles.

"Dig this coon's grave."

"Danny, let's just leave him here. We don't gotta . . ."

"Dig, or I'll bury you both!"

Charles did not follow his orders. He stood there, frozen from the inside out, unable or somehow unwilling to intervene. He hated himself now, and he would hold on to that hatred for a lifetime.

Danny began his tirade again. "What did you learn? You learn anything about that Polack? Who opened their mouth? Was it Lance? Was it someone Lance told?"

Another kick, this time to the upper arm.

"I don't know," Jon Jon grunted.

"You don't know who, or you don't know nothing?"

Jon Jon's entire demeanor changed at that very instant. The pain disappeared with a new goal in focus. He connected with Charles one last time. The only emotion remaining on his bloodied, filthy face was determination.

"I heard some things."

Danny threw his arms up and circled the area in celebration for having been right. "I fucking knew it! I knew it!"

When he circled all the way back, he was met with Jon Jon's deadly resolute stare.

"You know about the Polack? What did you hear? I only told Ricky and Alfredo, and they know better, so it was either Lance or . . . Was it you, Chuck? Who'd you open your big mouth to?" Danny took a frightening step in Charles's direction that was only stopped by the power of Jon Jon's voice.

"We already knew what you did to the Polack."

Danny spun on Jon Jon with his defenses up. "Me? What I did? I didn't do a goddamn thing. It was Lance!" Danny threw a finger up at Charles. "And this fucking mook! Do you know how he got rid of the body?"

"Danny." One word. One word of protest was all Charles could muster.

"My name is Detective Cochran."

"A fucking Fed. I fucking knew it."

"We know Lance killed him." All of Jon Jon's fear was gone.

Charles found the will to speak again. "Danny, he's lying. Does he have a gun? Wouldn't a Fed be carrying a gun?"

"We know that this gentleman here got rid of the body."

"'Got rid of the body'!" Danny burst into uncontrollable, insane laughter. "'Got rid of the body'? Is that what you call what he did?"

"He doesn't even know my name! He's lying!"

Jon Jon turned his deadpan glare back to Charles. "My name is Detective Cochran."

"All he's doing is repeating things you told him, Danny!"

"We know you killed the man." Jon Jon was trying to dig his own grave.

Danny straddled Jon Jon and wrenched him up by his shirt collar. "Are you lying? Why would you lie?"

"See if he got a badge. A Fed would have a badge."

"You murdered the Polack." Jon Jon hoped the punishment would come swift and end his pain.

Danny slammed Jon Jon's body down, whipping his head into the unforgiving earth. "I didn't do it!"

"He doesn't even know the man's name. He's saying 'Polack' because that's what you said."

"We know what you did."

Danny crushed his fist into Jon Jon's face, breaking his nose and one of his own knuckles at the same time.

Through a fresh river of blood, Jon Jon persisted. "You murdered the Polack. We're coming for you."

Danny stumbled up, cradling his right fist, and snatched the shovel from Charles's hand. "I didn't do it!" He put the sharp steel of the shovel to Jon Jon's neck. "I didn't do it!"

"Check his pockets!" Charles screamed through tears.

"We know . . ."

Danny lifted his foot to the top of the shovel's blade.

"No, God! Please, God!" Charles choked through his embarrassing, unforgivable stasis.

"You killed the Pol—"

Danny threw all his weight onto the shovel.

Charles blacked out and fell to the ground where he stood.

Danny sat down in silence before releasing a slow, methodical breath. When he rummaged through the dead man's pockets again, he found nothing.

There was no gun. No badge.

Everyone at the Grand Terrace that night had followed some path of the same reasoning to get there. The club was a mecca for jazz within the mecca for Black Americans, known as Bronzeville. Joe Louis or no Joe Louis, this place was hopping after Jersey Jim got put to sleep by the Brown Bomber. Everyone from "good friends" Clark Gable and Carole Lombard, to the top ranks of the Chicago Outfit, to the club's owner and Louis Armstrong's manager Joe Glaser, to Jasper and Valerie Carter were at the Grand Terrace tonight, because the resident bandleader, Earl "Fatha" Hines, was a personal friend of Joe Louis. It was no secret that Joe was notoriously low-key, but if he was going to make any stop at all before heading home to Marva at their apartment on South Michigan Avenue, it would be here. Everyone listening to Fatha's band of twenty-five blasting away on the tune "St. Louis Blues" hoped that at some point this evening, Joe Louis would pop in and give a shy wave of appreciation. No one expected a speech or for the new champ to hang around long, but stopping in for a wave didn't seem out of the question.

The room was alive with dancing and drunken revelry, both things

Valerie wanted to be a part of, but Jasper preferred to stick to the shadows, watching those who didn't know they were being watched. Valerie was feeling good, and it felt unwise not to take advantage of it. She stood by Jasper until her rhythm-keeping foot got the better of her. She downed her drink, pecked her man on the side of the mouth, and she was off to the dance floor. For all the time and energy consumed with moaning and worrying about her, when she was on, she was on.

Tonight she was fire.

Jasper watched as she boogie-woogied better than any hot tomato in the joint, and he loved every second of it. She shimmied and shook in her loose-fitted yellow gown, cut above the knee with layers of horizontal fringe that amplified all her wiggles in the sexiest ways. She danced with everyone and no one at the same time, occasionally shooting a wink back at Jasper to let him know how lucky he was that she was his. He didn't realize it, but a satisfied smile had crept to his face as he watched her show. She fox-trotted to a passing waiter and snagged a champagne flute from his tray, offering up a blown kiss as a tip, which he was happy to accept.

Jasper allowed his gaze to fall over the room. Black and white men and women doing the awkward mingle of being in the same space but not truly integrating, not like at home in Paradise Valley, anyway. Miss Lombard chatted with a blond girlfriend while her beau, Gable, tapped his heel and smiled at Valerie's moves. Even Hollywood stars coveted what Jasper had, and he liked it that way. The crowd's envy, no matter how innocent or debaucherous, only filled Jasper with pride in his wife. The mobsters looked slightly uncomfortable to be front and center to the evening's action. Joe Glaser sat next to Chicago boss Frank Nitti, and Jasper wondered if the Outfit still controlled Capone's 25 percent of this joint even with him being on the Rock in San Francisco Bay and all.

When "St. Louis Blues" ended, the crowd made a changeup. New people came to the floor, and the last batch took a seat to wipe their brows and grab another round. That's when Jasper found Fatha Hines leaning toward Valerie, who shouted into his ear. Fatha nodded and snapped his fingers to a band member, who fetched a handheld microphone with a long cord. Jasper folded his arms and settled his shoulder against the wall to watch his wife's impromptu show. He knew she could deliver, and he was excited to watch her win over a crowd.

Mr. Hines raised his hand from his seat behind the piano. He had the band's attention, and when his fingers hit the black-and-whites, the band bounced into "A-Tisket, A-Tasket." Valerie spun toward the audience, and a spotlight found her as she took a lap around the front tables, winking and smiling at the men and women who would soon be drooling. By the time she brought the microphone to her lips, everyone on the dance floor had happily acquiesced the space to accompany her from the sidelines.

"A-Tisket, a-tasket. A brown-and-yellow basket. I send a letter to my mommy. On the way I dropped it."

She highlighted her imaginary dropped basket by sticking out her ass and lowering herself farther and farther at the waist with each "dropped it."

"I dropped it, I dropped it. Yes, on the way I dropped it."

Her dress got shorter and shorter the lower she bent to pick up the imaginary brown-and-yellow basket. Holding the mic in her right hand, she batted her gown's fringe with her left, which was now very high on her thigh, giving those in the right seats more of a show than they had bargained for.

She popped back up, standing tall, pretending to be shocked at what the audience was looking at. She ate it up and so did they. Then she took the show to the crowd.

She swooped her hand over the slick, wavy hair of a lucky Black gentlemen, then moved to Gable and Lombard's table. He blushed, knowing full well that his celebrity made him a target. She held out her hand to be kissed by America's silver-screen heartthrob.

With a slight nudge from Lombard, Gable gave the crowd what they wanted and what Valerie demanded: he took her hand in his and kissed her fingers. The crowd hooted and hollered their reward, and Valerie moved on.

Maybe she was unaware of who the men at the next table were, but more likely she knew exactly what she was doing. She'd had enough liquid courage to make her adventurous and healthy but not enough to make her blind. When she bent at the waist this time, she aimed her curves toward the mobsters. The Outfit's muscle for the evening, future boss Tony "Joe Batters" Accardo, placed his hand on Valerie's hip and shoved her away with forceful disdain. Audible "oohs" came from the crowd, but she took it in stride and would have simply continued with the show if Jasper hadn't magically appeared at the table.

The whole club went quiet. Fatha Hines held up his hand to stop the band midsong, and everyone waited with held breath for Jasper's move. Each of the four mobsters at the table, boss Frank Nitti in the middle, looked up at Jasper standing above them with nonchalant dares in their eyes. Slowly, Jasper reached for Joe Batters's whiskey glass. He sniffed it, made an approving grimace, and shot it back, placing the empty glass down in front of the white goon.

Jasper spoke directly to Nitti. "You had us in the perfect place. You had all of Detroit in the perfect spot. . . ."

"Maybe you should take your seat, spook," Joe Batters interrupted.

"You had us asking if it was worth pushing back. Your rackets kept our profits low enough that we still needed to work for 'em but high enough that a good old-fashion turf war felt unnecessary . . . but then you had to go and push your luck."

"Do you want me to repeat myself, nigger?"

Jasper snatched up the empty glass in front of Joe Batters and violently spiked it to the floor between them. Shards flew in every direction to the sounds of more shocked "oohs" from the audience.

"Sure. Go ahead. Repeat yourself."

Jasper waited for a response, but none came.

"As I was saying, you went and pushed your damn luck. Charge us for the hooch and to deliver it too. It got me thinking. Do you know how much booze comes through the Canada-Detroit border?" Again, no answer. "Me neither, but I know it's substantial. Hell, your beloved Capone relied entirely on the Purple Gang during Prohibition. You used to pay Detroit! How on earth did that get flipped around?"

Preacher Carter brought his sermon to the people. "Here's another one for you. Who's the real boss of the Chicago Outfit?" Jasper circled back around to Nitti. "Certainly not this puppet."

The moans of the people signaled that Jasper may have gone too far.

Jasper looked into Nitti's seething soul. "Where's Paul Ricca? He's the one who calls the real shots, right? Does he know you're out tonight? Did he give you permission to stay up past your bedtime drinking Canadian whiskey that came through Detroit? Would he be ashamed if he knew you been gawking at my fine Black woman?"

A young Black stud in the crowd couldn't hold back the snortle that escaped his nose, causing a minor disturbance, but Jasper stayed focused on Nitti. "Last question for you. Who's in charge of Detroit delivery these days?"

Nitti finally decided to speak up. "I'm going out on a limb here, Mr. Carter, but it sounds like you might know the whereabouts of a young friend of ours named Valentino."

"No, sir, I'm sorry. That is not the correct answer." Jasper picked up where he left off, "The answer is me. I do. The delivery racket belongs to the Carters now. You hear? And if you keep your manners about you, like your sweet eye-talian grandmama done taught you, then we'll think twice about expanding into Chi-Town. . . . But it would be unwise to tempt me."

Jasper reached into his pocket and pulled out a money clip. He unfolded a ten-dollar bill and dropped it in front of Joe Glaser.

"That should cover the broken glass."

He reached back, and Valerie proudly took his hand, then he turned to the bandstand.

"You hot, Fatha Hines. You hot. If you ever make it out to Motor City, we gotta spot for you at Geraldine's. We'd be proud to have you."

As Jasper and Valerie made their exit, the crowd applauded in support of the poetry he just threw down. When the Carters were gone, Nitti and his friends settled up and donned their coats. That was enough embarrassment for one evening.

Fatha Hines raised his magical hand, and in moments the place was swinging once again to the grooving ditty "Bambino."

How so much had changed in one day was an impossible question to answer when no single member of the Carter family had all the details, but even though midnight had come and gone, the day was not over.

Mark Carter worked his Blue Streak Model 8 Linotype late into the morning hours. He was going to get that job at the *Chronicle*. Nothing was going to stop him. He was smart, though, and he knew not to give them everything at once. He hadn't removed the envelopes from his father's hiding place. He'd keep those for later. For now he believed he had a story big enough to get the attention of the union-backed Black periodical. Surely, they would see the value in a picture that Mark had taken earlier in the day of Governor Murphy shaking hands with one of Black Bottom's infamous Carter brothers.

PART THREE

PART
THREE

CHAPTER SEVENTEEN

The United Mine Workers union was at it again in 1914, and the National Guard was brought in to force the miners of the Colorado Fuel and Iron Company back to work. For nine months tensions rose until an eruption on April 20. The Ludlow Massacre. Gunfire lasted from breakfast to sundown, ending with a miners' camp in flames and dozens dead, including eleven children who suffocated in a pit dug beneath their tent. This was the start of the Ten Day War.

Jasper could see the writing on the wall and wondered why people were incapable of learning from their mistakes. It had only been three years since the disastrous 1911 coal strike in Westmoreland County, Pennsylvania, and this organized demand for better treatment would end no differently. Strikers were forced into tent cities, livelihoods were destroyed, and once again the United Mine Workers union would run out of money and give up.

Fortunately, Jasper had a new fire in his belly. The last couple years had given him something far more important to fight for than the right to dig rocks out of a smelly hole in the earth with a pickax: his wife, Valerie, and his baby girl, Sharon.

Valerie was a needed spark of life, and within months of them meeting, she was pregnant. When her father learned that another man had deflowered the daughter he regularly forced himself upon, jealousy took over. He beat Valerie till both her eyes swelled shut, and in retaliation, Jasper beat the old bastard into a coma. It was then that he decided to move the expanding Carter family away from Earlington, Kentucky.

The Carters settled in the East End of Xenia, Ohio, in a run-down two-bedroom home on none other than Jasper Pike. Jasper and Valerie shared one of the bedrooms with baby Sharon, and the other was divided by a dirty sheet nailed to the ceiling to give Lance and Rosalind, now twenty-three and thirteen, the illusion of privacy that their contrasting ages demanded for different reasons. Ben slept in the living room, and more frequent than not, a neighborhood girl named Margaret spent the night with him. Politeness and a dash of modesty from them both meant no one ever saw Ben and Margaret cuddled together in their undergarments. And no matter which of the bedroom dwellers woke up first, when they entered the living room, Ben and Margaret would already be dressed and their bedding folded neatly over the back of the sofa.

Jasper hadn't known if Xenia was close to any coal mines, but seeing his baby's smile locked him into the mindset that he would move anywhere and take any job, from shoveling shit to robbing banks, if it helped his family get ahead, and it was a tiny picture in an NAACP publication called *The Crisis* that led him to Ohio. The photo was of the most distinguished Black man he'd ever seen. He needed Ben's help reading the blurb under the picture, but even that was confusing. The man's name was a string of letters and periods, and his last name was just as odd. Did this man go by "Web"? "W"? How did you pronounce "Bois"? Further down was the equally strange word "Wilberforce," which was the name of a college for black folks where this man had once taught. Jasper studied this picture, the man's balding head, his manicured beard, the dignified upward angle of his chin, and his fashionable suit. This was the kind of man who could change the world for his family. Jasper held his own in the streets, but he felt insecure about his capacity for book learning, and Ben was his ticket. Xenia was close to Wilberforce College, and Jasper would work twenty hours a day if it meant Ben could get an education like the elegant man with letters for a first name. With Ben's brain and Jasper's brawn, their budding family's future felt bright.

With Ben distracted by Margaret and getting ready for his first day of college, Jasper out doing God knows what to earn some money, and Valerie dividing her time between baby Sharon and a bottle of gin, Lance was left to his own imagination. Then, when Rosalind finished her day at East Main, Xenia's colored high school, the two were a perfect recipe for trouble.

One sunny afternoon Lance and Rosalind ventured west on Main, right up to Monroe Street, the border of "their" neighborhood. The white side of town was a mystery, and Lance took a little thrill from walking right up to the line that made white people uncomfortable. That line could literally be Monroe Street, or it could be something like saying "How do you do, good madam?" in a British accent to a white lady passing by. Really anything to get a rise, and frankly, getting a rise out of white people was easy. What Lance couldn't understand was why more Black people didn't view their ability to make white people uncomfortable as a special power. Their mere presence could fluster white folks. It could make them leave, rob them of their ability to speak. Sometimes they'd even fumble and drop something, and for some reason, the wealthier they were, they funnier the reaction would be. Of course, they could also call their pale friends to a meeting at the closest hanging tree, but that's why Lance liked walking right up to the line. Going any further was dangerous, a lesson he learned that day: April 4, 1914.

Feeling emboldened by the combination of perfect weather and boredom, Lance took the lead, and Rosalind followed him westward, beyond Monroe Street. Half a block in and Lance was already wondering how far they could get. Why had no one stopped them yet? By the time they got to Collier Street, Rosalind's imaginary tether had shrunk so short that she tripped over Lance's feet.

Another block and a guttural laugh leapt out of Lance. "Whiteman Street? Is that a joke?"

Three white men smoking cigars half a block farther prompted a slight tug from Rosalind on the back of Lance's shirt, but he encouraged her with a glance, and they kept moving in the direction of the men, who stood in front of a barbershop at 49 East Main. When they noticed a couple of lost Black kids staring, they grew quiet and puffed their cigars. Lance and Rosalind froze. What would happen next? Would they get yelled at? Chased back toward Monroe Street?

"I heard niggers liked barbershops, but I'm afraid we don't got any garden shears here, son."

The smoking men chuckled, and Lance continued to stare in silence. Rosalind gave another gentle tug on her half brother's shirt.

A different man spoke up. "Come on, Al. Their heads ain't any more nappy than that thing you call a beard. All they need is your Dr. Scott's Electric Beard Curler."

This comment turned the men's chuckles into outright laughter at the bearded man's expense.

"Maybe with a bucket of coconut oil!" added the third racist gentleman.

Without warning, Rosalind turned and sprinted back in the direction of comfort. Lance would only be a few steps behind.

In less than fifteen minutes, they stood inside Fishback's New and Secondhand Store, about a block past Zion Baptist. It was mostly filled with clothes that nobody wanted, but there was one section of shelving full of gadgets that nobody wanted and a small area in that section for hair care items that nobody wanted. Will Fishback, who owned the place, was at the back of the room playing a piano that nobody wanted, but the sound of his song made Rosalind think that maybe he should keep it.

Lance had recognized the words as soon as the white man said them, and there they were on the shelf, scrawled across the handle of a little iron comb—"Dr. Scott's Electric Curler." He snuck it into his pocket, and the siblings walked out before Mr. Fishback even missed a note.

Valerie and Sharon were in their bedroom, daughter asleep with her bottle, mama "asleep" next to hers. Ben was out with Margaret and there was no telling when they'd pop in, so Lance and Rosalind needed to hurry. She had been shy during their outing to the west, but Lance's excitement was contagious, and all Rosalind really needed was a little convincing before the energy of a daring plan coursed through her veins. The plan? Straighten and soften her hair and then head east once again to see if they could make it all the way to the biggest intersection in town, where Main crossed Detroit Street.

Genetics is a funny thing. Even though it had the tendency to confuse a white person or two, Black people understood that sometimes the same Black mother and Black father could have three different children with three different shades of brown, from light to dark. Black people knew Rosalind was Black. They could see the features beyond the much paler shade of her skin. When you stood Rosalind and Jasper side by side, there was absolutely no denying they were siblings, and had their father, Charles, been standing between them, any passerby would know he was their missing link. White people, however, rarely looked passed the obvious: skin color and hair.

During their last summer in the Kentucky sunshine, Lance joked that some of the white men got darker than Rosalind. White skin was a weird thing. First it would burn, turn bright red, and sometimes blister, but then the reddish color would settle into a tan. Some got darker than others, but then, come winter, their skin went right back to pale, sometimes so pale that you could literally see their blue veins running under their skin. Rosalind would never be that pale, but those Kentucky summers proved she was light enough.

White people knew Rosalind was Black because they saw her with Black people. This meant it wasn't her skin keeping her from seeing the shops on Detroit Street—it was her hair. Her hair was black, but plenty of white people had black hair. The giveaway was that Rosalind's didn't blow in the wind or shake with the turn of her head. And this dumb, stolen comb wasn't doing a damn thing to help!

It clearly said the word "electric" on the handle, but there was no plug or wiring of any kind. There was no way for Lance to know this was a quack item, sold and marketed by a quack doctor. Rosalind had never been to a professional hairdresser, but she had watched through the window with intense jealous curiosity as more well-to-do Black women sat in the salon with expressions of near torture from all the yanking, pulling, and burning. That's how she knew to tell Lance to heat the comb on the coal stove. After burning the tips of his thumb, index, and middle fingers, he held the "electric" comb with a pot holder, but the heat alone wasn't showing much improvement. That's when they decided there was no other option but to follow the white man's advice. Coconut oil.

They escaped the house fifteen minutes before their plan would have been stopped by Ben. In fact, they passed on opposite sides of the street, but Ben was walking with Margaret, and they were so wrapped up in each other's presence that Orville and Wilbur could have flown by in one of their lawn-mower-powered bicycles with wings and the young lovers wouldn't have noticed.

Lance and Rosalind stood at the corner of Main and Monroe like they were George Poage at the starting line of the four hundred-meter hurdles in the 1904 games in St. Louis, where he became the first Black man to win an Olympic medal. Rosalind was wearing a pastel yellow Sunday dress, and her hair flopped around with each movement of her head. Whether that had anything to do with the stolen "electric" comb or the absurd amount of oil literally dripping onto her shoulders, they would never know. Tingling pricks of anxiety coursed through their veins, and energy flooded their legs. When Rosalind blasted forward, her wet hair bounced behind her, and a brilliant, joyous smile consumed her face. Lance was surprised she didn't need any further coercing and took off after her.

They passed Collier. They passed Whiteman. The white men were no longer outside the barbershop, but both Rosalind and Lance let out yelps of elated bliss as they sprinted by. When they got to Detroit Street, Rosalind spun around and screamed with a mix of terror and glee, overflowing with pride for her own disobedience to society's white standards, then kept sprinting west. The plan was to hit Detroit Street and turn back. Lance made chase and called out her name, but she only responded with more excited screams.

They hadn't even made it to King Street when a burly white man in a brown derby and bushy red mustache jumped from the doorway of a bakery and slammed into the side of Lance, sending him careening into the street.

"Not on my watch, boy!"

Rosalind spun at the boom of the man's voice and turned to find him standing over Lance and pointing in her direction.

"You're on the wrong side of town. And if I see you over here bothering white girls again, I'll string you up my own damn self."

Lance could see that Rosalind looked just as terrified as he felt but realized instantly that fear on her face while passing as a white woman only made the situation more dangerous for him. He scrambled to his feet and sprinted as fast as he could all the way home. The hurdles in this footrace had been more than he could handle.

Her white rescuer called out, "You all right there, little miss?" and then nothing for the next few hours felt in Rosalind's control at all.

Lance stumbled into the house to find the bedroom doors closed. He banged on both and screamed for help. Ben came out first, pulling his shirt on over his head. Seeing Lance afraid and frantic was contagious and left no time for anger or blame. That would come later and last a lifetime.

The police never patrolled East End, Xenia, and even if they had, how would they explain the situation without a backlash that would have lasting effects?

It took two full days to find Rosalind, and when they did, there was no way forward except to be prepared to leave Ohio immediately if needed. Valerie stayed home with the baby, and neither brother wanted Lance at their side. Jasper and Ben did, however, think it was smart to have a woman along to dull the edge of danger that their gender and the color of their skin carried in the minds of white people. Together, Jasper, Ben, and Margaret stood on the steps of the Soldiers' and Sailors' Orphans' Home.

The three-story redbrick administration building with its central bell tower combined all the terrifying feelings of church, school, and preposterous amounts of wealth. The grounds beyond were beautifully maintained but also large enough that there would be no escaping if one of the many possible negative outcomes of their visit came to fruition. The five-foot-nothing white woman who answered the door was polite, direct, and courteous. If she hadn't made purposeful eye contact with each of them, they would have assumed she was blind. Margaret did the talking. She explained as kindly as possible that there had been a mix-up and that their young, light-skinned sister had been mistaken as a white girl and brought there.

"Oh, how awful." The woman seemed to genuinely feel for their situation.

She reached behind herself to pull the door closed and then asked them to follow her. She led them quietly around the large building, where a group of identically uniformed girls picnicked and played in the grass.

"We've only had one new addition to our family here in over a month." She gestured to three girls sitting on a blanket in the grass. "Her. Just there."

"Yes, ma'am, that's our sister," Jasper spoke up.

"We do apologize for any trouble we may have caused," Ben added.

The woman responded with a loud and caring bellow across the yard, "Rose. Rose, could you please come here for a moment, dear?"

When Rosalind looked over, her hair fashioned on top of her head like a Gibson Girl, the laughter she shared with the white girls eating sandwiches vanished. As she cautiously stood and made her way toward the headmistress, Jasper and Ben spoke to each other through shared glances. *Rose? How'd she get her hair like that?*

"No need to be shy, Rose. These fine people seem to think you might be their lost sister?" The woman watched Rose for any signs of familiarity, but they were hidden by the building angst that currently controlled Rosalind's facial expressions.

Jasper held out his hand. "Come along, Rosalind."

Ben hurried with more pleasantries. "Thank you, ma'am. We'll get along and leave you to this beautiful day."

Rosalind's hand did not move to meet Jasper's.

"Rosalind. Come along now," he repeated.

The headmistress was now caught in the middle. "Rose, do you know these people?"

Rosalind mumbled too quietly to be understood and hung her head.

"Speak up, dear. Are these people your kin?"

Her head didn't rise, but her voice did. "No, ma'am."

"Rosalind!" Ben reacted too viscerally to her denial.

The woman's posture stiffened, and she planted herself a bit more firmly between the Carters and "Rose."

"What are you doing?! Come on now. We're leaving!" Jasper boiled.

"I don't know these people, Mrs. Claire." Then she turned to Ben. "I'm sorry." A tear welled in her eye that could be used as proof for either the truth or the lie. "I hope you find your sister."

"You go on now, child." With a small wave of the woman's frail hand, Rosalind went back to the girls watching from their picnic blanket. Then the headmistress used a powerful tone of voice that only mothers had—apparently all mothers, no matter their color. "I'm afraid I need to ask you all to leave the property before I'm forced to call the sheriff."

Margaret pulled at her dumbstruck boyfriend and his brother. If they were going to get Rosalind back, it wouldn't be now.

They attempted to send letters, both through the postal service and slipping them inside with a sympathizing Black woman who worked in the orphanage's kitchen on the weekends. No attempts resulted in a reply from their sister.

The next spring Ben and Margaret got married, but it wasn't the merry occasion it should have been because Rosalind still wasn't home. Jasper had hardened his heart to his sister, blaming her completely, believing that someday it would all backfire and she'd realize the error of her traitorous ways. A darkness surrounded Ben, which manifested itself as distaste for Lance, who he fully blamed for the loss of their sister. Valerie needed movement on the situation, either good or bad, because having no answer, no finality at all, was a worse level of hell than knowing for sure that they'd never see Rosalind again. It was out of character for him, but at Valerie's pushy, drunken request, Ben snuck his way onto the grounds of the orphanage and hid in a grove of trees near where he'd last seen his sister on the fateful day she'd denied their blood. He waited almost two hours in the shadows before a parade of frolicking white girls and one imposter came outside to enjoy a late lunch. When he spotted her, Ben's heart was pierced by the drastic change from thirteen to fourteen years old. Much of her hair was fashioned on top of her head, the rest taking the shape of loosely bouncing ringlets that framed her face. Ben knew the amount of work, not to mention product, that Black women went through to achieve these trendy European styles, but how had Rosalind managed to do so when the assumption must have been that her white hair shouldn't need the extra help to be this way? However she'd done it, he admired his sister's new, more mature appearance. He'd last seen a girl, and now the seemingly happy human he spied upon was a young woman.

Ben had collected a pocketful of rocks for the purpose of getting her attention. He could only throw them when no one else was able to intercept his desire to be seen. If it took him a month of sitting in the brush throwing rocks, that's what he'd do, but he got lucky. She wandered away from her friends to pick dandelions, and Ben took his chance. She looked toward the sound of a rock that landed nearby. When a second, then a third, tumbled into sight, she looked for where they'd come from, and there he was. On the off chance that she called the headmistress, Ben was prepared to run, but Rosalind slowly made her way over, careful to keep up the appearance of flower picking. She was growing accustomed to keeping her motivations secret.

She got within a whisper and stopped. She never looked right at him, instead fiddling with the flowers, pretending to be engrossed in a tree branch, stretching, anything but having a clandestine meeting with a Black family member. Ben had planned the entire mission but assumed he'd know the words to say when the moment came. He was wrong, and so Rose took the lead.

"I'm happy here. I have a roof that doesn't leak. All the food I want. Friends." She stumbled over her words a little when emotion tried to escape and got stuck in her throat. She wiped a single tear from her face and onto her uniform. "I miss you. All of you. And I feel guilty every day, but…" The tears began to flow more freely, from both Rose and Ben, who had yet to speak a word. "But I feel safe here. I don't live in fear."

"But if they ever find out …"

"They won't."

"But if …"

"Ben, they won't. . . . They won't." She punctuated her confidence with eye contact for the first time in a year.

"Don't they see you doing whatever you're doing to get your hair like that?"

"Mrs. Mueller, our headmistress, started helping me with it the day I arrived."

"She knows?"

"No." Rosalind let a smirking giggle escape, which she recognized as inappropriate for the circumstance, but she knew there was a painful humor to what had happened. "When I was brought here, I had all this coconut oil in my hair. After she helped me wash it out, my hair was frizzy, and she thought I was Jewish."

Ben joined her in the irreverent levity, careful to keep his volume down and remain hidden. He didn't know what to say. There was nothing he could say. The truth had been so far from anything the headmistress believed was possible that she made up her own truth.

Rosalind continued, "She told me I needed to fit in if I wanted to make friends here, and to her that meant keeping me supplied with oils and helping me iron my 'Jew-y' hair."

The comical absurdity of Rosalind getting help to hide her identity from the very person she was hiding it from ended with sighs that left space for the depression of their reality to settle in even heavier. Ben hadn't realized just how painful this moment would be, desperately attempting to memorize every wrinkle, every curve, every dimple in her face, knowing full well this visit would soon be over, and they'd likely never see each other again.

"How's Jas?" she asked.

"He's . . . He's angry."

This hurt, and Ben could see she wasn't prepared for it, so he tried some better news.

"Margaret and I got married. She's pregnant. If it's a boy, we're gonna name him Charles, after Dad." Ben knew it would cause a fight between him and Jasper, but . . . "Rosalind if it's a girl."

It was surprisingly sad to watch Rose realize the existence of her family's future that she'd never know. It looked as if she might even run to him in the shadows, and in that moment, Ben realized all his anger and sadness were selfish. At that moment the protective brother emerged. The protective brother who wanted the best for his sister.

The tears turned to quiet sobs as she choked out her only excuse. The excuse for it all. The excuse that made her new world make sense, but the excuse that would forever plague her.

"Being white is just . . . easier."

Ben released her from as much pain and regret as he could with two simple words: "I understand."

A whistle blew in the distance, and Rose spun around to see the other girls heading toward the dormitories.

"I have to go."

"I know."

She forced herself to turn away and felt the reality of "out of sight, out of mind." He was not out of her mind—he never would be—but it was certainly easier to walk away without being able to see him.

Life, the Carters would learn, didn't wait for anyone. Time continued to march forward. Ben got a remarkable offer to spend a semester
in Paris, and baby Charles joined the family, healthy and happy. Jasper, meanwhile, had enough stress and responsibility to drive a dead
man to drinking, but he would stop at nothing to put Ben in the same
league as W. E. B. Du Bois.

Eventually it was 1918, a huge year for Ben and the whole Carter
family. Margaret was pregnant again, Ben graduated from Wilberforce at the top of his class, and the family received a letter from their
cousin Minnie, who had settled in Detroit. With family already there
and manufacturing jobs ripe for the picking, it was hard to deny that
the time had come for the next chapter in their story. The Carters
were moving to Michigan, but first Ben needed to visit the grove of
trees at the orphanage one final time.

It was the last day of June, hot even in the shade. He brought a package wrapped in brown paper and waited until he saw the girls come outside. His breath was robbed when he saw the beauty and confidence that
seventeen-year-old Rose carried with her. At just the right moment, he
threw a single rock, and he could tell she heard it. When she turned, hiding her motivation, Ben was gone, and the brown package waited for her
at the edge of the trees. Written on the paper was the message "Be careful. Be strong." Inside she found a tin can labeled "Madame C. J. Walker's
Glossine and Pressing Oil." It was all Ben could do to help Rose on the
lonesome journey she had embarked upon.

While Ben was on his covert errand to deliver the going-away gift, Jasper and Margaret vowed to keep what they'd done secret forever. Never
again could they fall into each other as they had while Ben was in France.
Margaret loved Ben, and that was it for her till the end of time. Jasper
loved Valerie too, and she needed him. She was fragile. It had been a moment or two of weakness, and it could never happen again.

Detroit would be the new start they all needed.

CHAPTER EIGHTEEN

The sun and moon traded places seven times after the picture of Ben Carter shaking hands with Governor Murphy graced the pages of the *Chronicle*. The calendar on Rose's reception desk said it was Wednesday, June 30, 1937, and the group of men overflowing from Robert Peck's office and spilling into the hall were having an abnormally agitated conclave. Their crisp and pointed voices were heightened whispers that periodically turned to shouting before dropping right back to a volume of secrecy.

Rose had mastered taking advantage of alternate but equally feasible explanations for things that might otherwise have instigated too many questions for her comfort. So when her husband, Thomas, asked why she seemed so flustered and absent-minded, she blamed it on still being new at a high-powered legal office, and he fully accepted it as truth. *It's true!* she thought, or, at the very least, it wasn't a lie. There was a difference. Besides, telling him she'd had a run-in with her brother Ben, who she hadn't seen in . . . *The calendar. The last day of June . . . 1937*. It had been exactly nineteen years. Nineteen years to the day since the package of hair oil had appeared at the tree line of the Soldiers' and Sailors' Orphans' Home. She hadn't physically seen

Ben that day, so until two and a half weeks ago, it had been twenty-two years since she'd laid eyes on family.

"What do I care about the girl? She's not our client!"

"She's white, and she's a woman. If this gets to trial, who's a jury gonna believe? Charles Carter, a Negro charged with murder, or a helpless white . . ."

"Whore. She's a known whore, Carl. And a foreigner to boot."

The yelling lawyers quieted again. *Charles Carter?* He was surely family. *Was it Ben and Margaret's kid?* By keeping an ear aimed down the hall, Rose learned that Charles Carter and another man named Daniel Gaczynski had been charged and were in custody for the murder of Joseph Frolovski. She didn't know who this "whore" was, but she did know that another man, Lance Edwards, was picked up around the same time and that he and the "whore" were being held in a safe house because they could confirm Charles's involvement. *Lance? It couldn't be, could it? Why would his last name be Edwards?*

"Carl! We've got no body! We don't need to go further than that!" The yelling came back quicker this time.

"You don't think McCrea is gonna offer a cushy deal to whoever produces a body?"

"McCrea is on our side! The man testifies against cops to help Negroes, for crying out loud!"

"The Gaczynski kid says it's bodies, not body. Two. And that Charles is responsible for both. What if he proves it? What then, Bob?"

"Without a body, we don't know that Detective Cochran is really dead."

"What? You think he went AWOL? Are you willing to bet on it?"

There was plenty Rose didn't know. She didn't know that the photo of Governor Murphy hadn't impressed the *Chronicle* as much as Mark had hoped. She didn't know that Victor hadn't been seen by his family since the Shriners Parade. She didn't even know Mark and Victor existed! She did know Valerie and Margaret, or at least she had a long time ago, but she did not know that Valerie's health had taken a sudden turn after her and Jasper's trip to Chicago. And Rose knew absolutely nothing about how a couple of Chicago goons connected to Frank Nitti had shown up in Detroit to poke around Paradise Valley and Black Bottom to unravel what had happened to Valentino. But what Rose did know, she needed to tell. Rose needed to warn her estranged family.

The filing cabinets. The second drawer was the start of the letter C. Rose parted the papers so she could see the top page of Benjamin Carter's file. *Hastings Street. I can't be seen on Hastings Street.* She fingered to the next page. Next of kin—Jasper Carter. *Not Margaret? Wait, Conant Gardens? That's a little safer.*

Rose made a quick excuse for an early lunch, and no one objected. Too much was happening today to be bothered by the absence of the new woman who answered the phones. The phones could ring off the hook for all they cared. She retrieved her handbag from the bottom drawer of her desk, quickly touched up her Tango Red lipstick, and was out the door.

Standing on the doorstep of the Tudor Revival she found at Jasper's address made Rose unsure of her life's decisions. It was surely as nice as the place she and Thomas lived in. Had she given up too much to reach the same level of safety and comfort? She hadn't wanted to go to Ben's in Black Bottom because she was afraid of all the eyes on Hastings Street that would see her, afraid they'd somehow be able to see through her. Conant Gardens was a Black neighborhood too, the only difference being that it was more suburban. Black people's eyes could still see her; they were just hidden behind window curtains and picket fences. Suddenly "out of sight, out of mind" didn't feel so easy.

"Can I help you?"

The put-together Black woman in her early twenties who answered the door glared at Rose defiantly. If she had to ask the strange white woman again, her defiance would turn into aggression.

"Hello. Is this the home of Jasper Carter?"

"May I ask who's asking?" Sharon knew better than to offer up information without getting some in return.

"Someone who cares," Rose said, not knowing how to explain herself in the limited amount of time she had.

"Right. Okay. Uh . . . My daddy's not here, and my mama isn't feeling well enough for guests today."

"Valerie?"

Predictably, Sharon's head went to the side, and her hand found its position on her thrusted hip. "I'm sorry, ma'am, I don't know you. I'm glad you care, but I think you better . . ."

"I'm Rose." She stuck out a hand to shake. "Are you . . . Are you Sharon?"

Sharon glanced around as if a prankster's weird joke would soon be revealed. "Listen, lady. I don't know what this is, but I'm sure the cops would be willing to help me figure it out."

Rose's outstretched greeting hand flipped over to become a plea for more time. "No. I understand. I'm sorry. I'll only be a minute."

"Ticktock, lady. Ticktock."

"Charles."

"That's my cousin. What about him?"

"Ben's son?" Rose asked with hope.

"You really getting on my last nerve."

"Another man who was arrested, Daniel Gaczynski, is saying there are two bodies and that Charles killed them both. And one of them was an undercover Fed, so they'll stop at nothing."

"That's not true. Charles is innocent."

"I believe you—that's why I'm here—but there are two witnesses in protective custody who can place Charles at the scenes. A man named Lance Edwards and a Russian prostitute."

"Who are you, Rose?"

"This Gaczynski character isn't saying where the bodies are until he can cut a deal, but I don't think there's much time."

"Thank you." This stranger had transformed from white woman to angel before Sharon's eyes.

It was time for her to leave, Rose understood that, but she wanted more. "You said your mother is sick. Is she okay? Can I help?"

"My aunt Margaret is taking care of her. She'll be fine." Sharon knew her mother was anything but "fine," but as thankful as she was to this mysterious woman, it was too personal to speak about with a stranger.

"Okay, then." Rose smiled with longing in her eyes. "Goodbye, Sharon." Then she turned and walked back toward her Detroit Electric waiting at the curb.

Sharon watched in awe until Rose drove away, but then realized in an instant just how much work she had to do. It was time to move.

Ben usually went to the regularly scheduled meetings with Council-man Schwartz by himself, but today Jasper decided it was prudent to come along. Minnie told them something felt off as she led them down the hall to Schwartz, and when they entered, Ben understood why. The fat man, ornamented with his ivory-handled cane, usually had a selection of Minnie's women parading themselves before him. There were no women today. Just Schwartz's round body stuffed into an armchair, patiently waiting to do business.

Ben was visibly cautious—not that he liked seeing the women degrade themselves, but if Schwartz wasn't acting within the parameters of filthy and corrupt, then something else was afoot. Jasper, on the other hand, jumped right in with all the charisma needed to get from the man what they needed—information.

"Look at you, pip! Looking plenty rugged, as always." Jasper hung his hat on a hook by the door and pulled a chair up to Schwartz with a smile.

"Tell it to the women. I keep trying to convince them a round belly is a sign of wealth."

Jasper laughed some charm at Schwartz while Ben scooted another chair over to join them and pried just a touch. "No candy store today? Usually you're dizzy with a dame by now."

"Things feel a little different since the raid."

"You know about that, huh?" Jasper leveled with him. "We were pretty upset about it, but more than a few of Detroit's boys in blue are happy customers of Le Noir Palais, and we've been assured it won't happen again."

"Oh, I'm not scared of getting caught. I don't pretend to be more than a wet sock. The pickings just don't seem as desirable now that the Russky dame got picked up."

"I hear that." Jasper reached into his pocket for his gold money clip. "Well, we know you don't come by just to bump gums, so we can pay a little more until Minnie's selection is back to your liking. What do you say?"

"I don't want your money."

Jasper hit his first bump in the road and slid the cash back into his pocket.

Ben's turn. "You wouldn't be here if you didn't have something valuable, and we know you won't give up the lowdown without payment, so what's the bleed?"

"Minnie."

"What about her?" Jasper asked.

"That's what I want. That's the bleed."

The brothers went silent. Jasper got up to pace through the internal debate that broke out between his mind and heart. Was the honor of their cousin worth whatever information Schwartz had for them? Ben struggled too and closed his eyes to think.

"I heard the G-men found a hidden camera but no photos. I assume there are photos." The brothers remained silent. "Well, I hope you got some good ones of me. I always thought my best angle was from behind. Especially when I'm schtupping a colored girl."

Jasper and Ben were each sixty-forty on the Minnie decision but leaned in different directions. Unfortunately for Minnie, it was Jasper who spoke up first. "You got a deal."

Ben added an addendum, but it didn't make him any happier with the arrangement. "Is the intel you have for us worth the price? If it's not, there could be some trouble."

"It's worth it, Benjamin. For both of us."

Jasper retook his seat and leaned back. "Let's get to it, then, shall we?"

There was no longer a need to pretend they enjoyed one another's company, something Schwartz was pleased about, so he dove right in. "When the girls were interrogated, they said all kinds of crazy shit goes down within these walls."

"You would know, Schwartz, you would know." Jasper leaned in.

The councilman directed his next statement at Ben. "Some of them even swore they saw Frolovski here with Charles once."

"Are you playing games right now, or do you have something for us?" Ben asked.

"No, sir, I'm not playing games. I'm saving those for Miss Minnie."

It took a lot to blow Ben's gasket, and Jasper could see that his brother's motor was running too hot for comfort. Jasper stepping in to cool Ben down wasn't usually the way their river flowed, and when it did, Lance was always the reason, but Jasper recognized the signs nonetheless.

"For your sake, I think it's best if you get right to it."

"To me, the most interesting thing that the fine ladies of this establishment told the detectives was that not long ago, a flashy spender from Chicago came in, and no one saw him leave. Kid named Valentino. Ring a bell?"

This got both the brothers' attention, but Jasper stayed at the reins. "How worried should we be about this?"

"So far they ain't got a body, but if they find one, Izzy's kid seems dead set on pinning it on Charles."

"Charles didn't do it." That was as close to an admission as Jasper would let Ben get.

"Like you said, there ain't no body, so I guess we don't gotta worry about the Feds."

"Oh, I wouldn't be worried about the Feds if I were you. If Valentino's body turns up, you better hope they lock away your whole family for life, where at least you get a shower and three squares a day. No. No. No. If that boy's body turns up, it's Frank Nitti and the Outfit you gotta be worried about. We've all seen 'em around town. They're not exactly being secret about it. Not really their style."

The Carters moved toward the door, and Jasper grabbed his hat.

"No body. No crime. That's what you said, right?" Jasper's outward appearance was cool as a cucumber.

"That's correct." Jasper's hand was on the doorknob, but Schwartz wasn't quite done. "Now you just need to ask yourselves a few questions. First, are there pictures of Valentino in your collection?"

The prominently placed oil painting of the moonlit Parisian cityscape hanging nearby wasn't what it seemed. The dark shadow of a building had been carefully cut out of the canvas and replaced with a thinly woven black cotton fabric that, when lit from the front, appeared solid but was completely see-through from the darkened side.

The artwork hung over the top of a small, hinged piece of plaster, and in the dark closet on the other side of the wall had been Minnie's camera, a Kodak Junior 620, which was now property of the US government.

Schwartz continued, "Then ask, who did you tell, and who do you trust? Charles? The Russky dame? Lance?"

Ben's fiery eyes were aimed at Jasper, demanding that he open the door.

"We thank you for your time." Jasper ended the meeting without incident.

Minnie was waiting in the hallway when Jasper and Ben came through the door and pulled it closed again behind them.

"Is there something else? He already turned down all the girls, so why isn't he leaving with you?" Minnie asked.

Jasper answered as kindly as he knew how. "He didn't turn down *all* the girls."

"What the hell's that supposed to mean?"

The boys stared their cousin down until she understood.

"Me? You mean me? No. That ain't happening. I'm not your bargaining chip."

"Sometimes the job is ugly, Minnie. I'm sorry." Jasper was understanding but immovable.

"I said no, goddamnit!"

Scarily calm, Jasper stepped closer to Minnie, and she instinctually backed up against the wall. When his nose was nearly touching hers, he whispered, "You'll do it." Then he put his hat on and walked away.

Minnie was horrified and distressed, but she'd never let either brother see her cry. She was only able to mutter a single word. "Ben…"

His eyes were on the end of the hallway, where Jasper had disappeared. "Until Charles is safe, we gotta do what we gotta do." Then, as he'd done perhaps too many times in his life, Ben followed in his brother's footsteps.

Hank held open the door for Ben to join his brother in the back of the Series 70, and before he made it the three steps to the driver's door, Ben's question was already out in the open.

"Did you tell Lance?"

Jasper didn't even twitch.

Hank got in and turned the key. "Where to, boss?"

The brothers sat silently long enough for them both to understand two things: Lance did in fact know, and what the next course of action had to be.

"Hank, my man. Home to your cave or over to Geraldine's. You choose. You're taking a couple hours off while my brother and I wrestle with some family business."

Hank asked no further questions and pushed the gas. "Geraldine's it is."

Jasper knew the situation was no good, but Hank wasn't to blame. "Drinks are on the house today, Hank. Have one for me too."

A scared white man knelt in the middle of the dance floor at Geral- dine's. Charles knew the place was Geraldine's, but it also wasn't Geraldine's. The man's face was soaked in tears, his pants and the floor below him soaked in urine. Lance and Danny, but larger, distorted versions of themselves, stood over the man. They were screaming at each other in words Charles couldn't hear over his own thunderous heartbeat. Danny screamed violent, nonsensical words and raised the threat level with a gun pointed in Lance's face. A gun with a cartoonishly long barrel. Charles was somehow stuck in suspended animation, fully nude, desperately trying to run at them to stop whatever they were capable of, but his strung out, sinewy muscles were not capable of moving his arms and legs.

Staring down the barrel of Danny's mile-long gun stripped all the fight from Lance. He turned toward the crying white man kneeling at his feet, now drooling and begging, begging and drooling for his life. Danny cracked a lashing across Lance's back with a cat-o'-nine-tails, a short whip with broken glass and nails tied to the striking ends of leather. The gun had somehow transformed, and now Danny was Lance's master. He frothed gibberish at Lance that Charles understood to mean "kill him," but those were not the words. They weren't words at all.

His body aching and pulsing with energy but unable to move, Charles began to cry, and the tears that came were creamy, bloodred, and streaked down his body. His own wailing was too loud to hear Lance's screams as he gripped the white man's neck and squeezed with all his might, Danny all the while lashing and lashing at his back. When the man's eye popped out of its socket like a child's toy gun that fired a ball on a string, all of Charles's vision went bright white.

Now he was in the kitchen. It wasn't the kitchen, but he understood this to be the kitchen at Geraldine's. He was still naked and covered in the streaks of his blood tears, but now the dead white man was nude as well, his eye dangling on his cheek, body lying on the stainless-steel food prep counter with tools resting on his white skin. A rusty handsaw. Large bolt cutters. A set of pristine carving knives.

Charles looked at his hands to find holes had been drilled through his palms and thick twine strung through them and tied in knots. The string through his right hand pulled up against his own free will and then released tension, allowing it to fall on the handle of the rusted saw. Danny hovered above him, dressed in a brilliantly clean, shining white suit, working the strings attached to Charles's stigmata-wounded hands. With each violent yank, the saw dragged over the dead man's flesh. Blood splashed up, streaking Danny's face and suit as he yanked his puppet's strings. Charles lifted a leg sawed at the shin and dropped it into a gigantic meat grinder that hadn't been there just a moment ago but was also always there.

The string guided Charles's hand to the meat grinder's rotating handle. With each forced rotation, the leg dropped farther into the machine, and deliciously aromatic ground beef oozed onto the tabletop. The torture lasted all morning until the guard's baton raked across the cell bars, jolting Charles awake.

"Someone to see you, Carter."

He'd been out cold on the bench in his holding cell and was disoriented by having gone straight from the violent nightmare plaguing the inside of his eyelids to a visit from his cousin Sharon.

"Getting involved with a white prostitute wasn't your finest idea." Sharon started in on him.

"She didn't do anything wrong. Everyone's squealing to protect their own hides. The other girls pointed at Betty, that led them to me, I ratted Danny, and Danny pointed fingers at Lance and back at me."

"What did you tell them about Danny?"

"He killed Joseph Frolovski, Sharon. That man who was gonna run against Diggs."

"Can you prove it? That Danny killed him?"

Charles's head rolled between his shoulders. It wasn't that cut-and-dry.

"Did he kill the man or not?"

"Kinda."

"Kinda?! Goddamnit, Charles. He did or he didn't!"

He looked around, moved closer to the bars, and lowered his voice. "He made someone else do it, so, yeah, I blame him."

"You? Did he make you do it?"

"No!"

"Lance?"

"Not me. Okay? Just not me. I didn't do it. And it don't matter anyhow, because there's no body."

"How can you be sure?"

"I'm sure."

His tone shifted. Whatever it was, a lower pitch, a look in his eyes, she believed him.

"Great. Then Danny's bluffing about that one. What about the second body?"

The whiplash speed of his head turn gave Charles away, and he knew it.

"What's he saying? What's Danny saying?"

"I don't think you're in a position to be asking any questions right now, do you?"

"I didn't do it, Sharon. It was Danny. I swear it."

Once again, the mysterious tone, or look, or whatever, convinced her.

"I believe you, but I need to know that Danny can't lead them to that body either."

"We buried it."

"Where?"

His father and their attorney, Robert Peck, had told him not to say anything, and he struggled internally about giving up information.

"Where, Charles? The man was a Fed! You need to tell me where he's buried!"

"No. No. He didn't have a badge!"

She reached in, grabbed Charles's hand, and held it tight between their bodies. Face-to-face. As serious and urgent as could be, she whispered, "Is that going to be your defense? He didn't have a badge? Fed or not, do you know how easy it will be for pasty white Danny to convince them the evil Black man did it? Especially if he can lead them right to the body? Where is he?"

"Hey! No touching! Back up!" the guard yelled as he trotted over.

"Jesus H. Christ. You gotta be joking."

Sharon and Charles jolted apart, but Sharon couldn't leave until she had what she needed.

"What? You searched me! You know I ain't got nothing. What am I gonna do, slip him my bra?"

The guard pursed his lips in annoyance. "You got two minutes. Wrap it up."

That was all the time she needed. Two minutes later Sharon was strolling out of the station, repeating the directions to Jon Jon Cochran's body over and over under her breath to commit them to memory.

CHAPTER NINETEEN

Jasper's elbow was propped in the open window with Michigan drifting by at forty miles per hour, his flattened hand riding the current up and down, down and up, as Ben drove north on Woodward. It was an hour-long straight shot to Pontiac, the place they'd recently chosen to lay a young Chicago mobster to rest.

There was never going to be a situation in which Jasper flat-out admitted to being wrong, and Ben wasn't so petty that he needed to hear the words, but he did know there was a small window of time in which Jasper might be more open to suggestion.

"We don't know if they know where he is." Jasper didn't believe the words, but he said them anyway.

"Lance knows, so anyone could know, Jas, and that's a problem. He has to be moved."

This stopped Jasper's tongue. They'd been down this road many times, and he didn't have the mental space for it under the present circumstances. Neither brother was capable of understanding the other's feelings about Lance. If they could, perhaps they'd have a greater understanding of each other, but Jasper saw Lance as a blood responsibility given to him by their father, and Ben couldn't find it in his heart to forgive Lance for setting off a chain of events that lost them a sister. For all Ben's talk of community, Jasper couldn't comprehend his brother holding this grudge. For Ben, Lance was proof that blood was not a deciding factor in brotherhood. Hank was more of a brother than Lance would ever be.

Another five minutes of Michigan scenery flew by before Jasper spoke again. "While I'm sitting in hot water over here, there's something else I should tell you."

"You're keeping secrets?" Ben's half joke wasn't taken so casually.

"You mean like shaking-hands-with-the-governor kinda secrets?"

"That wasn't what it looked like."

"When it's on the front page of the rag, there ain't nothing that matters but what it looks like." Jasper understood optics, and he was quickly learning the importance of the press.

"You're right. I'm sorry." Ben was sorry, but he was also smart. He was giving over control to ease Jasper back in.

Jasper took the bait. "I asked Izzy to take care of Frolovski."

"What?"

"I didn't know he would pull Charles into it. I just didn't think Diggs had a shot against a white Polack."

It was too late for Ben to be angry about why Charles was in prison. He just needed his boy out. "So you do care about politics."

"Of course I care! But I ain't no fool, Benny! We just can't have our faces all over it. I know you were old enough to remember where we come from. Using up our reputation on politics or the UAW— it's risking everything. It could put us right back in the nightmare we worked so hard to escape."

"I'm gonna meet with Murphy and Leon Bates."

"No, you're not."

"Yes, Jasper, I am! It's just a meeting. What's the big deal? Watching you lately makes me think you're throwing out everything we got, anyway. If we're making risky moves, why not risk it for justice instead of cold-blooded murder?!"

"Power and strength work. Fear works." Jasper wasn't wrong. "Like it or not, brutality is how we got to where we are. We fought. Go ahead—give me an example of a peaceful picket line that worked, and not for people in general but for Black people. Any example."

Ben remained silent. It was hard to argue when he believed they were both right.

As the brothers drove toward Pontiac, Minnie peeked into Schwartz's room and told him to get undressed. The man giddily rocked himself up and out of his chair and feverishly started pulling at his tie and the top buttons of his shirt.

Minnie made the excuse of needing to freshen up and closed the door. When she came back five minutes later, she wore purple lingerie under a silk black robe, and Schwartz was naked, sitting on the bed. She presumed he was nude, anyway; it was impossible to tell with his gut resting on his thighs.

She strolled to the Victrola and put on Bessie Smith and Her Blue Boys' "Trombone Cholly," then slowly slinked over, letting Bessie's song do all the talking.

"Know a fool that blows a horn."

She pushed Schwartz back on the bed. Hard. And he liked it.

"He came from way down south."

Minnie climbed on top of Schwartz, straddling him under his belly and laying her body on top of his. His eyes were fixed on her cleavage pushed against him.

"Take out those Minnie titties for me, dollface," Schwartz demanded.

Minnie didn't listen. She produced a silk kerchief from under a bracelet and began tying his wrists above his head. The hardest part was not revealing how nauseating the smell from under his arms truly was.

"*I ain't heard such blowin' since I was born,*" Bessie crooned.

When the knot was secure, Minnie sat up and took in the gluttonous sight below her with a smile. He took in the sight of her too and was nervous he'd finish before the act even began.

"Fuck me already!"

And still Bessie sang. "*When that trombone's in his mouth!*"

Minnie's smile turned from sexy to mean behind her eyes, and a blanket of confusion stole the erection buried somewhere between Schwartz's legs.

"*He wails and moans.*"

Minnie lifted a pillow from the bed.

"*He grunts and groans.*"

And smashed it with all her weight onto his face.

"*He moans just like a cow!*" The song being spun successfully predicted Schwartz's muffled moans, and a few minutes later Bessie ended her tune as Minnie ended Schwartz's life.

Almost as soon as they had returned from Chicago, Jasper asked Margaret if she could help care for Valerie at home. When she arrived, the whites of Valerie's eyes were yellow, and she was passed out in her own vomit. She clearly needed more care than Margaret was capable of giving, and the moment had come for any and all last-ditch efforts, no matter how small or unlikely.

Margaret went to the cupboard for a can of applesauce to help soothe Valerie's stomach, and that's when it hit her. One of her customers from the market told her she cut the fat in her recipes with applesauce. Margaret only knew Neda in passing, but occasionally she mentioned the meals she cooked for a doctor and his wife in the University District. Neda could say no, and that would be an understandable possibility, but one look at Valerie, and Margaret knew she had to try.

Woodward Avenue made a loop around Pontiac as if it too couldn't wait to get back to Detroit, but just before the road began to round them back toward home, Ben took a right on University Drive.

"You speak truth, brother, but don't you believe some things, some ideas, are worth fighting for, no matter the cost?"

It seemed Jasper's window for being open to suggestion was closing. "How you gonna fix the world if you can't take care of your own family? Charles in jail? Victor changing his damn name?"

That hurt. Low blow. Ben didn't even know where Victor was anymore. "Because your kids are saints, right? Stephen's a walking tornado, and Mark aired family business in the papers."

Jasper had some psychological tricks up his own sleeve. He knew Ben would fight back with that Carter bite if he was punched below the belt, and that's what he needed from his brother.

"Stephen is rambunctious, that's for sure, but if anyone's to blame for Mark's actions, it's you. He told me the advice you gave him about journalism, about chasing any dream he wanted. Now, we can disagree on which level of bullshit 'chasing dreams' rises to, but who's to blame for putting family business in the paper? That's on you. Not up for debate."

Their destination, Oak Hill Cemetery, rolled into view. A left and then another right onto a twisting road that escorted them toward the back of the property.

"Getting into journalism isn't a bad idea, Jasper. Hell, we could use it to our advantage, but I agree, publishing the picture was sloppy. I'll have a talk with Mark and explain how he . . ."

"Or you can do what I already did. Tell the boy he was wrong and order him to make it right. Power, Ben. Strength. They work."

The car stopped, and both brothers sat staring out at the underdeveloped back acreage of the cemetery, and Jasper put the nail in the conversation.

"I shouldn't have told Lance. That was sloppy. This is me fixing it." With nothing more to add, he opened the door, rounded the car, and waited for Ben to pop the trunk so he could get the shovel.

The brothers took turns digging a hole next to the tombstone for Marjorie Abernathy, 1886–1937. When the shovel hit the coffin four feet down, they worked together to get just enough dirt off one of the long sides that they could wrench open the box. A testament to good embalming, Mrs. Abernathy still looked to be in peaceful slumber. The same could not be said for the body dressed in flashy burgundy pinstripes. The visible flesh of Valentino's head had already begun to liquefy.

As Jasper and Ben worked to pull Valentino from Mrs. Abernathy's coffin as carefully as they could to keep the body intact and placed it in the trunk of the Series 70, Mark was standing at the counter of Carter Family Printing, combing over his stack of stolen photographs.

The photos had a slight fuzzy blur caused by the camera focusing through and beyond the cotton fabric patched into the painting at Le Noir Palais, but not enough to hide someone's identity. Each image was labeled in Minnie's handwriting with a name and date on the back, and most encounters had two photos—one with a man's face clearly visible and another showing the same man in some gratuitous sex act or another. A picture labeled "Rev. Sam Truffaut" showed a skinny white man with his pants at his knees, holding the ankles of two Black legs above his head. "Nikolaos Savvides" was on all fours with a woman's face buried between his cheeks. "Hugo Cardoso," a chubby man with a bushy mustache and bald head, was bent over the side of the bed, being thrust into by a short, muscular Black man.

There were also photos of meetings. Men and women, but usually men, finely dressed, sitting in chairs obviously positioned perfectly for the camera's lens. Many of these photos showed Ben and/or Jasper off to the side, and a few had Mark's cousin Charles. Councilman Thomas Schwartz. Banker Cecil de Matteo. Assistant police chief Michael Blake. Judge Hyrum R. Bailey.

Mark stopped on the next photo with his father's words ringing in his head: *Make it right.* It showed his father and uncle Ben clearly visible in a meeting with a white man who the back of the photo identified as Valentino Locurto. The next photo in the stack showed Valentino on the ground and Jasper standing over him, holding something around his neck.

Make it right.

Mark lit a match, picked up both photos of Valentino, and set them ablaze. He watched until they were half consumed before dropping them into a metal wastebasket, where they burned to gray ash.

The next photo to catch Mark off guard was the first photo that Danny Gaczynski appeared in. He stood on the far right of the photo. Charles sat in a chair on the left, partially out of frame, but his face was unmistakable. Minnie's handwriting identified the man between them as none other than Joseph Frolovski.

Make it right.

Mark sat still and quiet for several minutes, and then his body started to move on its own, as if it knew the plan and didn't need his brain interfering. He took the photo to a small workstation on the back wall of the shop and slid one end into the paper cutter. He pulled the handle down, and Charles was out of the picture. The sliced end got the same treatment as Valentino's pictures, and then Mark took what remained of the photo, Danny Gaczynski and Joseph Frolovski, and moved to an oak desk with a green Royal typewriter.

His fingers typed with urgency. Mark was going to make it right.

Just over an hour later, the Series 70 was back in front of Geraldine's. Hank was asked to discreetly take care of a problem in the trunk. He could look if he wanted to, but Ben recommended against it. Jasper slipped him 350 dollars. "A fifty spot for you, brother." The rest was for Buck Hendrickson, who ran the crematorium at Detroit Memorial Park Cemetery. Hank was told to finish the last sips of his drink and that the keys were in the car.

Outside, Jasper offered Ben a ride home, but Ben had other things on his mind.

"I hear your words, Jasper. I want you to know that."

"And just what words are we referring to?"

"About family. About identity."

"I don't remember saying anything about identity, but I'll take credit if you're dishing it out. When's this Murphy-Bates meet and greet?"

"Later today. I can handle it."

"I know you can. You make me nervous, but you make me proud."

The brothers hugged it out, then Jasper got into his Lincoln LeBaron coupe and was off. The rest of the afternoon should be business as usual, and today that meant heading down to the river to make a deal with some dockhands about how best to enforce his family's new alcohol delivery tax. Ben started hoofing it the half mile north to the address his wife had shown him on a flyer for the Allah Temple of Islam. He hoped that in the ten minutes it took to walk there, he'd figure out what the hell he was going to say to whoever the hell answered the door.

Both brothers had failed to notice Sharon patiently waiting across Division Street from Geraldine's, blended in perfectly with the happenings of a normal Wednesday afternoon on Hastings. Her timing couldn't have been more perfect. Her uncle and father were separated and traveling in different directions, which meant Hank must be taking the car home that night. She had no idea he was already saying his final goodbyes and sliding his empty glass back to the bartender.

She jogged across the street and hopped behind the wheel of the Series 70 just as Hank stepped outside. The ignition cranked, and Hank jumped toward the passenger door, but when he saw Sharon through the window, the split-second pause to process his confusion was enough time for her to stomp the throttle.

Minnie stepped out onto the back steps of her Palais, her silk black robe tied tightly closed around her waist, and lit a Chesterfield. She wasn't much one for smoking, but she kept a pack tucked away for stressful situations. She hadn't given a single lick of thought as to how she was going to get rid of the dead fat councilman in her bed, and right then she didn't care. She was fine with watching the world burn, and if that's what came to pass, she'd be proud to have lit the match.

By the looks of it, she wasn't the only woman in the family making hasty decisions. Sharon came strutting up the side of the building and walked right by Minnie with so much in her head that it crowded her peripheral, the literal definition of tunnel vision. She swung open the barn door of the small lean-to shed and disappeared inside. After some rustling around, Sharon reappeared in the doorway with a shovel and let out a startled scream when she saw Minnie casually smoking her cigarette not fifteen feet in front of her face.

"A Carter with a shovel. I'm sure it's nothing." Minnie exhaled a waft of smoke.

Sharon rolled her eyes and started to speak, but Minnie's lack of interest was all-encompassing, and she cut her off.

"If you see Jasper and Ben, tell 'em I need to talk to 'em."

"I'm a little busy."

"I'm sure you are." Minnie snuffed her cigarette on the wall, tossed the butt, and casually walked back inside.

Sharon didn't have a second to spare. She was racing the clock against lawyers working deals behind closed doors, and soon that canary fink Danny would be lying his way to freedom and swallowing the key to Charles's cell. She marched back to the stolen car to drop the shovel into the trunk. A slimy, decomposing corpse and another shovel were not what she had expected to find.

"Fuck!" She leapt back, not knowing what to do. Heart in her throat, she looked around, and luckily there didn't seem to be anyone watching. She chucked the second shovel in with the body from a few feet away, then slammed the trunk using the full length of her arm to stay as far away as possible. This was certainly a kink in the plan, but for Charles's sake, Sharon needed to keep the plan in motion—kinks and all.

At a quarter to four, a golden yellow 1936 DeSoto Airflow pulled up in front of the Winston home on Birchcrest Drive. Margaret drove Valerie's car, Neda was a bundle of nerves in the passenger seat, and Valerie was asleep in the back.

Neda told Margaret to pull down the driveway and park as close to the standalone garage as possible, hoping it would thwart the looky-loos. Neither the doctor nor his wife would be home until five thirty or a quarter to six. Neda knew where a spare key was hidden but thought going into Thomas and Rose's home without them present was a step too far. They would just have to wait in the DeSoto.

Showing up unannounced was no doubt putting Neda's part-time employment in jeopardy, and she needed this job. Her first instinct was to say no, but Margaret begged her to come to Conant Gardens to see the state Valerie was in, and she conceded. Valerie looked to be on death's door and getting worse by the hour. Helping was the right thing to do, but Neda was stiff with fear, not knowing how she'd feed her grandbabies, six and eight, if she lost this gig. Margaret took one of Neda's worried hands, pulled it close to her heart, and vowed that if she helped, her girls would never go hungry as long as the Carters ran the Carter Market, "so help us God."

CHAPTER TWENTY

When he got there, Ben realized he knew 632 Livingstone. It was an old Masonic hall, but before Charles Diggs was a state senator, when he helped form the Michigan Democratic League, this was where they'd set up shop, and Ben had come to a meeting to see what it was all about. And if memory served, there had been a shoot-out with cops when the Moorish Science Temple of America had used the space. The Allah Temple of Islam used to meet in the hall over the Castle Theater on Hastings, but now they seemed to be taking refuge here after all their legal troubles with the city. There had even been horrific rumors of "voodoo" murders within the "cult," rumors that only felt more true to the readers of the *Detroit Free Press* when the group's mysterious leader disappeared, never to be heard from again.

Ben gave his 1908 wheatback a couple more nervous flips before dropping it back into his pocket and knocking on the door.

A man in a dark suit answered. "Assalamu alaikum."

Ben knew the appropriate response. "Wa alaikum salaam."

"Can I help you, sir?" the man asked, looking Ben up and down.

"I'm here to see my son Victor Carter. If he's here, I'd like a word with him."

The man nodded slowly in understanding. "Give me just a moment, brother."

He disappeared back into the temple, and in a matter of seconds, John, who Ben recognized from the Shriners Parade, where he'd last seen Victor, was standing before him.

"Assalamu alaikum" came the greeting.

But Ben's patience was already thin. "I'm sorry, can you please tell my son Victor Carter that his father would like a word?"

John looked to someone out of sight just inside the door. "Victor Karriem. Please." And then he turned his attention back to Ben, who was physically clenching and unclenching his fists to quell what was building inside him.

"My son's name is Victor Carter. After me, his father, Ben Carter, and his grandfather before him, Charles Carter."

John's cadence never rose above serene. "And it wasn't too many ancestors before the names of these men you speak that their white master bestowed his own name upon your family."

"It's a good name. It's a Christian name. It's a name I've spent my whole life trying to give some meaning. Some value. Honor." It was hard for Ben to look John in the eye for fear he'd lose his cool.

"Master Fard says our people 'have tried this so-called mystery God for bread, clothing and a home. And we receive nothing but hard times, hunger, naked and out of doors.'"

"I didn't come here to argue. In fact, I quite agree that God has done nothing for me. I just want what's best for my son. Can I please talk to my son?"

"Brother Victor is a good man."

"That's because I raised him up that way!" Ben was angry at his own outburst and took a step back to collect himself. "I'm sorry. I don't mean to cause a scene. My son. Please."

John, still calm and poised, saw an opportunity to spread the light. "Brother, the love you're showing right now is a love the devils all around us don't even believe our race is capable of. Standing here all of twenty seconds and you've proven Negro excellence beyond what the white man can ever admit. That's what we teach here. The Black man was the first man, and though he was lost, his tribe has now been found. We've been found. Victor Karriem has been found."

Ben exploded. "His name is Carter! His goddamn name is Carter!"

"Brother, it doesn't seem to me that you believe the lies that hold our people down. And that healthy anger inside you can be used; it can be channeled to help shine a beacon for more black sheep. The Black man is great. The Black man is capable of anything the white devil can do and better. And more!"

"Of course that's true, but we also need to live in the real world!" Ben begged.

"I think you mean the white world."

"No, sir, I do not. I mean the real world, where we gotta eat, pay our rent, look out for one another, and hopefully build something up that we can leave for our children when we're gone."

John smiled. "When you put it that way, it seems our paths are already aligned. I know who you are, Brother Ben, and from what I've seen, the only differences in our personal beliefs are booze and gambling."

The levels of anger and annoyance building in Ben were stunning. He couldn't remember ever getting this worked up so quickly. "Go ahead and add sacrificial killing and boiling people to that list. How dare you?"

"For an educated Negro, I'm surprised how easily you believe what white newspapermen put in print." John's attention was interrupted by the person hidden just inside the door. After a few hushed words to the side, he addressed Ben once again. "I'm afraid Brother Victor isn't interested in visitors today."

Ben spoke through his teeth. "Brother Victor needs to tell me to my face."

Before John could respond, a man's voice was calling out Ben's name. It was Hank. He was out of breath and drenched in sweat, running up Hastings in his direction.

"Boss!"

The last time Hank had sprinted for Ben's help, the dry cleaner's had been ablaze, but Ben needed to see Victor. "Tell my son to come tell me to my face."

"Sharon took the car! She stole the car!"

His attention was fully divided, one side anchoring him to the Islamic Black man blocking him from his son, and the other to the new information that could topple the entire Carter dynasty.

Hank made it to Ben's side a dripping mess. "She just got in and drove away."

"Before the . . . ? With . . . ?"

"Yes, sir, she got the car before I was even out the club."

Ben growled at John, not out of anger toward him but because of an inner hatred that he had to leave without seeing Victor, since his niece had no idea there was evidence flopping around in the trunk of the car she stole that could get them all killed.

Things that needed to happen were happening, but Jasper was having the kind of day where nothing came easy. First Schwartz and Minnie, then the trip to Pontiac, and when Jasper got to the docks to negotiate with a stuttering fool named Lester, the young punk had the audacity to say that 1 percent had been a special price for Valentino, but for Jasper the take would be 2 percent. That cost could easily be funneled to the clubs, but for Jasper, it was the principle of the matter. Lester had given an out-of-towner a better deal than a man from the neighborhood, and Jasper could only assume it was because of his skin. But he assumed wrong. Lester wanted more because Jasper was scarier to work for than Valentino. More fear, more money.

Then, on his way back to the LeBaron, Jasper found a couple of Chicago hooligans waiting for him. He recognized the man who did the talking. It was the one they called Joe Batters, the one who had shoved Valerie at the Grand Terrace, the one who threw racist names at Jasper and was warned with a glass shattered at his feet. Batters didn't seem to recognize Jasper, and if he did, he didn't care.

"It's nice to see a smooth wheat like yourself understands a good racket."

"What racket is that?" Jasper was willing to play.

"It don't seem like a lot to the distributors, but you take a few pennies from each bottle delivered, and you got yourself a damn good take. We know. It used to be ours." Batters sat right on the edge of threatening.

"Just trying to make a buck."

"No. No. You figured it out. Sure, your approach is a bit obvious, but it's still good business, right? Especially this UAW stuff we hear you're nosing into."

Jasper was confused as to how this thug knew anything about his family's nonexistent relationship with the UAW.

"Unions. Biggest racket out there, am I right? The mob called by another name. Taking pennies from people whose main problem is not having enough pennies. Genius."

"My family ain't involved with the UAW."

Jasper excused himself and drove off, but the day wasn't ready to let up just yet, and less than three minutes later, as he passed Lucky's Drug Store, Jasper hit his limit for keeping it cool. Stanley Moore slammed out onto Hastings with Stephen Carter's upper arm wrenched tightly in one hand and a Smith & Wesson hand ejector revolver in the other. Stanley tossed the boy toward the curb, and the LeBaron slammed to a stop in the middle of the street, blocking traffic. Jasper leapt out, still holding residual heat from his encounters on the docks.

"Whoa! Whoa! What happened? What's going on?" Jasper placed himself between his youngest son and Stanley.

"Sorry, Dad."

"Boy, what trouble you got yourself into now?"

Stanley answered instead. "This ruffian of yours stomped into my store, telling me from now on I need to pay him a weekly cut to ensure customers continue drinking from my soda fountain."

"What?" Jasper spun on his son, who hung his head.

"When I told him to scram, he pointed this at me." Stanley held up the gun.

Jasper snatched the pistol from Stanley. "You get this from the printshop?"

Stephen refused to answer, but Stanley kept at it.

"Oh, it's not hard to see where he got it from."

Jasper aimed his irritation at Stanley. "Excuse me?"

Stanley yelled at Stephen, "I been giving you and your gutter-rat friends free soda tastings for years, and you point a rod in my face?"

"What's got into you, son?" Jasper asked, genuine concern bleeding through.

"You stay out of my store, you understand me, you little hoodlum?"

"Hey, maybe cool it with the name-calling."

Stanley didn't know when to quit. "Chip off the old block if you ask me."

"What's that supposed to mean?" Jasper was fed up with them both now, but the one he didn't share blood with needed to watch his mouth.

"Just keep your bum son out of my store."

The back of Jasper's hand connected with Stanley's face, and a switch was flipped. It would have been best if Stanley had gone straight inside right then, but he was stunned.

"This what you trying to be?" Jasper shouted at Stephen, then hit Stanley again. "You trying to be some kinda gangster?"

Stephen's face hardened, and in a teenage act of defiance, he challenged his father with direct, unapologetic eye contact. This small gesture of provocation opened Jasper's floodgates, and he brought his other hand, the one holding the revolver, down on top of Stanley's head.

"This the life you want? You think this is glamourous?" Jasper kicked Stanley's fallen body. "Answer me, boy! Is this the life that you want?"

Stephen boldly turned and walked away from his father's disgusting act of violence.

Watching him go, Jasper finally noticed the stopped traffic and crowds of sullen-faced men and women who had witnessed the unrighteous beatdown of Stanley Moore, one of Black Bottom's most stand-up citizens. These people, this community, knew Jasper Carter, but hearing rumors and bearing witness were different, and now their eyes were truly open.

As Stanley's blood stained the sidewalk, Ben was back at Geraldine's, trying to make sense of why Sharon had taken the car, and waiting for his rendezvous with Bates and the governor. Bates seemed to think the Carter family's influence in their community might give the governor the political safety he needed to further back the UAW and go head-to-head with Henry Ford. Ben was glad to have the man's confidence but wasn't so sure it was earned.

Sharon followed the memorized directions she got from Charles and found the spot where he and Danny had buried federal agent Jon Jon Cochran. Sharon didn't stop to think about the morbid and heinous act she was performing; she simply worked like she always worked. A task needed completing, and she did it. She dug out the shallow grave and dragged the filthy body by the legs to the back of the Caddy, Jon Jon's head flopping behind, only connected by an inch of flesh.

Then she turned her attention to the trunk, and she was far enough off the beaten path that speaking to Valentino's body at full volume had no consequences. "I don't even want to know who you are or what in Baby Jesus's name you're doing in Uncle Ben's trunk, but..." She strained to roll the decomposing body out, landing him directly into the hole that had been dug for Jon Jon. "When Danny tells the coppers where the dead Fed is at and they find you? It ain't gonna look too good for Danny G."

It took all her might to lift the dead weight of Jon Jon's body up into the trunk. When it fell in, Jon Jon's head fully separated, bounced off the rear bumper, and rolled a few feet away.

When Sharon looked at the man's blood and dirt-caked face, her stomach flipped over and her chin quivered, but she had to shove any human feelings back into the cold pits of detached apathy. Charles was in jail, and the clock was ticking. Using as few fingers on each hand as possible, Sharon lifted Jon Jon's head and dropped it into the trunk with his body.

Meanwhile, Rose pulled in behind the yellow car in her driveway. Her first thought was of mild panic that she'd mixed up her days or forgotten a social gathering: book club, Thomas's poker night, drinks with the Taylors from the next block over. Rose opened her door at the same time that the passenger side of the mystery car opened and Neda revealed herself with nervous hesitation oozing from her face. Neither woman said anything for three seconds as their minds made thousands of calculations. Neda ran through all the terrible outcomes of bringing Margaret and Valerie here and how to best mitigate the situation, while Rose made a mental tally of everything in her cupboards and how to combine the ingredients into some light refreshments for Theodore and Susan Taylor, who she must have forgotten about.

All mental calculations stopped when the head of a woman in the back seat popped up, the back door opened, and the woman dry-heaved over the pavement. Rose and Neda were both startled, and the situation grew infinitely more complex when the driver's door opened and Margaret Carter emerged.

"Excuse me, ma'am, I'm terribly sorry, but my sister is very sick."

Margaret's words were enough to assure Rose that she hadn't been recognized—not yet, anyway. These women hadn't known each other all that long in Ohio, and Rose had only just been a prepubescent girl, but standing here now, decades later, whole lives later, Rose knew Margaret instantly.

"I beg you not to be upset with Neda, but she mentioned your husband was a doctor."

Still silent, Rose slowly rounded her car and crossed between their fenders to get a look at the face of the heaving woman who was hidden by the suicide back door of the yellow DeSoto. Her hand jumped to her mouth. She and Valerie had known each other much longer, all those years ago. They had first met in Kentucky when her brother Jasper had rescued Valerie from an abusive father. Her charade was over. She was finally going to be outed.

"Colored doctors say there ain't much they can do. It's her liver," Margaret explained.

Valerie lifted her head and looked right into Rose's eyes. There was a flash of recognition, but it disappeared entirely as another wave of nausea coursed through her body. A false alarm.

"I've been getting worse fast. It's probably my time, but . . ." Valerie became mildly weepy as her words trailed off.

"Is there a chance your husband might take a look?" Margaret hated how hard it was to ask. "We can pay."

"Luck" was the wrong word. This was bigger than luck. Stars had aligned. Margaret had made this bold move for the love of her sister-in-law and Neda had agreed for the love of her community, but none of the visitors in the driveway of Thomas and Rose Winston understood that Rose's willingness to help was rooted in the exact same reasons: sisterhood and community.

"Way to force my hand, Ben" were the first words Governor Murphy said when Ben opened the back door to lead him into the main room, where Leon Bates, Shelton Tappes, and John Conyers were already sitting around a couple dining tables pushed together near the stage. Ben apologized for the photo in the paper as they entered, and Murphy started in without so much as a greeting. He was a slight man, but he took charge. A natural leader.

"My friends, you know I believe in your cause, but I wasted a lot of political goodwill with the GM fight."

"We won, sir. I would hardly call that 'wasted,'" John Conyers corrected.

"We did. We certainly did, but we're bankrupt. After a battle like that, you have to scratch some backs and pull some strings. You gotta earn some 'attaboys' and put them in the bank for later. When you have enough, you fight. But right now? I'm sorry to say, I'm all out of 'attaboys.'"

"Anyone else know what this white man talking about? 'Attaboys'?" the young Tappes asked his partners before turning to the governor himself. "Mr. Governor, Your Honor, Your Majesty—sorry, I'm not sure how to address you—but we're not fighting for a pat on the back. We're demanding better treatment from the rich, ruling white class."

"And if I lose the next election because I fought a battle I knew I couldn't win? What then? Can you be sure whoever replaces me will be as willing to meet with you? With your community? Let alone actually accomplish anything for you?"

"You're not doing anything 'for' us." Tappes always spoke truth to power but hadn't yet honed the art of winning good graces. He wasn't getting any of Murphy's "attaboys."

Leon Bates came to the rescue. "That's why Ben is important to the equation. He proved he can energize a substantial voting bloc. Black Bottom residents will follow his lead."

"Don't sell me too hard now. We barely got Diggs in."

"'Barely' counts, Ben!" Leon turned his argument back to Murphy. "I'm not saying it'll be easy, but if we energize the Negro vote statewide, we can cancel out any votes you lose when you step in and help us unionize Ford."

Ben had to interject again. "I feel okay about how loud my voice is in Black Bottom. That helps in a single district, but statewide?"

"You're a natural leader, Ben. And the truth is . . ." Conyers struggled to say it in a way that wasn't hurtful. "We can tour you around for some speaking engagements and campaign stops, and we believe you can get more than just the Negro vote."

The truth made Tappes smile. "White votes, Ben. We think you can get some white votes too. You speak their language. You sound just like them."

Ben was aware that people thought the way he spoke was "white," but he refused to act differently just to fit into someone else's mold. The education Jasper afforded him meant too much, and the way he spoke was a byproduct of that education. It was a gift from his brother. And it certainly didn't make him any less Black.

Leon continued, "With Ben's help, we believe we can keep you in office, and all we ask is for you to work that same magic on Ford that you did with the other manufacturers."

The eyes of each of the four Black men burrowed into Murphy. They could see the physical signs on his face and in his posture that he thought this plan was at least worth considering, but there was another problem.

"I don't enjoy making my job harder. There are rumors your family does more than 'energize' voters to get a win. Charles is in jail. Did he do it, Ben?"

Hank had been smoking out front when Jasper pulled up. "Boss" was the title he honored Ben with, but he'd never disobey a direct order from either brother, and Jasper told him to stay outside. From the other side of the saloon doors between the bar and the back room, Jasper had heard most of the conversation, but this felt like as good an entrance as any.

"My nephew didn't kill anyone, but that don't mean he won't go down for it. Legal system's far more corrupt than the auto industry. And you're right to be scared of Ford. He plays dirty, and it would be devastating if he got his hands on some dirt about you and your 'friend' Ed Kemp."

Without another word, Murphy turned and saw himself out through the back entrance he had come in through. Just like that, Jasper killed any deal that may have come from this meeting of the minds.

"Jasper!" There was a lot packed into Ben's saying of his brother's name.

"I had a change of heart." Jasper turned to the UAW trio. "Get."

The three beaten men left the same way Murphy did, and before Jasper and Ben could have it out, Hank was in the room to tell them Sharon was back with the car.

Out front they found her standing by the Series 70, filthy from head to toe.

"Minnie wants to see you."

"Stealing cars now?" Ben wanted answers.

"Is anyone at all concerned that Charles is in jail on murder charges? Or are you too busy trying to get charges of your own?"

She jammed the key into the trunk and swung the lid open.

They glimpsed the decapitated Black man inside, and Jasper slammed the lid closed. "Who the fuck is that?"

"Oh, him? He's a Fed that Danny killed and Charles helped bury."

Jasper had some sarcasm of his own. "May I ask how we earned the pleasure of his company?"

"I made Charles tell me where he was so I could move him before Danny tried to bargain himself out and put Charles in the hot seat."

Ben spoke barely above a whisper. "What about . . . Where's . . . ?"

"You mean the other body? Right! Well, when Danny sings, the coppers will find a completely different body, and my hope is they light him up in the chair."

"Get inside and clean your ass up."

She charged into Geraldine's, leaving Jasper, Ben, and Hank stunned at how little they had known.

"You still got those Benjamins Jas gave you?" Ben asked.

"Yes, boss."

"Same plan, then. Get this over to Detroit Memorial. Charles Diggs owes us one," Jasper added.

"Yes, sir."

Before Charles Diggs got into politics, he owned the House of Diggs, Black Bottom's most successful funeral home. Years ago he had taken it upon himself to help create Detroit Memorial Park Cemetery, a place for Black families to bury and honor their loved ones in peace and not be relegated to the worst plots and undesirable times and days because white services took precedence. After throwing their weight behind Diggs's campaign and getting their hands dirty in the process, it was logical for the Carter brothers to believe Detroit Memorial was a good place to get rid of some evidence. They were sorely mistaken.

When Hank arrived, bribe in hand to cremate the body in the trunk, Buck Hendrickson turned him down flat. He wasn't going to call the cops, but he made it fully clear that he had no desire to, as he put it, "get my Black ass dragged into some Carter family bullshit."

Hank drove the Caddy to his brother Earl's junkyard and parked it behind a couple of busted up Ford Model As and a rusted John Deere Model B. He didn't have a plan yet, but there was no scenario in which Hank would let Ben down. He'd sleep on it, but as he slept, the Carters' problems only grew.

CHAPTER TWENTY-ONE

The next morning, Thursday, July 1, 1937, when the *Chronicle* hit the doorsteps of its subscribers, it included the article "Missing State Senate Candidate Photographed with Purple Gang's Danny Gaczynski" by Mark Carter. The photo that accompanied the front-page story showed Joseph Frolovski and Danny, only Danny, meeting at a known brothel. No one would ever be able to prove that Charles had been at the edge of the camera's field of view in a portion of a picture that Mark had destroyed.

Jasper got the paper off his stoop just after 8:30 a.m. He brought it inside and started making coffee for himself and Sharon, who was sleeping in. At the top of his mind was where the hell Valerie could be. Her car wasn't there when he got back last night, and she was still gone. He boiled water, poured it over the coffee grounds in the bottom of the jug, waited a full five minutes for it to settle, then poured the black liquid through a strainer into his cup. Not until then did he sit and open the paper. Less than two minutes later, coffee unsipped, Jasper had a shotgun and the pistol he confiscated from Stephen, and he was racing to Carter Family Printing.

Ben hadn't slept more than a wink or two because, like Valerie,

Margaret never came home. It was a strange start to a bitter day. Ben's house felt empty. Charles was sleeping in his cell, and no one knew exactly where Victor was currently spending his nights. Stephen was sound asleep on one of the sofas in the living room. It had become a habit for his nephew to sleep there, but Ben knew last night's stay was due to the beating Jasper had given Stanley Moore. As Ben got dressed, he decided the first step to making amends on the family's behalf would be to pay all of Stanley's hospital bills.

He walked to Congress Street, but Hank wasn't in his usual waiting spot with the Series 70. This made sense, all things considered. As he ducked into the corner bodega to satisfy his addiction to the stock section, it was the front page of the *Chronicle* that leapt up at him from the stacks of papers. The familiar setting of the photo. The byline "by Mark Carter." The Gaczynski name in black and white. Ben sprinted out and ran as hard as his legs would carry him in the direction of the printshop.

A black 1934 Studebaker Commander turned onto Hastings right in front of Jasper's LeBaron. The car drove too slowly for Jasper's anxiety, but he couldn't get around it. He beat his steering wheel and honked, but the car didn't speed up or pull over to allow him to pass. Jasper had religiously followed Dillinger in the papers, and he knew this car could race because it was the same make and model of a getaway car used by the nation's onetime public enemy number one, only two years newer. There were just a few more blocks to the printshop, but Jasper raged inside to move faster.

As he approached the painted storefront windows alerting passersby to CARTER FAMILY PRINTING, Jasper pulled to the curb and jumped out, silently cursing the car that had delayed him. That's when time slowed. The Studebaker's window rolled down, and a tommy gun pushed through. Rapid-fire shots rang out, and the windows of the shop burst into raining glass. Wood on the door splintered and exploded. Then the driver of the slow car floored it. Jasper had a decision to make: run back to his ride and make chase, or investigate the devastation. If only he'd read the headline before his coffee had fully brewed.

Ben was a block and a half away when he heard the string of shots. Mere seconds later the Studebaker was flying past him and skidding into a right-hand turn to get lost in morning traffic downtown. When he got to the printshop, the bullet-riddled door was wide open. Ben found Jasper inside, cradling Mark's limp body on the floor. He was rocking and hyperventilating, but something about the sight of his baby brother in the doorway gave Jasper permission to release his rage. The screams that followed, like those of their burning father long ago, would haunt Ben's dreams till the day he died.

It's in times of pain and suffering that human beings show the qualities that allowed the species to inherit the Earth. That effect is quadrupled within subsects of the population deemed less-than by the majority. The deeper into Paradise Valley—or even more so, Black Bottom—the more likely residents understood that the only people they could rely on were themselves. The moment the shots were heard, before they even knew who the victim was, neighbors shifted into gear. The initial reactions were not oceans of tears or blinding anger; those feelings would come later. First came dutiful reverence forged in communal pain and put into motion by brotherly and sisterly love.

A man and woman who Jasper and Ben didn't even know the names of were the first to arrive. They took the responsibility of easing the traumatized father and uncle away from the carnage and covering Mark's body, then they quietly and respectfully delegated jobs. One by one bystanders were sent to fetch a pastor, a funeral director, cleaners for the gore in the shop, and a carpenter to fix the shattered glass, mend the door, and patch the dozens of holes. Mrs. Jackson and her son Thad, a Geraldine's regular, would coordinate fresh-cooked meals to be delivered to the Conant Gardens home for at least a week, and over the next month, no fewer than fifteen pies would be anonymously left on the doorstep with notes of condolences. All these tasks were, of course, done for free, no matter the cost of materials or supplies, and even though it was well known that the Carter family lacked a belief in the Christian God, pews would be full on Sunday to pray for the family, to pray for the community. The people of Black Bottom knew that in times of tragedy, thoughts and prayers came after actions. After all, one person's action could be God's answer to someone else's prayer.

Jasper and Ben had already left the scene in the collective hands of their loving and capable community by the time Assistant Chief Michael Blake arrived to investigate. Good thing, because had Jasper laid eyes on Blake that morning, he wouldn't have had the restraint needed not to wind up in a cell next to Charles.

Ben drove Jasper home in the LeBaron. They needed to get to Sharon, Stephen, and heaven forbid, Valerie, before those with good intentions alerted them first. Sharon came to the door when she heard the car pull up, and she knew something terrible was headed her way. Her father and uncle were dressed in stoicism but had failed to hide their devastation. When Jasper wrapped his arms around his firstborn, he was only able to force a single word from his throat.

"Mark."

Sharon's face melted into a silent, pained wail as she curled into Jasper's embrace like the small child he couldn't help seeing every time he looked at his baby girl. He'd never felt so weak, but as she soaked up every needed ounce of love and protection from her father's arms, Ben could see that his brother had never been so strong.

When Margaret pulled up in the DeSoto, she recognized the disturbance on her husband's face. The worry about why she and Valerie hadn't come home the night before vanished. All that mattered now was getting to Valerie and using the least devastating combination of words possible to say that her child had been murdered. Margaret apologized for her disappearance, explaining how bad Valerie had gotten and where they had been all night, but none of that mattered anymore. If her liver didn't kill her, the news they bore would.

Margaret went inside to grab some extra clothes and a toothbrush for Valerie, then she drove Sharon to the Winstons' in the DeSoto. On the way, Sharon read Mark's article aloud, and the subtext was as clear as the printed words: Mark died attempting to save Charles.

Ben followed in the LeBaron with his heartbroken brother riding shotgun. Since the day Jasper had met Valerie, his life had been about protecting her from the pain and sorrow of her world. Now faced with delivering a message that would crush her already fragile soul, Jasper was prepared to burn down the city if that's what it took to get revenge.

The cars rolled into the driveway on Birchcrest, and four more Black bodies got out and approached the front door of the white couple's home. Thomas answered as Jasper reached for the doorknob and stepped outside to stop the parade.

"I'm really sorry. I want to help, but I can't have a house full of Negroes just . . ."

"Is it better for your neighbors to see a bunch of Negroes camping on your front porch?" Jasper paid no attention to the man's hand physically pushing against his sternum.

Thomas stepped aside and watched with worry as Jasper, then Sharon, then Margaret, then Ben stepped by. As they entered the living room, Neda came down the stairs, and Margaret made the introductions. Jasper approached the nervous woman with outstretched arms that invited both of her hands into a gentle embrace between them. There were signs that his tears would soon return, but he'd make them wait just a bit longer.

"Thank you, Neda. It's no small thing, what you done. If there are any consequences for your loving actions, me and my family are here for you."

She wanted to say thank you, but no words came. All Neda could produce was a small nod of acknowledgment.

Then Jasper turned his head to Thomas. "Sir, I appreciate you. We haven't had any luck at our own hospitals, and white establishments have been . . . less than accommodating."

Thomas was nervous but friendly. "Your wife is an alcoholic, Mr. Carter."

"That's true; I won't deny it," Jasper said, chewing on the inside of his own lip to stop himself from hitting the man. "But the doctors we've been able to meet with over the years say it's her liver, but nobody's got any way to fix it. They say diet. They say climate. They say it's something you're born with."

"They're all correct, but each for different people. For your wife, it's her drinking. She has what not too long ago was called 'gin drinker's liver.'"

"I hope you'll forgive me for doubting you, but, one, it's my wife, and, two, doctors have told us booze ain't the problem. They've literally prescribed whiskey to make her better."

Thomas was shaking with endorphins, but his education and experience were finally taking control away from his casually racist fear. "I never believed in the temperance movement, Mr. Carter, but the medical science was crystal clear before Volstead was the law of the land, and now all the data collected since the end of Prohibition is definitive proof that alcoholism leads to liver failure. Tax dollars and lobbyists have convinced doctors to promote other actual causes of liver disease. They are bending over backward to say it's some other attribute of an alcoholic's lifestyle and not the alcohol itself, but the data states what emotional humans don't yet have the guts to say—alcohol leads to liver failure."

By the end of his rant, Thomas was feeling confident again, but Jasper's next words would put him in a situation that would bring back all his insecurities.

"Okay, so then all she has to do is stop drinking, and she'll get better?"

"No. I'm sorry. Your wife's alcoholism led to liver failure. Past tense. Her liver has failed."

"What are you saying, doc?" Ben asked quietly.

"Valerie doesn't have long. She's dying," Thomas answered just as softly.

Margaret's turn: "How do we turn this around?"

"Maybe years ago, maybe even just last year if she'd stopped drinking altogether, but now? I'm sorry. She's going to die . . . soon. All anyone can do now is make her as comfortable as possible." The silence that fell over the room was as definitive as the words Dr. Winston had spoken.

"May I see my wife, please?"

Thomas felt Jasper's grief, and it was the first lesson in a long personal journey of rewiring his brain away from what white society had indoctrinated him to believe about the Black race.

"My wife, Rose, is tending to her now." Thomas gestured to the stairs. "Second door on your left."

Jasper led the procession up the stairs, and when he got to the door and looked into the room, every muscle in his body halted. There sat his wife's nurse, Dr. Winston's Rose, and undeniably his baby sister, Rosalind, all grown up. She sat with a cool rag on Valerie's head, holding her hand as she slept.

Ben squeezed by, concerned by his brother's frozen reaction to whatever sight he beheld. "Oh my God," and he too became a statue.

The barricade of stunned Carter men in the doorway injected a moment of dread into Sharon, who feared the worst for her mother. She pushed fully through into the room.

"You? Daddy, this woman came to our house looking for you yesterday. She knew things about Charles's case."

When the others slipped into the room, Margaret joined Ben's side just in time to hear him whisper his sister's name under his breath.

Margaret had spent an evening and the entire night in this room with Valerie, and Rose had been a nearly constant presence, but it wasn't until she heard her husband utter "Rosalind" that the truth flooded her brain. Rosalind had only been an energetic little girl the last time she'd seen her. There had been a strange familiarity with the wife of Neda's employer, but now she saw it. Margaret was able to see through the maturity that the years had added to the girl who was now a woman. She was able to see through the disguise of light skin made lighter with makeup. She was able to see her husband's lost sister hidden in plain sight in a white world.

Rose cleared her throat and spoke up to steer the attention away from herself. "She's in and out. She's gotten so much worse, even since she arrived yesterday."

It was true. Valerie looked like hell on a hot day. Eyes sunken. Sweating. A sick tint to her dark complexion. Standing at the back of the small crowd in his spare bedroom, Thomas remembered the words of the ancient Hippocratic oath sworn by physicians for hundreds, if not thousands, of years—a part of which stated it was his duty to cure anyone, "whether mistress or servant, bond or free."

"If there's a minister of some kind you wish to . . ."

"There is not," Jasper interrupted.

"Then I suggest saying your goodbyes. Rose, let's give the family some time to . . ."

Jasper interrupted once more. "No. Stay." He looked with sad kindness at Rose. "Please."

Rose stood, offering Jasper the seat next to Valerie. Jasper sat and took up both his wife's hands. She attempted to adjust her body, contorting her face in discomfort, then opened her eyes, which were now wilting sunflowers.

"Hey, baby," she said, her eyes already closing again. "I hate you seeing me like this."

"If I'm the judge, you always the foxiest catch in the room." He smiled, wiping a tear.

Jasper took in the whole sight of his wife, the mother of his children. There had been symptoms on and off for years—sometimes she had even been bedridden—but he'd never seen her like this and was shocked it came on so fast. Her arms and legs were swollen, and her stomach was fully distended.

Sharon was still caught between her dying mom and whoever these white people were. "Excuse me, but how do you know my family? How exactly did we end up here?"

Thomas quietly answered for his wife to preserve some sort of respect for the dying. "It seems my wife has some access to a legal matter concerning your family at the law office where she works as a secretary. She knows now that it was a mistake to interfere. We do apologize."

"My mama is laying up in your bed because some white lady overheard some things at work? This ain't making any sense. What am I missing?"

Margaret took this one. "Crazy coincidence. It's a small world. I knew Neda worked for a doctor, and we didn't have anywhere else to go."

"Who's that?" Valerie asked without opening her eyes.

Sharon went to the other side of her mom's bed and knelt. "It's me, Mama. Sharon. I'm right here with you. We're all right here with you."

"Sharon?" She turned her head back toward Jasper. "Jas, don't be bringing my babies to see me like this. You tell Sharon, Mark, and Stephen that I love 'em, okay?"

"Mama, I'm right here!"

Sharon's presence was confusing Valerie, but she took comfort in Jasper's hands. "I don't want them remembering their mama like this."

"That's okay, baby. You'll see them when you're up on your feet again."

"I ain't worried too much about our Sharon. Ain't nothing ever gonna stop her. She's strong." Valerie's face was pinched in pain. "But don't be too hard on Mark, Jas. He's so smart, but the boy is fragile."

These words for their already dead son were a stabbing jolt to Jasper's heart. "I won't. I'll go easy on him."

Sharon shed angry tears as her mother continued.

"God help us all with Stephen. Whenever that boy acting up, you just remind him I'm looking down on him. I don't know if it'll help, but it's worth a try."

Jasper's face was drenched. "I love you."

"I love you too, baby." Valerie's head relaxed into the pillow. "I need to sleep."

Jasper kissed his wife's hand, then her forehead. He swallowed back his emotion and nodded to the crowd. It was time. He stood and ushered everyone out to let his wife sleep. Last to leave, Jasper stood in the doorway, fighting the urge to look back one final time. He knew this was it, the end of their brilliant and thrilling ride together, but in a final, seemingly insignificant act, he didn't turn back. She had said she didn't want her family to remember her this way, and he would honor her by forging mental images of her laughter, her dancing, her kisses, and the light in her eyes every time she saw one of the three children she bore for them. Those would be the images he clung to as he shut the door and followed his family downstairs.

When he reached the first floor, Jasper had already decided on a plan, and no one was going to stand in his way.

He zeroed in on Rose. "What do you know about my nephew's case?"

Rose looked to Thomas for permission, but he spoke instead. "It's really not appropriate for my wife to have . . ."

"She told me Danny's trying to work a deal by pinning two murders on Charles." Sharon wasn't asking permission from anyone.

"I'm sorry. I simply can't have Rose interfering in . . ."

"She also told me that Lance and Betty are in protective custody, and they can place Charles at the crimes."

"Please!" Thomas raised his voice. "I'm sorry I haven't been able to help your wife, your sister, but there's really nothing . . ."

"Enough!" Rose blurted loudly. Then she timidly collected her nerve and looked at Jasper, then Ben. "This man they have in the safe house, this Lance . . . Is it . . . ?"

Jasper lowered his head in shame as Ben nodded. It was Lance. Their brother. Rose's brother. Jasper stepped forward, facing Thomas. His voice was steadfast and collected.

"Sir, you said all we could do at this stage was make my wife comfortable. Do I assume correctly that you have access to morphine?"

Thomas had had enough. "Mr. Carter, it's time you and your family . . ."

Rose cut her husband off again, this time with her actions. She went to a small rolltop desk where Thomas always placed his things when he got home from work. She undid the brass buckle on his brown leather briefcase and pulled out what looked like a zippered leather book and held it out to Jasper.

"Absolutely not."

"Please be quiet now, Thomas," Rose said without looking at him.

Fully caught off guard by Rose's disobedience, Thomas clammed up.

Jasper slowly stepped up to Rose but did not take the case that he understood to hold morphine. "Do you know the address of the safe house?"

Rose nodded solemnly.

"If family ever meant anything to you at all . . ." Jasper's sentence didn't need to be finished for his desire to be understood.

"Small green house on Fullerton Avenue. 4830. Russell Woods area," Rose answered, still holding the morphine for him to take.

"Good. Now I need to ask you a favor." He pushed her hand with the zippered case back toward her own body. "Please make my dear wife comfortable. . . . Very comfortable." Jasper turned his head to Thomas, whose mouth had dropped open. "And don't you dare let me find out you stood in the way of my wife's comfort."

Then Jasper walked out the front door, and one by one his family and Neda followed until only Rose and Thomas remained.

She didn't look at her husband when she started across the room.

"Rose! Absolutely not!"

She didn't look back at him when she started to climb the stairs.

"You stop this, and you stop it now!" But he wasn't actually going after her.

Ignoring her terrified white husband who stood in the parlor screaming orders, she sat in the chair next to her Black brother's sick wife and unzipped the case of mortal comfort.

Resolutely, she twisted the needle onto the end of the syringe, selected the vial labeled "morphine," inserted it, and pulled the plunger back to fill the cylinder.

"Dammit, Rose! Whatever you're doing, you stop this right now" came the voice from the lower level.

Rose was an obedient housewife, but Rose was not currently present. At the moment Rosalind was helping her brother humanely end his wife's suffering by pushing the opiate into her arm and holding her hand as she breathed her last breath.

CHAPTER TWENTY-TWO

Mentally, the next few hours felt like floating through a thick, catatonic fog, but Father Time blanketed the Carter brothers as he'd sometimes been known to do, and life flew by entirely too fast for either of them to think beyond instinct. The specific tasks before them made it easy to work together within the large overlapping portions of their Venn diagram. Jasper strove to protect their family's standing in the community while Ben was ready to start down the path of helping the community to protect their family. They were focused, they were matter-of-fact, they put aside their emotions, and as each new piece of information presented itself, they adapted on the fly; they bobbed and weaved as masterfully as Joe Louis himself.

Jasper's LeBaron coupe and Valerie's DeSoto landed outside Geraldine's, where plans were put into play. Hank, who'd been waiting, quickly informed them that Buck over at the crematorium had flat-out turned down the incineration of a decapitated federal agent. For now, he'd hidden the Series 70 and its incriminating cargo, but it was still a problem that needed to be taken care of. Ben recognized an opportunity to align with the Chicago Outfit, and Hank was tasked with finding Joe Batters and inviting him for a face-to-face.

"Not here," Margaret added.

The family couldn't afford for Geraldine's reputation to be embroiled in whatever might go down in a high-stakes meeting between Detroit and Chicago. Sharon suggested Le Noir Palais and stated again that Minnie had said she needed to see Jasper and Ben.

"You heard the safe house address?" Jasper quizzed Sharon.

"4830 Fullerton Avenue. Russell Woods."

"Drop Neda off and get Stephen," her father ordered, then she and Neda took off in the DeSoto.

Knowing full well what his brother was setting in motion, Ben felt justified that Jasper finally saw Lance as the threat to their family that he was. Jasper could smell a hint of righteousness on Ben and almost shouted to stop the DeSoto, but he knew what had to be done, had to be done. He accepted both credit and blame at the same time for this stubborn, eye-for-an-eye rigidness that for the most part Ben kept at bay, but Jasper didn't like the way the quality looked on his kid brother, who he held to higher standards than himself.

Ben kissed Margaret and told her to go to Charles. "Make sure he's okay and tell him to hold tight. We're working it out."

Margaret took the LeBaron, leaving Jasper and Ben to hoof it over to the Palais.

On the way, Jasper expressed his anger at Buck. "After what I did for Diggs? After what Charles got caught up in?" But that was all the complaining he had time for. "Do we need to worry about your Caddy?"

"I trust Hank. He said it's hidden, so it's hidden. We can figure it out later."

As they stepped up the walk toward the Palais, Minnie was waiting on the porch, still wearing her silk black robe from the day before. The woman was confident before she had a drink, but after three, she topped the swagger of her Carter cousins. The affectionate, happy manner she greeted them with told the brothers something was up. They climbed the steps and entered the grand salon populated by a handful of men being plied with whiskey by Minnie's girls to loosen their wallets.

Jasper got to business. "We're expecting some VIPs from Chicago, and we need to make sure they're well taken care of."

Minnie's laugh was on the edge of rude. "Oh, I know how you like to treat VIPs from Chicago."

"Minnie, please just get our room ready." Ben wasn't in the mood.

"Sorry, cousin. Room's occupied."

"Then move them to another room."

Minnie dropped her phony good cheer. "If you want your damn room, then get on in there and move that fat fuck's body. I suggest being discreet, because this empire you think you're building is a whorehouse of cards."

Ben's hurt feelings leaked onto his face. "What are you doing, Minnie?"

"You thought I'd just fuck you out of your problems? Go to hell. . . . But first, clean up your mess. He shit himself after he stopped breathing."

Jasper's face was a solid rock. "You don't know what you're playing with, cousin. Careful."

"I don't?" Minnie's rude laugh came back. She turned and sauntered to the room's bar, where the attractive bartender was already making her next drink. She called over her shoulder, "You don't think I had copies of every photo the G-men confiscated? Oh, I know exactly what I'm doing."

Thirty minutes later Schwartz's body was stuffed into the closet. Perfume had been sprayed and the windows opened, but hints still lingered in their nostrils. As the sheets were stripped and the mattress flipped, Sharon was across town behind the wheel of her mother's yellow DeSoto, parked in front of the safe house with Stephen at her side, giving meaning to the seat commonly referred to as "shotgun."

Stephen opened the door and stepped out, glancing up and down the street. He held a Remington Model 29 down the side of his right leg to keep it as hidden as a thirty-inch barrel could be when carried by a pint-sized fifteen-year-old hit man.

Sharon watched with the motor running as her kid brother disappeared around the back of the small green house. Thirty seconds later she heard two pops, one for each witness, but as Stephen walked back to the car, she could see that the life behind his eyes was the third victim. On the way to Minnie's to report the job complete, Sharon made a pit stop on a dirt road, and Stephen disposed of the weapon down a well.

Hank showed up with Joe Batters and three tough tagalongs, and Minnie drunkenly waved them up the stairs with grand, queenly gestures. Once inside, the showdown began. Jasper and Ben sat in high-backed chairs on one side of the room with Hank standing over Ben's shoulder. Batters sat in the center of the golden-cream sofa with the ornately carved armrests with his crew standing at his flanks—two on his left, one on the right. Both sides of this negotiation were ready to attempt the angle of "the enemy of my enemy is my friend," and that required every word spoken to come with a certain level of caution.

Batters began. "We were deeply sorry to hear about your boy."

Jasper was unsure how to respond but kept himself composed. "Was Valentino your blood?"

"He was not." Batters reassessed the air in the room. "But he was a young member of our crew, and our crew is our family."

"We don't have a crew. Only family," Ben added, as even-keeled as his brother.

"Well . . . Frank Nitti and the Outfit send their condolences to you and your wife."

"My wife is dead."

The four members of the Outfit shifted uneasily with the new information, and the Carters let them stew in the hard silence until they felt ready to move the negotiation forward.

"Word on the street is the Gaczynskis got both our boys," Jasper planted.

"That the word?"

"That's the word," Ben confirmed.

Jasper laid it out. "What they did to Mark was public. If we go after Izzy now, Blake and his keystone cops will march straight to our door."

"What exactly are you proposing?"

Ben picked it up. "If Valentino was 'family' like you say, then you have as much reason to take care of Izzy as we do. Reasons that aren't so public."

Joe Batters studied the Carter brothers—Jasper, Ben, then back to Jasper. Revenge? Sure, but that wasn't enough. There had to be something more. "Valentino was a big earner, and we were hoping for some kind of . . . compensation for our loss."

Jasper, of course, expected this. "The Gaczynskis run the largest numbers game on the east side. If you deal with Izzy, seems only fair that you get his business."

Joe Batters nodded slowly and pursed his lips in thought, but before he vocalized an actual decision, Jasper continued.

"There's a condition."

"What kinda condition we talking?"

Jasper drew his line in the sand. "The rest of Detroit is ours. That's the compensation for *our* loss."

"And one more thing . . ." When Hank spoke up, it shocked Joe Batters as much as it shocked Ben and Jasper as much as it shocked Hank himself, but he'd already overstepped his bounds, so there was nothing left to lose by finishing his thought. "My mama plays the numbers, and she's feeling lucky."

Jasper and Ben both shot eyes at Hank, and for a moment no one in the room knew which way his outburst would fall, but the slightest impressed smirk momentarily flashed on Jasper's face, and he turned back to Batters for a summary. "You get Izzy and take over the numbers. We get the rest of Detroit. We both get retribution for our losses." Jasper ended with a tossed finger in Hank's direction. "And you honor one more bet from the mother of our friend here."

Joe Batters checked in with the men over each of his shoulders, then stood and stuck out his hand. "Deal."

After rising from their chairs to heartily shake the hand of the man who would one day sit atop the entire Chicago Outfit, Jasper, Ben, and Hank escorted their new partners out of the Palais. The sun was setting, and Minnie sat at the far end of the porch sharing a smoke with some of her girls while keeping an ear on her cousins' conversation.

"I'm sorry, boss. That wasn't my place."

"A boy's gotta take care of his mama. I assume you got something cooking?" Ben was curious.

"I sure do, boss. I sure do," Hank confirmed, adding only his contagious laugh. "He-haa!"

With all due respect, Jasper wasn't ready for gaiety. He wouldn't be for a long time. "We're counting on you, Hank. You got a plan for the cargo in the Caddy?"

"Yes, sir, I do."

It was then that Sharon and Stephen rolled up in the DeSoto. Jasper trotted down the steps and moved toward the car. Stephen's door opened first, and he sprinted toward his father, weeping freely over the loss of his brother. Weeping freely over the loss of his mother.

Weeping freely over the complete loss of his innocence. He crashed into Jasper and hung on for dear life. Sharon slowly walked over and joined them, but her tears didn't start to fall until the three of them were locked in a hug of the only remaining members of their nuclear family.

Ben, Hank, Minnie, Minnie's girls—they all watched as the violent sobs of the teenager, a man too soon, only grew. The orders Jasper had given may very well have protected the family, but in the coming years, they would drive a wedge between father and son, between Stephen and sanity. Right now, though, all Jasper could do was cling to his boy, to his daughter, and to the hope that he was strong enough to make up for all his wrongs.

Watching them finally helped Ben see his brother's point of view. Lance *was* their brother, and his murder would have a far more profound effect on the Carter family than any lingering grudge or minor inconvenience that having him around had ever done. And yet, once again, Jasper was teaching Ben a lesson.

"I got some work to do. You good, boss?" Hank asked.

Ben looked over at Minnie, who was actively watching him back, and spoke loud enough for her to hear. "Jasper and I got some skeletons to take care of here at the Palais before we call it a night."

Hank made it to his brother Earl's junkyard, where he set his part of the plan in motion like clockwork. He spent two solid hours shining and polishing up the Series 70. When he got to the trunk, Hank pulled out a bottle of perfume he'd gotten his mother for her birthday. He'd pay her back soon enough. He furiously pinched the little ball to mist the scent over the decapitated body, but the stench quickly got the better of him. There was no option but to twist off the top and dump the whole bottle in.

By 11:15 Hank and the Caddy were out back of the distribution center of the *Detroit Free Press*. He banged on the door till Earl's wife's uncle Walter answered the door. He explained who he was and that he was desperate to bring the paper to his boss, who needed a distraction from the loss of a family member.

"Paper won't be ready for hours."

"He only ever reads the stock pages. I don't understand any of it myself, but he loves it. That section is just yesterday's numbers, right? So maybe that section's already done? Can you help me out?"

By 11:38 Hank was parked outside the Checks Cashed, thankful that the lights were still on inside. He opened the acquired stock section and found the table of numbers he remembered from Izzy's office. He traced his finger to "Jan. 1 to date," then followed the line of dots to the corresponding nine-digit number: 493,968,262. He had always been good with numbers, but it had never counted like it counted now. He spent three minutes, till 11:41, listing those nine digits over and over again in his head, committing them to memory.

He had no idea that a block north on Gratiot, Jasper and Ben were parked in the DeSoto, watching when Hank got out of the Series 70 and started pounding on the door to the Checks Cashed.

"What the hell is he doing?" Ben asked rhetorically.

Jasper had no idea either but was willing to "Trust, brother. Trust."

The door opened and Hank disappeared inside, and by 11:49 he had convinced Izzy Gaczynski that he hated the Carter brothers for forcing him to commit sins against "the Heavenly Father and Jesus Christ almighty."

"I just can't do it anymore. I wanna leave this town behind and go back to Georgia, where I'm from and where I belong."

Izzy was tired and ready to go home after a long day. "How is it dat you think I can help you, Hank?"

Hank needed this to work bad, real bad. He needed this Purple gangster to see an easy mark and swallow the bait, hook and all.

"Well, sir, my mama done gone to see this gypsy woman in Savannah, and she took my mama's hands, and she started speaking in tongues, but ya see, mixed up in all the gibberish were numbers that she said clear as the day is long. Nine of 'em." Hank was laying it on thick, almost too thick. "Nine numbers. Just like your numbers. 493,968,262."

"You wanna play da numbers? Why didn't ya say so?" Izzy pulled out a receipt book. "Drop me doz magic gypsy numbers again."

"493,968,262."

"How much you got?"

"That's the thing, sir. I ain't got nothin' but a need to get back to my mama."

"So ya wasting my time is what ya saying?"

"No, sir, I come wondering if I could bet with this." He held out Ben's keys. "This here is a 1937 Cadillac Series 70, in pristine condition if I do say so myself."

"Dat's Ben Carter's car."

"Yes, sir, but if these magic numbers do what I think they gone do, then I'll be long gone before that sinning fool even know his tin can's missing."

Now Izzy was interested. His vendetta against the Carter brothers was enough to keep him at work as late as needed.

"Dat ride is worth over two thousand five hundred bones. Ya know I can't do full market value."

"If I just give ya the keys, what do you say about lettin' me play those gypsy numbers and givin' me a receipt for a thousand dollars?"

Izzy countered immediately. "Seven fifty."

Hank's act of pretending to be disappointed in the deal certainly wasn't going to get him an Academy Award out in Hollywood, but it was enough for Izzy.

"Well, if that's all you can give me, then I guess I gots to take it."

Izzy wrote "$750" on the receipt next to the numbers Hank had memorized from tomorrow's paper and slid it to the edge of his desk.

"Just so it looks all official, I was wondering if maybe you could sign it?"

The fun had worn off now and Izzy was ready to go, but he felt the quickest way to his bed was to sign the damn paper. It was the least he could do for what was essentially stealing his enemy's car.

At 11:55 Jasper and Ben watched as Hank exited the Checks Cashed building and left on foot.

"Okay, now he's got my attention," Jasper said aloud.

Then at midnight on the button, Izzy came out of the building, got into the Series 70, and drove away.

"Trust, brother. Trust," Ben said before he started the car and moved it to the back alley behind the now-empty Checks Cashed building. They needed to work fast.

Assistant Chief Blake was currently searching Izzy Gaczynski's home for evidence in the murder of Mark Carter, and when the mobster pulled into his driveway twenty minutes later, he was interrogated by the waiting cops.

"This your vehicle?"

"Whaddya think, I stole it? Fuck you. I bought this off a coon. Got it for less than half its worth."

"It's nice. Can I look inside?" The officer motioned to the trunk.

"If dat's what it takes to get you out of my goddamn house so I can get some sleep, be my guest."

Izzy tossed the keys to the officer, who popped the lock and lifted the trunk. The combination of the sight and smell literally pushed the officer back, grabbing at his nose.

"Holy shit! Blake! You need to see this."

By sunrise Izzy was booked for the murder of FBI agent Jon Jon Cochran, who was found decapitated in the car Izzy now swore wasn't his. When Danny got word of his father's arrest, he panicked and came clean with information about the body he'd been trying to use for leverage. Of course, when he told his story about how Charles had decapitated the Black bartender, the officers were confused because they already had that body, and it was not buried in a shallow grave just north of Brighton, but rather in his father's trunk.

Naturally, they ran a squad car out to the location Danny pointed them to, where they found the decomposing remains of one Valentino Locurto, a member of the Chicago Outfit that the *Chronicle* had just yesterday published a picture of alongside none other than Danny Gaczynski.

It was perhaps the sloppiest of Jasper and Ben's covert actions, but when Detroit PD's day shift came on duty, it was time to start methodically rummaging through the lives of Izzy and Danny Gaczynski to add to the piles of incrimination being stacked against them. If it wasn't already a lock-them-up-and-throw-away-the-key situation, it became one when the Checks Cashed on Gratiot was searched, and an unsuspecting rookie opened the broom closet to discover the buck-naked body of a dirty Detroit city councilman named Thomas Schwartz.

CHAPTER TWENTY-THREE

The thing about a Friday night is that it doesn't care how good or bad the week was. It only knows the week is over and it's time to celebrate. Friday night told hardworking men and women to let loose, and many of them made it a point to specifically swing by Geraldine's on the second of July 1937.

A tradition that is far more common among the Black population of America than the white is the celebration of life through death, and the people of Black Bottom and Paradise Valley were highly aware of the tragedies that had befallen their community only the day before. Yes, this meant it was a time for mourning, but death shines a light on the value of life, and that called for song, laughter, and the undeniable power of a community coming together.

Geraldine's was full to the max with a rotating congregation of well-wishers paying their respects to the Carter family with hugs, handshakes, dancing, crying, laughing, and, of course, partaking in a drink or two and leaving a larger-than-normal tip for the cast and crew.

All the important players swung through, and on the surface, everyone was having a damn good time to the sounds of Hank Jones on the keys, with a string of guest musicians who came up for a song or two at a time. But as is always the case, everyone has a deeper story just beneath their merry exterior.

Jasper and Ben sat like sultans in their regular booth. They smiled and small talked; they schmoozed and gossiped. Even though the room came to them, it was them who worked the room.

So much evidence had piled up against the Gaczynskis that Charles was released after being told not to leave the area in case they needed to talk to him. That was fine by him, because where else in the world would he want to be besides Geraldine's, where friends and strangers alike were showering him with love for being free? He was a changed man after the things he'd witnessed, and now that he knew his cousin Mark had lost his life for publishing the photo and story that helped prove his innocence, he was determined to live up to the gift he'd been given and the guilt he would never shake. Not all the events of what went down while he was locked up made sense to him yet, and frankly, that's because he'd been told different stories by different people.

Charles had asked Sharon to make sure Betty was safe, and to her credit, even though she knew she was breaking her brother's heart, she confessed to him that she and Stephen had been tasked with eliminating witnesses who were able to paint him guilty: their uncle Lance and his Betty Bell. He hadn't even had time to take in the loss of the woman he loved before he privately got the story from Stephen as well. Two shots had been fired in the house. One got Lance, but the other took out the agent stationed with him. Stephen had checked every room and certainly would have ended her life, but Betty was not there.

Did Sharon know Betty was alive? If so, why did she want Charles to believe she was dead? The truth that none of them knew was that originally, Betty and Lance had been in the same location, but one of the cops on duty felt it was "inappropriate" to hold a Black man in the same safe house as a white woman, especially one who claimed to be pregnant. Charles didn't know why Sharon would lie to him, he didn't know where his Betty was now, and he didn't know that in seven-and-a-half months, she would give birth to their daughter.

Sharon hadn't spoken to Stephen. She didn't think she needed to. They'd both been there, and she assumed that one of the two shots fired had taken Betty down. She understood Charles being upset with her, but something she couldn't comprehend was how much love and attention Charles was getting when he was the reason the family had been neck-deep in pig shit and he had nothing to do with digging them out. She had done that. She deserved more. Sharon was owed acknowledgment, but all she got was a kiss on the head from her father. Maybe her actions had been overshadowed by the deaths of her mother and brother. That made sense, but then again, she felt like Jasper and Ben were now subtly treating Stephen as if his actions had been more praiseworthy. Did she need to kill someone to get respect?

Victor was alive and well, better than well, if you asked him, but as hard as Ben and Margaret wished he'd walk through the door of Geraldine's that night, he would not. Ben would never say this to Jasper, but he secretly wished Victor had been killed instead of Mark. As a father, it was somehow easier to accept that your son was gone from the earth, that he'd been taken, stolen from you, but Ben had to exist knowing his living son had actively chosen to disown him, gotten rid of his name, and refused to even come to the door and explain his decisions face-to-face, man-to-man. No, Victor was just gone, and the heaviness of no definitive ending was almost too much to bear. The news of the murder of his cousin made Victor even more confident that his new family at the Allah Temple of Islam, a family who actively stood for Black excellence and preached the Black origin of man, was where he belonged. Even if it meant cutting ties with the men and women who had raised him strong and independent enough to choose his own path to begin with.

Margaret couldn't see the pain Jasper felt; he was good at hiding it, too good, but she knew it was there. As she made the rounds from table to table, person to person, she occasionally looked back to where he sat next to her dear, dear husband, and she struggled to shake both the desire to comfort Jasper and the fear of falling into his arms again like she had done all those years ago. Ben was a good man, a strong man. Ben had a moral compass led by a heart that wanted good for all. Ben had given her a life, beautiful children. She belonged with Ben. Not Jasper. Jasper . . . Jasper.

Minnie left her girls to run Le Noir Palais so she could come pay the respect that decency and decorum said she should. She was lively, and everyone she graced with her company fawned over her, but the number of New York sours Ben watched her chug down that night made him wonder if her liver would one day need a shot of morphine to make her "comfortable."

They were not the only white couple at Geraldine's that night, but Rose and Thomas Winston looked the most out of place. Oddly enough, it was Thomas who had insisted they come. As socially terrifying as it had been to have a house full of Negroes that ended with a euthanized patient, it didn't take long for his nerves to settle with the realization that Jasper had the bravery to make the merciful choice for his wife. Would he have had the same courage? If a law firm the size of Canfield, Honigman & Peck, where Rose was now a receptionist, was openly representing Black clients, why was he scared to help Black patients? As he drank his scotch neat and looked around the club, Thomas felt the whisper of guilt on the back of his neck. Everyone understands that an apology without changing the offending behavior is not an acceptable apology, and that night Thomas decided that guilt must be the same. Feeling guilt without making amends, without attempting to repair, without reparations, made Thomas part of the problem.

For Rose's part, she thought Thomas felt, and looked, self-righteous, but who was she to make such an accusation? She lived every aspect of her life as a lie to obtain a false sense of security. She couldn't blame Thomas for deciding to help, even if it was from the comfort of his generational wealth and the safety of a redlined neighborhood, because she was protected by the same things. She wasn't yet willing to face the consequences of her big lie, but couldn't she be more helpful to the Carter family, to her family, from the white side of society? Maybe that was an excuse to stay hidden. Maybe she got a perverse thrill from it. Maybe knowledge was needed that could only be obtained from white society if white society believed they were only in the presence of white society. For now she would stay hidden, and her brothers Jasper and Ben didn't seem to mind the idea of having a spy on the inside. Word spread fast to each member of the Carter family, but that night at Geraldine's, no interaction between the Winstons and the Carters came close to revealing Rose's true identity. No one could know. Not even Thomas.

Leon Bates showed up with John Conyers and Shelton Tappes. Their resolve to fight the Ford Motor Company was strong, and Ben couldn't ignore the bite in the pit of his stomach telling him that what these men stood for was worth a hundred Battles of the Overpass. These were relationships that he needed to water and prune. They felt the same way about Ben but hadn't yet spilled the beans on their next plan—asking Ben to run for office. Their only concern was that rumors were spreading that Victor had joined the Black Muslims and how that might affect a campaign.

Chicago came too; after all, they were partners of sorts. Tony "Joe Batters" Accardo dropped an envelope stuffed to the gills on the table.

"I hope you'll pass our congratulations on to your man Hank and his mother. They got every single number," Batters said with a sly wink.

"They're good people." Ben glanced across the room to his friend Hank Malveaux, who his eyes closed, held a whiskey and swayed to the sounds of Hank Jones at his piano.

Jasper spoke with the slightest edge in his tone. "I heard you put an offer on the Checks Cashed. That was fast."

"We're anxious to get home. Not that Detroit's not great and all, but it's not for me. We'll be sending someone out to head up the numbers next week."

"Have the terms of our deal been met?" Jasper asked, not backing down an inch.

Batters chuckled to one of his enforcers and leveled a finger at Jasper. "You got balls. I like that. I'm sure the papers in the morning will be proof enough that we're square."

Batters walked out of Geraldine's less than five minutes later, confident in what Jasper and Ben didn't yet know. As the paddy wagon transporting Izzy Gaczynski from booking to holding turned left from Bates onto Randolph Street, the timer reached zero, and the bomb's blast lifted the vehicle off the ground and tossed it to its side. The left foot of the innocent driver had to be amputated, but there was no saving Izzy. He was gone.

The ticktock of the clock never stopped. Soon this night would be over. The pain of losing family members would never go away completely, but it would grow more tolerable. Jasper and Ben rebuilt the dry cleaner's and started a couple more businesses with the Carter name too. Even though a crematorium hadn't helped out this time, it seemed like one could come in handy, and as a legit business model, the world was full of potential clients. The second new business was inspired by Mark Carter. He had proven the power of the news media. In one story he set Charles free, took away Danny's play for freedom, and became a martyr for his own cause. This power could be used for good or evil, but however it was used, Jasper and Ben felt they should have a seat at the table. And thus the *Paradise Gazette* was born.

Of course, the future wasn't guaranteed, something both Mark and Valerie taught them so poignantly. The Carter family needed to plan for obstacles seen and unseen, and there was one such concern Jasper and Ben each had but which they kept secret from each other: women. Often mistakenly attributed to William Shakespeare, there was a William Congreve quote from his play *The Mourning Bride* that Ben had read at Wilberforce: "Heaven has no rage like love to hatred turned, nor hell a fury like a woman scorned." Ben's secret concern was a building animosity, dare he think jealousy, aimed at Charles, coming from the direction of his niece, Sharon. Jasper's worry was his assumption that Minnie had photographic evidence that his and Margaret's physical relationship had not fully ended back in Ohio all those years ago. There had been one slipup. One. But one was enough if Minnie had clicked the button on her camera. These were problems for sure, but problems for another day. Tonight was about family, here and gone, and bearing witness to just how far they'd come.

They had no money to spare for renting a room halfway in Findlay, Ohio, so they agreed to drive straight through. The old Model T Town Car that Jasper rebuilt got about seventeen miles to the gallon, so the ten-gallon gas tank meant filling up at least twice on their trip north over the eastern route of the Dixie Highway. Lance said he had some things to take care of, but he'd join them in Detroit as soon as he could. The brothers didn't know if this was true or not, and frankly, Ben hoped not. Jasper held out hope that his brother Lance would show up but didn't argue, as the car was just big enough for six, since two of them were tiny.

Jasper and Ben took turns driving, and Valerie shared the back seat with Margaret, who was seven months pregnant with the child she and Ben would either call Victor or Victoria. The little ones, Sharon and Charles, tested their parents' patience by constantly climbing back and forth over the front seat.

It was an all-day affair that Ben had insisted start at six a.m. After ten hours, two fuel stops two stops for food, three breaks for Margaret to stretch, and what felt like well over a hundred trips to the privy, the Carter family was turning onto Hastings Street for the first time.

Jasper pulled over so he and Ben could step out and smell the air.

"What do you think, Jas?" Ben asked, rubbing his lucky penny between his thumb and forefinger.

"Ready or not, here we come."

With a bit of fear and some excitement, one by one, Valerie, Margaret, Sharon, and Charles quietly joined Jasper and Ben to take in the sights of the place they would now call home.

It felt like freedom.

Black Bottom felt like freedom.

ACKNOWLEDGMENTS

The more I grow and realize the improbability of nearly every one of life's achievements, the deeper my humility becomes, and the more thankful I am for the people who, for better or worse, decide I'm worth supporting.

I owe everything to the incredible humans that are my chosen family, who not only support but encourage my continued gamble to explore the world in story form.

I am thankful to Patrik Bass, Francesca Walker, Judith Curr, and the team at Amistad for their acceptance and guidance. To Tiaka Hurst for trusting me with the story that ultimately became *Sins of Survivors*. To Adel Nur for always being a positive and energetic force, willing to stand behind any idea I pitch, big or small.

My eternal gratitude lies at the feet of Blair Underwood. He is a giving and caring creative partner that I'm sure has spoiled me for future partnerships. Always generous with his time, passion, and love for character and story, Blair has been a defender, a champion, a collaborator, a foundation. My only hope is that I may somehow be worthy of the support he's thrown my way.

ABOUT THE AUTHOR

Joe McClean spent his childhood in the wetlands of South Carolina and his adolescence was baked in Phoenix, Arizona, where he first discovered his love for telling stories.

After studying Shakespeare in college, nepotism from a general contractor uncle in New Jersey , delivered the education that would keep Joe fed while he chased his artistic dreams. Over the years, his days swinging a hammer dwindled as he studied at the Royal National Theater in London, acted with a national-touring children's theater, and wrote, produced, and directed numerous short films and two independent features films—*Life Tracker* and *The Drama Club*. Soon after joining the Writers Guild of America, he wrote and produced his third feature film, *Viral*, which was directed by and stars Blair Underwood. *Sins of Survivors* is Joe McClean's first story told in novel form.

Joe lives with his wife and son in Los Angeles, where he still chases dreams, occasionally supplemented by swinging his trusty hammer.